SUBLIME

Praise for *Sublime*

———

"Sexy, scary, and creepy as hell,
Sublime will both seduce you and send chills down
your spine. A beautiful, haunting read."

—Tahereh Mafi,
New York Times bestselling author of *Shatter Me*

"A romantic and unforgettable story of first love."

—Kami Garcia,
#1 *New York Times* bestselling author of *Unbreakable*
and coauthor of *Beautiful Creatures*

ALSO BY CHRISTINA LAUREN

The House

SUBLIME

CHRISTINA LAUREN

SIMON & SCHUSTER BFYR

NEW YORK   LONDON   TORONTO   SYDNEY   NEW DELHI

SIMON & SCHUSTER BFYR

An imprint of Simon & Schuster Children's Publishing Division

1230 Avenue of the Americas, New York, New York 10020

SIMON & SCHUSTER BFYR is a trademark of Simon & Schuster, Inc.

For information about special discounts for bulk purchases, please contact Simon & Schuster Special Sales at 1-866-506-1949 or business@simonandschuster.com.

The Simon & Schuster Speakers Bureau can bring authors to your live event. For more information or to book an event, contact the Simon & Schuster Speakers Bureau at 1-866-248-3049 or visit our website at www.simonspeakers.com.

Also available in a SIMON & SCHUSTER BFYR hardcover edition

Cover design by Lizzy Bromley

Interior design by Hilary Zarycky

The text for this book is set in Stempel Schneider.

Manufactured in the United States of America

First SIMON & SCHUSTER BFYR paperback edition October 2015

2   4   6   8   10   9   7   5   3   1

The Library of Congress has cataloged the hardcover edition as follows:

Lauren, Christina.

Sublime / Christina Lauren. — First edition.

pages cm

Summary: "Lucy and Colin discover they have a connection on the grounds of the private school they attend, but Lucy has a startling secret"—Provided by publisher.

ISBN 978-1-4814-1368-8 (hardcover)

ISBN 978-1-4814-1369-5 (pbk)

ISBN 978-1-4814-1370-1 (eBook)

[1. Dead—Fiction. 2. Ghosts—Fiction. 3. Supernatural—Fiction.
4. Love—Fiction.] I. Title.

PZ7.L372745Su 2014

[Fic]—dc23

2013038763

*To a writing partnership and friendship that gets stronger
with every book*

ACKNOWLEDGMENTS

This book feels like it's been in this secret corner of our hearts for so long and now it's out in the world! (We can only hope it behaves itself and doesn't eat crackers in your bed.)

Our agent, Holly Root, has been along for this entire journey, and no doubt all three of us are doing a ridiculous happy dance seeing this labor of love in print for the first time. Our editor, Zareen Jaffery, wanted to acquire this story long before any of our other books saw the light of day, and we have a special throne in Christina Lauren Wonderland reserved for her for loving Colin and Lucy so long ago, and for making them so much stronger with every edit. Thank you, Lizzy Bromley, for our beautiful cover. It still takes our breath away. Thank you to everyone at Simon & Schuster Books for Young Readers—especially Katy Hershberger, Chrissy Noh, and Julia Maguire—for welcoming us with so much enthusiasm! Let's go get matching ring pops.

Our prereaders have seen this book so many times, I'm

sure they don't even really know which version is final, and so sorry for that! But on the upside, we love you endlessly: Alison Cherry, Martha Henley, Erin Billings Service, and Anne Jamison. Thanks as well to the kindly critical eyes of Myra McEntire, Gretchen Kopmanis, and Tonya Irving. Thank you: Lauren Suero for being the most fabulous assistant, Nathan Bransford for giving a world of writers a clear road map and a set of tools, and always to Tahereh Mafi for the assurance that the only thing in our way was time. We adore you.

Thanks to John Donello for the mentoring, the friendship, the endless giggles, and of course, for the spark of an idea that turned into a book.

Finally, thank you to our husbands and kiddos for keeping up the enthusiasm from the day we wrote the first word of *Sublime* to this very moment. Right now.

Lo, there's only a thirteen-minute wait for the Tower of Terror.

C, then let's skip over there together and outline as we go.

sublime

1. (*adjective*) transcendent; complete, absolute

2. (*transitive verb*) to cause to pass directly from the solid to the vapor state

A slumber did my spirit seal;
I had no human fears:
She seem'd a thing that could not feel
The touch of earthly years.

No motion has she now, no force;
She neither hears nor sees;
Roll'd round in earth's diurnal course,
With rocks, and stones, and trees.

—SIR WILLIAM WORDSWORTH

SUBLIME

Chapter 1 · HER

THE GIRL IS BENT INTO ODD ANGLES WHEN
she wakes. It doesn't seem possible that she could
have been sleeping here, alone on a dirt path, surrounded by leaves and grass and clouds. She feels like she
might have fallen from the sky.

She sits up, dusty and disoriented. Behind her, a narrow
trail turns and disappears, crowded with trees flaming garishly
with fall colors. In front of her is a lake. It is calm and blue, its
surface rippling only at the edges where shallow water meets
rock. On instinct, she crawls to it and peers in, feeling a tug of
instinctive pity for the confused girl staring back at her.

Only when she stands does she see the hulking buildings
looming at the perimeter of the park. Made of gray stone,
they stand tall over the tips of fiery red trees, staring down
at where she's landed. The buildings strike her as both

welcoming and threatening, as if she's at that in-between stage of awake and asleep when it's possible for dreams and reality to coexist.

Instead of being afraid, she feels a surge of excitement tear through her. Excitement, like the sound of a gunshot to a sprinter.

Go.

She slips down the trail and across the dirt road to where the sidewalk abruptly begins. She doesn't remember putting on the silk dress she's wearing, printed with a delicate floral calico and falling in wispy folds to her knees. She stares at her unfamiliar feet, wrapped in stiff new sandals. Although she isn't cold, uniformed students walk past, wrapped in thick wool, navy and gray. Personality lies in the small additions: boots, earrings, the flash of a red scarf. But few bother to notice the wisp of a girl shuffling and hunched over, fighting against the weight of the wind.

The smell of damp earth is familiar, as is the way the stone buildings capture the echoes of the quad and hold them tight, making time slow down and conversations last longer. From the way the wind whips all around her, and from her precious new memory of the trees in the woods, she also knows that it's autumn.

But nothing looks like it did yesterday. And yesterday, it was spring.

• • •

An archway looms ahead, adorned with tarnished green-blue copper letters that seem to be written from the same ink as the sky.

SAINT OSANNA'S PREPARATORY SCHOOL FOR GIRLS AND BOYS

GRADES K–12

EST. 1814

Beneath it, a broad iron sign lurches in the wind:

And whosoever shall offend one of these little ones that
believe in me, it is better for him that a millstone were hanged
about his neck, and he were cast into the sea.
Mark 9:42

The campus is larger than she expects, but somehow she knows where to look—right, not left—to find the grouping of smaller brick buildings and, in the distance, a wood cabin. She moves forward with a different kind of excitement now, like walking into a warm house knowing what's for dinner. The familiar kind. Except she has no idea where she is.

Or who.

Of the four main buildings, she chooses the one on the left, bordering the wilderness. The steps are crowded with students, but even so, no one helps her with the door, which seems intent on pushing her back outside with its own weight. The handle is leaden and dull in her grip, and beside it, her skin seems to shimmer.

"Close the door," someone calls. "It's freezing!"

The girl ducks into the entryway, breaking her attention from her own stardust skin. The air inside is warm and carries the familiar smell of bacon and coffee beans. She hovers near the door, but nobody looks up. It's as if she's any other student walking into a crowd; life keeps moving in the roaring dining hall, and in a blurred frenzy, she stands perfectly still. She's not invisible—she can see her reflection in the window to her right—but she might as well be.

Finally, she makes her way through a maze of tables and chairs to an old woman with a clipboard who stands at the doorway to the kitchen. She's ticking items off a list, her pen pressing and flicking in perfect, practiced check marks. A single question perches on the girl's tongue and sticks there, unmoving, while she waits for the old woman to notice her.

The girl is afraid to speak. She doesn't even know herself, let alone how to ask the one question she needs answered. Glancing down, she sees that her skin glows faintly under the honeyed light fixture, and for the first time it occurs to her to worry that she doesn't look entirely . . . normal. What if she opens her mouth and dissolves into a flock of ravens? What if she's lost her words along with her past?

Get it together.

"Excuse me," she says once, and then louder.

The woman looks up, clearly surprised to find a stranger standing so close. She seems a mixture of confused and, eventually, uneasy as she takes in the dusty dress, the hair tangled with leaves. Her eyes scan the girl's face, searching as if a name perches near the back of her mind. "Are you . . . ? Can I help you?"

The girl wants to ask, *Do you know me?* Instead, she says, "What day is it?"

The woman's eyebrows move closer together as she looks the girl over. It wasn't the right question somehow, but she answers anyway: "It's Tuesday."

"But which Tuesday?"

Pointing to a calendar behind her, the woman says, "Tuesday, October fourth."

Only now does the girl realize that knowing the date doesn't help much, because although those numbers feel unfamiliar and wrong, she doesn't know what year it should be. The girl steps back, mumbling her thanks, and reclaims her place against the wall. She feels glued to this building, as if it's where she'll be found.

"It's you," someone will say. "You're back. You're back."

• • •

But no one says that. The dining hall clears out over the next hour until only a group of giggling teenage girls remains seated at a round table in the corner. Now the girl is positive something is wrong: Not once do they look her way. Even in her moth-eaten memories she knows how quickly teenage eyes seek out anyone different.

From the kitchen, a boy emerges, pulling a red apron over his neck and tying it as he walks. Wild, dark curls fall into his eyes, and he flips them away with an unconscious shake of his head.

In that moment, her silent heart twists beneath the empty walls of her chest. And she realizes, in the absence of hunger or thirst, discomfort or cold, this is the first physical sensation she's had since waking under a sky full of falling leaves.

Her eyes move over every part of him, her lungs greedy for breath she doesn't remember needing before now. He's tall and lanky, managing somehow to look broad. His teeth are white but the slightest bit crooked. A small silver ring curves around the center of his full bottom lip, and her fingers burn with the need to reach out and touch it. His nose has been broken at least once. But he's perfect. And something about the light in his eyes when he looks up makes her ache to share herself with him. But share what? Her mind? Her body? How can she share things she doesn't know?

When he approaches the other table, the schoolgirls stop talking and watch him, eyes full of anticipation.

"Hey." He greets them with a wave. "Grabbing a late breakfast?"

A blond girl with a strip of garish pink in her hair leans forward and slowly tugs his apron string loose. "Just came by to have something sweet."

The boy grins, but it's a patient grin—flexed jaw, smile climbing only partway up his face—and he steps out of her grip, motioning to the buffet against the far wall. "Go grab whatever you want. I need to start clearing it out soon."

"Jay said you guys did some pretty crazy stunts in the quarry yesterday," she says.

"Yeah." He nods in a slow, easy movement and pushes a handful of wavy hair off his forehead. "We set up some jumps. It was pretty sick." A short pause and then: "You guys might want to grab some food real quick. Kitchen closed five minutes ago."

Out of instinct, the girl glances to the kitchen and sees the old woman standing in the doorway and watching the boy. The woman blinks over to her then, studying with eyes both wary and unblinking; the girl is the first to look away.

"Can't you sit and hang out for a few?" Pink-Haired Girl asks, her voice and lips heavy with a pout.

"Sorry, Amanda, I have calc over in Henley. Just helping Dot finish up in the kitchen."

He's fascinating to watch: his unhurried smile, the solid curve of his shoulders and the comfortable way he slips his hands in his pockets and rocks on the balls of his feet. It's easy to tell why the schoolgirls want him to stay.

But then he turns, blinking away from the table of his peers to the girl sitting alone, watching him. She can actually see the pulse in his neck begin to pound, and it seems to echo inside her own throat.

And he *sees* her, bare legs and arms, wearing a spring dress in October.

"You here for breakfast?" he asks. His voice vibrates through her. "Last call . . ."

Her mouth opens again, and what spills forward isn't what she expects; nor does she dissolve into a flock of ravens. "I think I'm here for you."

Chapter 2 · HIM

A WEEK LATER

COLIN HOVERS NEAR THE DOOR, STARING down at the fingers sticking out of the end of his newly set cast. They're big and awkward—some are crooked from the older breaks he'd never had set. His knuckles are wide, his skin scarred from cuts and scrapes left to heal on their own. Today his fingers look swollen. Abused.

He's finally managed to get the door open when his boss confronts him.

"Colin," Dot says, her face set in a grim line. "Joe called and told me you've been at the infirmary all morning." She doesn't need to add, *Don't bother making an excuse*, or, *I knew this would happen again.*

He exhales a shaky breath, and it condenses in the cold

air in front of him. "I'm sorry, Dot," he says, letting the door close behind him.

"Why are you apologizing to me? It's your arm in a cast." She clears her throat, her expression softening as she touches the plaster. "Broken this time?" He nods. "So why are you showing up for work?"

Her apron is drenched. She's been doing dishes again, and Colin makes a mental note to kick Dane's ass for not finishing before he left for class.

"I was coming to tell you I can't work for the next two weeks." The words burn as they come out. Working in the dining hall makes him feel less like a charity case.

"Only two?" She cocks her head and looks straight at him, catching the lie.

"Okay, four." He fidgets, starting to reach to scratch his neck with the hand of his broken arm, and then winces, working to not grunt some cusswords in front of Dot. She was his mom's best friend and the closest thing he's had to a grandmother for the past twelve years. The last thing he wants to do is upset her.

"And you haven't been to basketball in three weeks," she says. His eyes widen, and she nods. "Yep, I know about that. Talked to Coach Tucker a week ago; he says they cut you from the team."

"Come on, Dot. You know that kind of stuff isn't my thing."

Dot narrows her eyes, considering him. "What *is* your thing, exactly? Defying death? Driving the rest of us to drink, worrying about you? I've always loved your fire, kiddo. But I'm not going to tolerate any more of this insanity."

"It's not insanity," Colin says against his better judgment. "It's biking."

"Now, that's a bald-faced lie. It's tricks and props and jumping from train cars to the tracks. It's riding *on* the train tracks and across bridges made out of rope over the quarry." His head snaps up, and Dot nods forcefully. "Oh yeah. I know about that, too. You could have died out there. When will you realize you can only be so reckless before it's too far?"

Colin curses under his breath. "Does Joe know?"

"No." He hears the layer of warning in her voice, the unspoken *not yet*. "Slow down. The tricks, the racing. Everything. I'm too old to lose this much sleep worrying about you." She pauses, considering her words before speaking. "I know seventeen-year-old boys think they're invincible, but you more than anyone know how quickly people can be taken from us. I'm not going to let it happen to you."

He bristles slightly, and Dot reaches for his arm.

"Just promise you'll be more careful. Promise you'll think." When he doesn't respond, she closes her eyes for a long beat. "I'm cutting down your spending account and revoking your state parks pass. You're grounded to school property until I say otherwise." She glances at him, probably waiting for him to explode, but he knows it isn't worth it. Since Colin's parents died, Joe has kept Colin under his roof and handled the official details of Colin's meager inheritance, but Dot has the unofficial final say. The two of them give Colin miles of rope to proverbially hang himself and are always there to cut him loose when he almost does. This has been coming for a long time.

He nods, hooking his bag over his shoulder before walking into the kitchen to cross his name off of his dining hall shifts. The marker squeals in the silence with a sound of finality, and he can feel the pressure of Dot's attention on his back. He hates disappointing her. He knows how much she worries about him; it's a constant, obsessive loop in her mind.

It's why he hid in his room with a broken arm last night instead of going straight to the infirmary. It's why Dot and Joe will never, ever know half the stupid shit he's done.

Pulling his hood up against the wind, he grips the handrail as he climbs the steps of Henley Hall. The metal is cold and familiar beneath his palm, colder even than the autumn air that snakes around him. White paint has started to flake away, the surface marked with the scars of tires and skateboard axles—most of them his. The beginnings of rust bloom around the edges. What little sleep he got last night was broken up by stabbing pain; now he's just sore and tired and not sure he can deal with today.

He pushes through the door, and emptiness greets him; the space ticks dully with the synchronized rhythm of the clocks at either end of the long hallway.

The halls don't stay empty for long, though. The bell rings, and he turns the corner to find Jay pressing a girl against a locker outside class, a set of red-tipped acrylic nails running through his dirty-blond hair.

Jay looks back as Colin approaches, smirking at him over his shoulder. "About time you got here, slacker," he says. "You missed the world's most painful calculus class. I could practically hear my brain bleeding."

Colin nods his chin in greeting, lifting his cast. "I think I'd have preferred calc over this."

"I wouldn't be so sure." Jay's latest conquest reluctantly leaves as he and Colin walk into the classroom. Students continue to file in around them, and Colin drops his bag at a desk inside, bending to dig for his assignment.

"So you were right," Jay says, motioning to the cast. "Broken?"

"Yeah." As quickly as he can with one functioning arm, Colin finds his paper and stuffs everything else back in the bag.

"Joe and Dot read you the riot act?" Jay's been at Saint Osanna's as long as Colin has—since kindergarten—and knows just as well that Dot has never appreciated the two boys' particular thirst for adventure.

Colin looks at him pointedly. "Dot did."

Jay straightens. "Did she ground your fun money?"

"Yeah. And I'm restricted to school property indefinitely. Thank God you took my bike to your parents' house last night or she'd probably take that, too."

"Brutal."

Colin hums in agreement and hands his assignment to the teacher. What kills him the most is that this ride wasn't even that dangerous. A week ago he jumped from the lip of the quarry onto a boulder at the base and came home without a scratch. But yesterday he couldn't land even a rookie jump without wiping out.

"Hood off, Colin," Mrs. Polzweski says. He pushes it off and shoves his hair back from his eyes as they move to their desks.

Just as the second bell rings, *she* walks in. The girl from the dining hall. Colin hasn't seen her in a week, and he hasn't been able to stop thinking about what she said just before she ran out the door.

I think I'm here for you.

Who says shit like that? He'd tried to call after her, but she was gone before the words dissolved in the air in front of him.

She slips through the noisy room and takes the seat in the row next to his, moving her eyes to him and then quickly away. Her arms are empty, no books or paper, no backpack. A few people watch her sit down, but she moves so fluidly, she seems to already have joined the rhythm of the room.

"If you can't ride for a whole month, we're going to need a plan," Jay whispers. "No way can you be stuck inside that long. You'll go insane."

Colin hums, distracted. It's crazy; the girl seems other-worldly, almost as if a faint sheen of light surrounds the exposed skin on her arms. Her white-blond hair has been brushed free of leaves, and she has these badass black boots laced to her knees with a French-blue oxford tucked into the navy uniform skirt. Her lips are full and red, her eyes lined with thick lashes. She looks like she could rip through the wool of his trousers with only a dirty word. As if feeling him watching, she pulls her legs farther under the desk, her arms closer against her body.

Jay pokes Colin right above his cast. "You're not going to let that little cast stop you from having fun, are you?"

He pulls his eyes from the girl to look at Jay. "Are you kidding me? There's tons of other ways to get in trouble without leaving the grounds."

Jay grins and bumps Colin's good fist.

Mrs. Polzweski organizes her stack of papers at her desk, ignoring the flurry of hushed activity: books being opened, pages turning, and students grumbling, the occasional cough, a pencil being sharpened somewhere. The girl sits, staring ahead, looking like she's trying as hard as she can to not be noticed.

Where has she been?

In the periphery, Colin sees her thin fingers reach for a pencil that someone has left on the desk. She turns it over and over in her hand, as if the movement requires practice, examining it like she suspects it's a magic wand.

Colin doesn't think he's ever seen such light hair before. When she tilts her head slightly, inspecting the pencil, her hair catches a dusty sunbeam, making it seem almost translucent. The strands twist and spill over shoulders that are hunched forward and wrapped in a shirt that's too bulky for someone so delicate. She looks like a shadow of a girl. A shadow wearing a cap of sunshine.

As if she can feel him staring, she turns, an involuntary smile lifting the corner of her mouth. Her dimple makes him think of giggled pleas, mischievous promises, and the taste of sugar on his tongue. Gunmetal eyes meet his, and the color is alive, churning like an angry ocean, pulling him in.

He lets himself drown.

Chapter 3 · HER

THE ONLY PERSON LOOKING AT HER IS THE same boy whose face has haunted her all week, with wild dark hair that needs to be cut, an arm in a new cast, and eyes that pierce her, amber and fierce.

"Hi," she rasps, tucking away her smile. Her voice is rough because this is the first time she's used it in six days. The first time she used it since she spoke to him and then burst from the dining room, intending to run into town to find the police and tell them she needed help. She could get only as far as a hulking metal campus gate a half mile down the gravelly road. Each of the three times she tried to escape, one step past the gate put her right back on the trail where she woke up, as if she'd stepped into a skipping song.

The boy's gaze narrows and slips across her cheeks, over

her nose, pauses at her mouth. He blinks once, slowly, then again. "Where did you go?"

Nowhere, she thinks, envisioning the empty shed she found in the middle of a barren field beside the school. It was as deserted as her memory bank, after all, and seemed the perfect home for a girl who has no name, no past.

After being inexplicably drawn to this school building every morning for a week, she finally grew brave enough to steal a uniform, walk inside, and sit down.

"You disappeared," he says.

She shifts in her seat, glancing at his mouth. "I know. I wasn't quite sure how to follow up my stunning opening line."

Laughing, he says, "Here," and pushes his open textbook closer to her.

She blinks, the phantom trace of a pulse racing inside her throat at the way his eyes move over her face, the way he purses his lips slightly before smiling.

"Thanks," she says. "But I'm okay. I can just listen."

He shrugs, but doesn't move away. "I think we're covering the history of labor-management relations today. Wouldn't want you to miss out on the full experience."

The girl isn't sure what to do with his attention. She suspects, from the way her skin seems to be aching to move closer to him, that he's the reason she's drawn here every morning, just as she found herself in the dining hall that first day. But he seems so sweet, almost too open, like she's a strip of paper dragged through poisoned honey and this perfect boy flies innocently around her. How good can a girl be when she doesn't need to eat or sleep and keeps finding herself snapped back to school grounds every time she tries to leave?

He continues to stare, and she shifts her hair over her shoulder, lowering it like a curtain between them.

"Colin?" It's a woman's voice, clear and authoritative.

The pressure of his gaze on her lifts. "Sorry, Mrs. Polzweski," he says.

Now that the girl knows his name, she wants to whisper it over and over.

"Who are you, honey?" the teacher asks.

The room is a vast bubble, silent and pulsing with expectation, and the girl realizes this Ms. Polzweski is speaking to her.

But with the question hanging in the air, a man's voice speaks in the girl's mind.

"I bet you didn't know your name means light," he whispered, *lips too close to her ear.*

"I did know," she wanted to say, *but the hand on her throat made it hard to even draw breath.*

"Lucia," she remembers in a gasp. "My name is Lucy."

The teacher hums in acknowledgment. "Lucy, are you new?"

Something inside Lucy stirs at the sound of someone else

saying her name. For a heavy moment, she feels real, as if she's a balloon and someone has finally weighted her to the ground. Maybe a girl with a name won't float off into the sky.

Lucy nods, and a phantom heat burns across her cheek where Colin's gaze settles again.

"You're not on my roll, Lucy. Can you go to the office to check in?"

"Sorry," Lucy says, fighting panic. "I just started today."

Ms. Polzweski smiles. "You need to make sure to pick up your add card. I'll sign it."

Lucy nods again and slips away, wanting to disappear like a shadow into black.

Lucy knew she'd be told to go, but she doesn't even know where the office is and isn't quite ready to brave the outdoors and the winds that weigh more than she does. And here her feet seem grounded anyway, keeping her from leaving. She sits at the end of the hall, knees to chest, waiting for the next tug of instinct to pull her up and forward.

A door opens and closes shut with a quiet *click*.

"Lucy?" It's one of the only two voices in this world that she's connected to a name—Colin—and it's hesitant and deep and quiet. It cuts straight down the hall, and his lanky figure moves just as smoothly, straight to her. "Hey. Do you need help finding the office?"

She shakes her head, wishing she had something to gather to take with her so she could look purposeful and less like a lost girl sitting on the floor. Instead, she stands and turns, watching the lines of wood flooring weave a path in front of her as she walks away. She knows how it would go, anyway: He would walk with her, notice how she fights the wind, ask if she's okay. And how would she respond? *I don't know. I only remembered my name five minutes ago.*

"Hey, wait."

She reaches a door, but it's locked. She tries another beside it. Also locked.

"Lucy, wait," Colin says. "What are you looking for? You can't go in there. Those are janitor closets."

She stops, turning to face him, and he's looking at her. *Really* looking, like he wants to capture every detail. When their eyes meet, he makes a strangled sound, narrowing his gaze and leaning closer to look. Her eyes are murky green-brown; she's stared at them for hours in an old mirror, hoping to remember the girl behind them.

"What?" she asks. "Why are you looking at me like that?"

He shakes his head. "You're . . ."

"I'm what?" What will he say? What does he *see*?

He blinks again, slowly, and she realizes it's just something he does: an unselfconscious, unhurried blink, as if he's capturing an image of her and developing it on his lids.

"Intense," he murmurs.

With that word, the other man's voice appears in her head again, an echo from the same intrusive memory. *"You have to know how intense this is for me."*

She stumbles back, eyes wide.

"Are you okay?" Colin reaches for her arm, but she's already turning, hurrying away.

With lips wet and pressed to her ear, he asked, "Are you afraid of dying?"

"Lucy!"

A flash of her reflection in a crisp blade of silver. Breath smelling of coffee and sugar, cigarettes and delight. Cool water lapping near her head. A knife, drowning in her own blood, the feeling of being pried open.

She bursts through the side exit, sucking in a huge gasp of sharp, autumn air.

So that's who she is. She's the girl who isn't alive anymore.

Chapter 4 · HIM

THERE'S THAT NEW GIRL," JAY SAYS THROUGH
a mouthful of sandwich.

Colin follows his gaze and grunts, noncommit-
tal, as Lucy glides across the soccer field. When she's alone,
she's statuesque, long lines and slim profile. When she gets
closer to the other students, she shrinks in on herself: shoulders pulled in, head down.

She reminds him of himself after his parents died and he
didn't and the sadness and guilt felt like a crushing weight
under his ribs. He didn't know how he was supposed to
weather it. When people tried to talk to him at first, it made
him wish he could turn into air and disperse in a thousand
different directions. Lucy carries that same kind of bewil-
dered fragility.

It's been three days since she showed up in his class,

offered the most achingly vulnerable smile he'd ever seen, and then ran away again. Nobody talks to her. Nobody looks at her. She has no books, or even a backpack. She looks at every building as if she's trying to see through its walls to what lies inside. She always touches the outstretched arm of the statue of Saint Osanna Andreasi as she passes through the darkest corner of the quad, pulling back as if she's been burned before reaching out to touch it again, carefully. No one ever touches the statue—it's said to be haunted—but Lucy does. Colin has never seen her with anyone. Lucy doesn't even go to the same classes every day. She kind of hovers around campus.

He feels like a total stalker for knowing these things when everyone else seems content to let her be. Most new students get a schedule of classes and let the tide carry them. Lucy seems determined to remain disorganized.

At least she looks more peaceful today, as if she's enjoying the weather before it all goes subzero. It's still a bit on the cool side, but she never wears a jacket. Thin blue fabric wraps down the length of her arms. How can she be warm enough? She must live off campus, he reasons. Maybe she left her coat at home.

"She seems weird, though," Jay says.

This catches Colin's attention, and he looks over at Jay, wondering what he means. Two nights now Colin has fallen asleep thinking about Lucy's mood-ring eyes. Does Jay notice too? "Weird, how?"

Jay shrugs and takes another bite, propping his feet on the wall of the arts building. His dirty sneakers blend into the gray concrete. "She's been in my English class a few times. Doesn't talk much."

"And her eyes, too."

Glancing at Colin, Jay asks, "Eyes?"

"Never mind. They're . . . I don't know. Different."

"Different? Aren't they, like, brown or something?"

Colin mumbles, "Maybe gray," but his heart is thundering. He's pretty sure if he says, "They're like melted metal," Jay will actually have a T-shirt made for him with the words I AM A DELICATE POET printed across the chest.

"Brown hair, gray eyes," Jay says as if reciting the ingredients for average. Colin pauses with his sandwich partway to his lips. He turns to Jay and follows his gaze again, making sure they're both looking at the same girl. They are.

"Brown?" Colin asks, motioning to where she's reached the edge of the field. "That girl over there?"

"Uh, yeah," Jay answers. "The same one you've been staring at for the last twenty minutes."

Lucy's hair isn't brown. It's not even close. Colin watches her again and shivers, pulling his hood up.

Colin wonders if it should freak him out that Jay sees

brown hair when he sees almost white-blond. But, with a strange rush of warmth in his limbs, he finds he likes that he sees her differently. It feels strangely surreal, and it occurs to him that this reaction might come from the same part of his brain that turns on when he looks over a cliff and instead of thinking, *Back off,* he thinks, *Pedal faster.*

"Amanda said they saw her walking down by the lake," Jay says.

"The lake?"

"Yeah. She's new; wouldn't know the stories, would she?"

Colin nods. "No, she wouldn't know any of that."

The stories are as old as the buildings here: Walkers out in daylight, wandering lost and confused. A man in military uniform sitting on the bench near the lake. A girl vanishing between two trees. Sometimes a student will claim a Walker tried to talk to them or, worse, grab them. But it's all ghost stories, a legend built on the morbid history of the school. The Catholic institution was built on grounds where deceased children of settlers were buried before the survivors made their long trek through the mountains, but in the first week the school was open, two more kids died in a fire that burned down the chapel. For years, students claimed to see the two lost children standing by the newly erected statue of Saint Osanna, or sitting in a pew in the rebuilt chapel. The legend lived on, and over time, the population of Walkers grew in the students' collective imagination.

It's a morbid history, Colin knows, and the students keep the stories alive because it makes the school interesting and makes them sound brave. But even though everyone swears they don't believe the Walkers exist, only stoners and drunk kids given a dare on Halloween hang at the lake or deep in the woods. Or dumbasses like him and Jay, who are doing shit they don't want to get busted for. Of course Amanda would be the one to have seen Lucy there.

Jay pulls his feet from the wall. "You like her."

Colin bends and ties shoelaces that don't need tying.

"It's cool if you like her. She's not ugly or anything, but she's . . . I don't know. Quiet." Jay takes a long pull from his water bottle. "Which isn't always a bad thing. Amanda would never shut up. God. Was she always talking when you guys were—"

"Dude." Colin doesn't want to think about another girl while he's watching Lucy. It feels wrong, like comparing a river stone to a ruby.

"She totally was," Jay guesses, and makes a yapping gesture with his hand. "Oh, Colin, Colin, Colin," he gasps in a high, breathy voice.

Colin doesn't reply, choosing instead to shove a handful of chips in his mouth. Jay actually does a fairly good Amanda impersonation.

"Have you talked to her?" Jay asks.

"Amanda?"

"New girl."

Colin shrugs and wipes his palms on his jeans. "Once or twice. Last time I tried, she ran away."

"That's because you're a dick," Jay says with a punch to his arm. "A nice dick. But still a dick."

Colin pauses before balling up his garbage and tossing it into the trash. "You called me a nice dick."

Jay winks at him, but two seconds later punches his good arm again. "So are you going to talk to her, or what?"

Colin shrugs, but of course he knows he will.

"All right, lover boy," Jay says, stretching his arms over his head. "This chat's been great, but I told Shelby I'd meet her behind the school."

"You're a walking cliché."

Jay cycles through girls the way Colin goes through bike tires. Only used for a few, wild rides. Ignoring the comment, Jay juts his chin toward where Lucy has turned and is walking back toward the quad, only twenty or so feet away. "She's coming back."

For a brief moment, Lucy's eyes catch Colin's and hold on. And even though he thinks she's been watching him, too, suddenly she's walking faster and veering away from where he sits.

"Make me proud," Jay says, clapping a hand on Colin's back before walking away.

Colin stands and crosses the soccer field, accelerating his long strides to catch her. He has no idea what to say. It doesn't feel the same as approaching one of the girls from school, the girls who knew him when he was five and couldn't write the letter *S*. The girls who knew him when he was ten and wore the same Han Solo shirt for an entire week. The girls who, lately, never seem to say no. This feels like approaching an exotic snake on a trail.

As if she knows he's there, Lucy turns and looks at him over her shoulder.

"Hey," he says nervously, shoving his good hand into his pocket. The fingers of his other hand twitch at his side.

She frowns and keeps moving along the grass.

"I didn't see you eat anything," he continues, moving into step beside her. "Weren't you hungry? Dot makes the best grilled cheese." Lucy gives only a small shake of her head, but the response is enough to make something like hope spread in his chest. "Are you cold? I have a fleece in my room. . . ." He cringes inwardly. That sounded like a bad pickup line.

They walk for another minute in silence, leaves crunching beneath the soles of their shoes. Although it's weird how quiet she is, for some reason he doesn't feel ignored, either. "Did you move here?" Ducking his head, he smiles at her. "It's like you just showed up one day."

There's a slight falter in her steps but nothing else. Colin studies her profile: creamy, pale skin and bee-stung lips that stick out in kind of a hot pout.

"Where did you go to school before?" he asks.

Lucy picks up her pace but doesn't answer. He's decided to give up and turn away when she slows, motioning to his cast. "How did you hurt your arm?"

He flexes the fingers of his left hand on instinct. "On my bike. I didn't quite land a jump."

"Does it hurt?" she asks. Her voice is scratchy, like she was at a show last night screaming her head off. He imagines her dancing alone, rocking out, not giving a crap what anyone thinks.

"Nah. I've had worse. Broken bones, fractures, concussions, stitches. You name it. This is nothing." He stops talking abruptly, realizing he sounds like a frat boy bragging about slamming a beer can against his forehead.

Lucy frowns again. "Why would you do those things if you keep hurting yourself?"

Without thinking, Colin says, "For the rush? The burst of adrenaline? That feeling you get when you do something that reminds you you're alive?"

Lucy stops in her tracks; her face goes blank and her arms wrap protectively around her stomach. "I have to go."

"Wait," he says. But it's too late. With long, determined strides, she walks away.

Chapter 5 · HER

ONCE LUCY REMEMBERS WHAT HAPPENED TO her, a tangle of other memories connect, plugging together bundles of fine, tenuous synapses. She remembers her loud, barking laugh, forever-skinny arms, and hair so straight it slipped right out of clips and bands. A gift for chemistry but also art, fear of dogs, and a love for the smell of oranges.

She remembers the face of her first teacher, but not her father. She remembers her favorite torn jeans and a Cookie Monster sweatshirt she wanted to wear every day when she was little.

In other words, she remembers nothing that tells her anything about why she's here instead of floating on a cloud somewhere, or beneath the trails and pavement, dancing in flames.

And it's that question—*why am I here?*—that begins to eat away at her quiet, composed shell. Questions burn on her tongue, wanting to be screamed into the cold. But she knows there's no one to answer them. She's spent hours since she woke trying to understand what she is. If she's back where she was killed, then is she a ghost? And if she is, then how can she wear clothes and open doors and even be seen? Is she an angel who came crashing through the clouds and landed on the trail? Then, where are her wings? Where is her sense of purpose?

Her chest aches with the tickling anxiety that she could disappear as quickly—and mysteriously—as she appeared. Somehow, the idea of leaving and being sent elsewhere is more terrifying than the idea of staying here as a shadow. At least here is familiar. Elsewhere might be the stuff of night-mares: stitched-together monsters and blue-black darkness, yellowed claws and misery.

So much about this strange life doesn't make sense. There's the statue in the quad, the one with the outstretched arms and heavy marble cloak draped over her shoulders. Lucy is convinced she's touched it a hundred times before, but now it doesn't feel . . . right. Or at least, it feels more right than stone should. The first time, Lucy let her hand linger on the delicately carved fingers, trying to remember the exact moment she'd felt it before and marveling at the strange texture. But last time she jerked away, convinced she felt a faint warmth beneath the marble skin and certain one of the fingers had moved. Other students make a wide arc around the statue when they pass, but to Lucy, it beckons.

It feels like one more thing that separates her from the students around her: Her skin turns almost translucent in the sunshine. Normal objects like pencils and stones fascinate her when she stares at them, but when she picks them up, they grow dull in her hand. She's solid enough to wear clothes, but they weigh a good deal more than she does and she never loses awareness of them: stiff and touching her everywhere. Her mind is full of questions and empty of memories. It's as if she's been dropped here and is waiting, suspended, for her fall to make a sound.

The *unknown* of it all sometimes slips in and makes her feel breathless, tight in the chest, panicked. In those moments, Lucy closes her eyes and shuts out everything but the quiet. She's here, a ghost in girls' clothing, haunting this private school; she should just get used to it. But she doesn't want to haunt anyone. She wants to be tangible and solid. To sleep in a dorm and eat in the dining hall and flirt. With him. All she wants is to be near him.

And he seems to want it too. Colin follows her everywhere, and where she feels as if she's built of a million questions and doubts, he seems to be only instinct, happy to simply be near her. His presence raises a warm, soothing hum beneath her skin. He's behind her as she walks down the halls between classes. Sometimes he walks beside her and talks about—*everything*—even though she rarely answers what he asks. He's stopped offering to share his lunch. He's stopped offering to share his books. Since that first day in the hall, he's never tried to touch her. But he hasn't yet revoked his company.

She isolates herself at school because she feels so *other*. She's unable to throw away the clothes she woke up wearing, but they feel like a hook to another place, piled in the corner of the old shed she's found. Every time Lucy looks at them, she knows she wore them when she lay buried somewhere. The new, stolen uniform hangs limp on her bony frame. She tells herself to keep going to classes because, really, what else does she have? At least here, she can be near him. And the closer he is, the more she relaxes. Is it dangerous to want so much to know someone without first knowing yourself?

She pretends she's wandering the campus—not seeking him out—but is flooded with a wild, charged excitement when she finds him in the parking lot near the security gates, riding a BMX with the other guy she always sees with him. His friend—Jay, she remembers—is good-looking, a bit shorter but wiry, with a constant smirk. His gaze slips past her to focus on Colin as Lucy approaches. Then Jay stands on his pedals and moves away.

"Hey," Lucy calls, and she thinks she's said it too quietly, but Colin's head snaps up and his eyes go wide. She sees his face every time she closes her eyes, but the reality of him in person still surprises her.

He pedals over, too-long limbs and too-long hair, hopping off his bike while it continues to come to a skidding stop only inches from her legs. He looks impressed that she hasn't stepped back. "Hey, Lucy."

She swallows, unprepared for how intimate it feels when he says her name. "How can you bike with a broken arm?"

He shrugs, but something is illuminated behind his eyes, and she recognizes it as joy. "We're playing around to see if I'll be able to hit a trail later this week."

A small tug in her chest. A flutter. "With one arm?"

"Yep." He grins, and the combination of the wonky bottom tooth that overlaps its twin and the small metal ring hugging his lip make her blink and look away so she can process his answer. "My legs are fine, and I only need one good arm to steer."

She nods and smooths the wisps of hair off her face. "Are you following me?"

She expects embarrassment or defensiveness, but he laughs, wiping his forehead on the sleeve of his noncasted arm. "Am I following *you*?" His eyes move to his bike and then back to her, playful. "Not at the moment."

She's embarrassed, fighting a smile. "You know what I mean."

"I do," he says. "And yeah, I guess I have been." He pauses while he looks at every part of her face. "I mean, we both know I have been."

His smile widens then, invading every feature and making his eyes brighten last, and best. She wants to stare at him. Long lashes drop slowly as his eyes close, as if developing another image. She loves his blink. It's a strange fascination she has, but she wants to ask him what he sees behind his lids.

"Why?" she asks.

"Why am I following you?"

She nods, and his playful smile disappears. "I don't know."

"You don't look at me the way the other students do," she says.

He studies her in that way he has, like every day is made up of hundreds of hours and he's not in any hurry to wrap up his inspection. "How do other students look at you?"

"They don't."

He shrugs and his eyes soften. "Then they're idiots."

Every inch of her skin aches to be near him, but the doubts roll back in, gray as rain clouds. He has no instinct to protect himself from the strangeness of her. Is she supposed to believe he hasn't noticed that she's different? "You shouldn't follow me. I'm not who you think I am."

He rolls his eyes. "That's kind of dramatic."

"I know it is. That's my point."

He moves closer, expression soft. "Did you come here to find me and tell me to stop coming to find you?"

She shrugs, fighting another smile.

"That seems like a poor use of your lunch break. You could have waited for me to find you later. It's in my plan, right after chemistry."

"Seriously, Colin. You shouldn't—"

"It isn't that easy," he interrupts. All teasing is gone from his eyes as he looks up to the sky, and he's blushing hotly, slowing himself down. His voice drops to barely a whisper, and he admits, "I don't know why, okay? I just want to get to know you, and I can't seem to stay away."

Lucy drinks in his full lips, his hungry expression, and his earnest attention and tries to keep it safe somewhere inside. "Colin."

He exhales a puff of air, saying shakily, "What?"

She looks away, up at the dense autumn storm clouds now beginning to form, green with electricity and heavy with rain. "Like you said, I'm a dramatic girl." She smiles, feeling her skin hum with electricity at the way he's hanging on her every word. "Don't boys hate that?"

"Usually." He licks his lips, tracing the shape of the silver ring.

"Seriously though," she says, dragging her gaze away from his mouth. Her chest, it aches. "I don't even know what I'm doing here."

He sees something in her eyes that keeps rejection from clouding his face. He blinks once, nods slowly, as if he already knew this about her. "Okay."

He stares at her as she walks away; his focus is like a point of heat on her back. Did she really tell him to stay away? Now, as if there's a magnet behind her and she is composed of shards of scrap metal, she feels almost irresistibly pulled backward. Ahead is the cabin at the edge of campus, and a man in khakis and a sweater stands on the porch, stretching in the crisp air. A small plaque at the foot of the walkway leading to the home reads:

WILLIAM P. VERNON MEMORIAL RESIDENCE

Joseph Velasquez, Headmaster

As she passes the path to the steps, the man she assumes is Joseph R. Velasquez doesn't even nod or smile or somehow acknowledge her. His focus is on the lot behind her, where she's left Colin and Jay horsing around on their bikes.

His eyes narrow, and what looks like exasperation moves through his body, deflating him.

"Colin Novak!" he yells, irritation thickening his voice. "The doc said no riding!"

Pressure builds inside her chest, a balloon that fills with some indescribable need until it's so strong, so *full,* she fears her ribs might crack beneath the strain. She feels *angry.* But she has no idea why. And as his words echo past her to the quad, bouncing back and joining the whispers of Colin's name that repeat in her thoughts, the man glances at her, horror appearing on his face before the sturdy porch groans and in a sharp snap, wood planks splinter. It happens so fast, but in Lucy's mind it feels like each event occurs in slow succession: wood cracks, Velasquez pitches first forward and then back as his legs break through the porch and he falls beneath. His surprised cry echoes across the lawn.

The balloon bursts, and relief seeps into each corner of her body. She breathes again, gasps as if it's the first breath she's ever taken. And she's horrified. Lucy scrambles up the steps and reaches for his hand before immediately pulling back. She's never touched anyone, not in this body. She doesn't even know if she *can* be touched. Instinct presses her back. He looks up from where he landed, waist-deep under the porch and grimacing in pain.

"Go away," he says, pleading with her.

She takes another step back, hands moving to cover her mouth in silent apology. But her face is unrecognizable beneath her fingers, as if heat and anger have torn away her skin.

"I don't think I can pull you out," she says, too quiet, aching with apology but unwilling to move closer, almost as if an invisible wall stands between her and the wounded man. He looks at her in awe, and she steps back, holding her hands up. "I'm afraid to try in case—"

Shouts from the lot reach her, and footsteps pound down the sloping lawn. Colin, with Jay close behind him, shouting, "Joe! Oh, my God, Joe!" Colin buckles when he reaches the gaping hole in the porch, and he and Jay struggle to heave out a dusty and injured Mr. Velasquez.

There's blood and torn fabric, and Lucy is oddly fascinated with the way the red blooms thickly through the fibers of his pants and pools beside Colin on the porch.

"I'll . . . go get someone," she says.

"Get Maggie," Jay says to her, tearing a bit of his shirt and tying it around Mr. Velasquez's leg.

"Maggie?"

"Campus nurse. Hang on. I'll go with you. You got this, Col?"

Colin nods numbly and watches as she steps away and begins backing down the stairs. "What happened, Lucy?"

"He fell through," she answers simply.

Crimson blood almost reaches Colin's leg, and he scoots back before it touches him. Looking back down, Colin says quietly, "We'll get you fixed up, Joe."

Lucy turns to leave, uneasy with the odd sense of responsibility she's feeling, remembering the way Mr. Velasquez reacted as if her face told him something terrible was about to happen. Beside her, Jay is already scrolling through a list of names on what she's learned is a phone with a bright, colorful screen. "I'll walk with you," he says.

Lucy had been confused at first when she'd seen students staring down at and tapping the front of what looked like a tiny TV. She'd never seen anything like it in her life. *I'm not from here*, she thought. *I'm not from* now. She wonders what would happen if she tried to take one, to use it to call outside the school. Would the dialed call bounce back into the school grounds, too?

They head back down the trail in an uneasy rhythm as Jay passes on the details to Maggie, and Lucy works to match his frantic pace. The lawn rolls ahead, stark and so green it almost looks unreal. Will they walk to the infirmary together? Will she be required to explain how a seemingly sturdy porch simply caved in under the weight of a small man? For once, Lucy wishes the earth would open up and reclaim her, the girl with no answers.

She turns and looks over her shoulder to where Colin remains bent over Mr. Velasquez, speaking quietly.

"Why is he so worried?"

"Did you not see the man up to his chest in porch? The *blood*?" Jay asks, a hint of sharp amusement in his voice.

Lucy nods, tucking her chin and staring at the brilliant green grass bending only slightly beneath her feet. Her words echo back to her and sound ridiculous. "Of course. I didn't mean he shouldn't be worried."

"No, I know what you mean. He's more worried than most students would be, I guess." Jay ducks to meet her eyes. "It's just that Colin miraculously survived this horrible accident that killed his parents. So accidents kind of freak him out. Plus Joe's his godfather and, like, his one remaining semi-family member left on the planet."

Chapter 6 · HIM

COLIN'S BEEN IN THE INFIRMARY MORE TIMES than he can count, but he's rarely been the one sitting beside the bed while someone else babbles under the influence of painkillers.

"Like a demon. Or a ghoul. Or . . . something whose face melts," Joe mumbles.

"Everything's okay now," Colin reassures his godfather. Joe has been rambling about demons for almost an hour. "It's the morphine."

The door from the hallway opens and Maggie comes in, carrying fresh bandages and a glass of water. She's barely in her thirties but has the wisdom of a much older woman. It shows in the deep set of her frown and the persistent worry lines on her forehead.

"How's he doing?" she asks Colin.

"Still going on about a face-melting demon, but he seems better."

Maggie hums, lips tight, and pulls the sheet down to check Joe's bandage. "We should take this one to the hospital, to be sure."

"I'm fine," Joe growls, suddenly coherent. "We're not driving two hours for something you can do better here."

"I can stitch you up, but this is deep. You'll have a nasty scar."

"I'm staying put. Don't have anyone to impress with my flawless skin."

"Chicks dig scars," Colin says, and ducks when Maggie pretends to smack his arm.

Joe groans when Maggie peels away the blood-soaked bandage. Colin looks away, wincing. The cut is deep, but clean now, and Colin swears he saw a hint of bone. Maggie shoos him to the other side of the room while she stitches Joe up. His stomach turns at seeing Joe like this: obviously old, vulnerable.

"Get out of here, kid," Maggie says, lifting her chin toward the door. "You're green."

"I've . . . never seen him like this."

"Mm-hmm. And how do you think he felt seeing you worse off more times than any of us can count?"

Colin knows she's right. He can remember being here or

in the hospital after a nasty crash on his bike, with several broken ribs and a huge gash on his scalp. He'd wondered at the time if he were going to die. It seemed so matter of fact to him: Either he would, or he wouldn't. It was simple. He never considered how they might feel to lose him.

"Go on. Get some sleep. I got this," Maggie says.

Colin looks at the man on the bed. "You good, Joe?"

Joe grunts as Maggie ties off a stitch. "I'll be back to work tomorrow," he says.

The nurse laughs. "The hell you will."

Colin is startled awake when Jay returns to the dorm room. Dim light from the hall slips across the walls and is gone just as quickly.

"You'd better be alone," Colin says into his pillow. It's been a crazy day, and the last thing he wants to deal with tonight is one of Jay's girlfriends sneaking into their room. If caught, all three of them would get demerits.

"I'm alone. Dude, I'm so tired."

Colin hears the rustle of fabric, Jay swearing as he trips, and the muffled clunk of keys and shoes hitting the rug. The mattress across the room creaks as he collapses on his bed. He moans something and rolls onto his stomach.

Jay's breathing evens out, and Colin opens an eye, trying to see the clock next to the bed. It's four in the morning, somehow both too early and too late to easily guess where Jay's been.

"Where were you?" he asks. Jay doesn't answer and he asks again, louder, reaching with his good arm and throwing an empty water bottle toward Jay's side of the room.

Jay startles, lifting his head slightly before dropping it down again. "I'm sleeping, man."

"Shelby?" Colin asks.

"Nah, she's such a scene queen. Not to mention insane."

Colin rolls his eyes and adds a snort so Jay hears his scorn even if he can't see it. All the girls Jay dates are insane.

"How's Joe?"

"His leg's pretty cut up," Colin says, scrubbing his face. "But otherwise he seemed okay when I left."

"He's, like, seven thousand years old," Jay says. "And nothing keeps Joe down. Not even his whole fucking porch collapsing with him on it."

"He's seventy-two," Colin grumbles. "And he's lucky. Half an inch to the left and he could have bled to death."

Jay answers this with the appropriate weight of silence. Sometimes, when the planets align, even he realizes when a smart-ass comment is unnecessary.

"Oh," he says with more enthusiasm. "I saw your girl."

"What?"

"Lucy. I saw her on my way here. She was sitting in front of Ethan Hall. I asked her if she needed help, but she said no."

"First of all, she's not my girl—"

Jay groans into his pillow.

"Trust me," Colin counters, opening his eyes to stare at the ceiling, wide-awake now. Scattered above him are glow-in-the-dark stars and a model of the solar system. His dad made it for him before he died, and it's followed Colin to every bedroom he's ever had. He sighs, rubbing his hands over his face again and wondering who this strange girl is and why in the hell she was sitting outside alone at four in the morning. "She told me to leave her alone."

"Christ." Jay groans. "It's like you know nothing about women. They all say shit like that, Col. They have to. It's, like, hardwired into their brains or something. They say that stuff to feel less guilty about wanting us to jump their bones. I thought everybody knew that."

"That's the kind of reasoning that will earn you a cell mate ironically named Tiny," Colin says.

"If I'm wrong, then why did I get laid last night and you were here with a pile of laundry and your hand?"

"I think that has less to do with me and more to do with the poor choices being made by the female students at Saint O's."

"Ah, right," Jay says thickly, already half asleep. He falls silent, and eventually his breaths even out. Inside, Colin is a tornado, unable to stop thinking about Lucy and why she might be sitting outside in the cold.

On that first day, she said she was here for him, and although he doesn't understand what that means . . . maybe part of him does. Clearly she looks different to Colin than she does to Jay, and it's hard to pretend that doesn't mean something. In fact, he's trying his best to ignore the caveman-asshole feeling he gets when he thinks that she's somehow his, but she's the one who put it out there, planting the idea like a tiny dark seed inside him.

And now he can't sleep. Great. Careful not to wake Jay, he grabs two hoodies and slips out of the room.

Lucy is exactly where Jay said she was, sitting on a bench in front of Ethan Hall with her back to Colin, facing the pond. In the low light, the water looks strangely inviting, smooth and dark and calm enough to make the moon and thousands of stars come see their reflections. Mist curls along the edges, like fingers luring its victims into the frigid blackness.

With a deep breath, he closes the distance between them.

"Hey," she says, without turning to see him.

"Hey."

Finally, she peeks at him out of the corner of her eye. "What are you doing up?" she asks. Her voice is always so raspy, like she doesn't use it much.

"Couldn't sleep. What about you?" As expected, she doesn't answer, so he places the sweatshirt on the bench next to her. "Jay said he saw you out here. I thought you might be cold." She's still wearing the plain blue oxford, and no way is it warm enough.

"Is that why you came out here?"

"Maybe." He rubs his hands together, blowing into them, and glances over at her.

"How is Mr. Velasquez?"

Colin wants to burst out in song he's so happy she's speaking to him. "He's going to be okay. By the time I left, he was back to his old self, insisting he could work from bed if Maggie would let him. I'm pretty sure Dot will be in the infirmary forcing food on him every twenty minutes."

Lucy stares at the pond for several beats, and Colin wonders if they've gone back to the silent game until she says, "Dot is your boss, right? You seem close to her."

"She is my boss." He smiles at her tentative efforts at making conversation. "But she's always been kind of like a grandmother to me."

"So, your kind-of-grandmother runs the kitchen and the headmaster is your godfather?"

"God-fahhthaahhh," Colin says in his best Brando, but Lucy only gives him an indulgent tiny-dimpled smile. "My parents died when I was little. They were teachers here and were close to Dot and Joe, who was a history teacher at the time. Dot hired me in the kitchen when I was fourteen, but she's been feeding me since I was five. I try and hang out with her as much as I can—like help her out on baking nights and stuff."

"I'm sorry your parents died."

He nods once. His stomach tightens, and he hopes they can move on from this topic. He doesn't want to think about his mother's spiral into psychosis, or the accident, or any of it. Almost everyone here knows the story, and he's grateful he never really has to tell it.

"And you've lived here since you were five?"

"We moved from New Hampshire when my parents got jobs here. They died when I was six, and I lived with Joe until I moved to the dorms freshman year." He bends so he can see her face more clearly. "What about you? Does your family live in town? I thought you were a commuter, but . . ." He trails off, and her silence rings back to him.

"Colin . . . ," she says finally.

Hearing her say his name does things to him. It gets him thinking of ways to make her say it again, and louder.

She looks up at him. "About what I said yesterday . . ."

"You mean the part where you asked me to stay away and here I am, finding you in the middle of the night?"

"No, not that." She sighs, tilting her head up to stare at the sky. "I'm glad you're here."

Well, that's the complete opposite of what he'd expected.

This girl is about as hard to read as a Cyrillic text. "Okay . . . ?"

The amount of attention she's giving the stars makes him wonder if she's trying to count them. Does she see something there that he can't?

"I shouldn't have said what I said yesterday. I want you around me. It's just that I don't think *you* should want to be around me." She takes a deep breath, like she's readying herself for a hard admission. "And now I sound crazy."

He laughs. She totally does. "A little."

"But I guess what I'm going to say *is* kind of crazy."

He stares at her, focusing on the way her teeth rake across her bottom lip. He already knows there's something different about her. And there's most definitely something strange about *them*. It's not until he's here, in this moment, that he realizes how much he's resisted thinking about how weird everything has been. After his mother's breakdown and the resulting death of both of his parents, he'd learned how to guard his mind so carefully, never lingering too long on his morbid history or—eventually—anything even mildly worrisome. The idea that there might really be something strange about Saint O's always struck Colin as legend, a way to make new kids behave, to lure the thin stream of tourists to the town nearby in the summer. But there's something paradoxical about sitting with an odd stranger at night next to a foggy pond that makes you see things more clearly.

Even so, his body fights the clarity. Colin can feel his thoughts clouding, letting go, as if he's supposed to not care how strange it seems. This time, he pushes back, listening instead to the rational side of his brain and sliding away from her the tiniest bit. He's always known Lucy wasn't a normal girl. Her hair is blond to him, not brown. She never seems cold; she never seems to eat. She's so . . . *different*. And when her eyes meet his and they are a slow, grinding, *anxious* gray—filled with metal and ice, worry and hope, and wholly unlike anything Colin has ever imagined before—he wonders for a flash if Lucy is even real.

Chapter 7 · HER

HER THROAT IS TIGHT, ALMOST AS IF INVISible hands strangle down the words inside her. But it isn't some strange, supernatural force urging her to keep her death a secret. It's fear, plain and simple.

Her murder—the blood and death and unanswered screams—is the sharpest memory of her life. She has no idea how much time has passed since she died, or whether anyone in this town was alive when it happened. A boy she kissed? A favorite teacher? Her parents? But after the week of wandering the grounds, of not knowing her name or who bought her the shoes on her feet, of feeling a rising panic stirred up by the sheer emptiness inside, knowing something about her life—even that it's over—was a bittersweet relief.

But whereas the human rules are always so straightforward—priority number one: stay alive—rules after death are a complete mystery. Was she somehow responsible for what happened to Joe? It feels that way. Worry fills her hollow chest with an icy chill at the thought that she could hurt someone without meaning to.

Now one thing is for sure: The only thing keeping her from being completely alone in this world is the nervous boy sitting next to her. And she *does* have a story to tell. It might be short and unreal and full of holes, but she can't keep it from him much longer. The question is whether he'll want to have anything to do with her once he hears.

"Lucy?" Colin asks, ducking to reclaim eye contact. "I didn't mean to make you feel like you have to talk. You don't have to tell me anything you don't want to."

"No, I'm putting the words together." She smiles weakly at him. Swallowing down her apprehension, she begins. "I woke up by the lake a few weeks ago." She points behind them, over her shoulder. "The day I saw you? I had only just stumbled off the trail."

His first reaction is silence, and it reverberates dully between them. She chances a look at his profile; he's squinting as if translating the words in his head. "Sorry. I don't know what you mean," he says finally. "You fell asleep out there? In the woods?"

"I *appeared* there," she says. "I don't know if I fell from the sky, or materialized out of thin air, or if I'd been sleeping there for a hundred years or a day. I woke up with no memories, no belongings, nothing."

"Really?" he asks, his voice high-pitched and shaky. He meets her eyes then, studying. She sees his expression cloud with something. Anxiety, maybe fear.

"Please don't be scared," she whispers. "I'm not going to hurt you." *At least, I don't think I am.* She slips her hands into her lap, as if they might be capable of something she hasn't yet discovered.

He shifts back, his angular jaw clenched tight, and it's clear in his expression the thought hadn't occurred to him until she'd said it.

She shakes her head. "Sorry, I'm not doing a good job explaining. See, I think I know why I don't remember anything and why it's hard to pick things up and why I don't need food or sleep or—your sweatshirt." She looks up at him, waiting for him to say something, but he doesn't. Licking her lips, her eyes pulsing with anxiety, she says, "I'm pretty sure I'm dead."

Chapter 8 · HIM

COLIN STARES AT HER, PART CONFUSED, PART horrified. "Okay?" he says, eyebrows slowly rising. Half of his mouth tilts in an unsure smile. *This can't be happening. It can't.* "Dead, huh?"

He blinks, pressing his hands to his eyes. He's officially lost his mind.

"Yeah." She stands and walks a few steps toward the pond.

Colin watches her as she gazes at her reflection and wonders if a dead girl would even have one. "So, when you said you're here for me, you mean, you came back from the *dead* for me?"

He can see her nod even though she faces away from him. "That's what I mean."

Dread, heavy and cold, settles between his ribs. *No, please no.* "But if you're dead, how can you open doors, or"—he points to the sweatshirt in her arms—"hold my hoodie, or even wear the school uniform?"

She shrugs. "I don't know. I'm pretty sure I look the same. Still tall and knobby. But I'm less clumsy." She looks over her shoulder and smiles at him sadly, then turns away again. "But I think I feel different, less solid, less . . ." She trails off, shaking her head. "Just *less*. I remember dying, but I'm here. That's all I can tell you."

Her long white-blond hair reaches the bottom hem of her blue shirt, and she looks so eerily beautiful in front of the pond with the perfectly sliced half-moon directly overhead. Suddenly the idea that he's losing his mind doesn't seem so impossible. Colin wonders if Lucy is even really here.

"Lucy, what color is your hair?"

She turns, a confused smile on her face. "Brown . . . ?"

With this, he drops his head into his hands and groans.

Lucy walks over, sitting beside him on the bench. "Why did you ask me that?"

"It's nothing."

She reaches out and takes his hand, but he immediately drops it, shooting up from the bench and wiping his palms on his thighs. "What the *hell*?"

His hand tingles where it touched hers, the sensation slowly fading into buzzing warmth. She felt like static, like charged particles in the shape of a girl. Colin stares at her and then puffs his cheeks out as he exhales.

"What is going *on*?" he murmurs, looking beyond her and up at the sky. He's suddenly remembering every burnout kid that's come back from the woods with a story about something they saw. How his mom used to talk about . . . *God*, he can't start thinking about that. The idea that Lucy is a Walker is impossible. The idea that Walkers are *real* is even more impossible. But either scenario makes him nearly choke with panic. Because if Walkers aren't real, then he is insane. And if they *are* real . . . then maybe his mother wasn't crazy after all.

And right now, in every other way, he feels sane. He does. He remembered to grab a jacket before he came outside; he's wearing shoes. He thinks he's speaking coherently. When he looks around, he doesn't see anything amiss—no spiders crawling up his body or stars weaving in the sky. Just a brown-haired girl who looks blond to him, says she's a ghost, and feels like static heat.

That's it. He's insane.

"Why didn't I think about it more?"

"Think about what?"

He waves a hand, blindly indicating the area around her head. "Your hair is blond, and Jay says it's brown. And your eyes? Oh God. What is going on?"

"My eyes? My hair?" Lucy bends to catch his gaze. "I look different to you?"

He shrugs stiffly. It feels like there is a stampede of horses galloping in his chest.

"I look different to you and it didn't freak you out *before*?"

"Not until now." He groans. "I guess I didn't want to think about it. I don't ever want to think about it."

"Think about what?"

"Nothing. Forget it." He shoves his hands into his hair, pulls.

"What did my hand feel like?" she asks, more insistent now.

"Um . . . ? Like . . ." He shakes his head, trying to find the right words. "Energy . . . and buzzing . . ."

She offers her hand again. After staring at it for what feels like an eternity, he steps forward, breathing heavily, and takes it. In his grip, her touch snaps against his skin before settling into a warm, vibrant hum. His voice shakes when he says, "Like energy and air? Um . . ." The hum begins to fill him with a longing so intense he feels disoriented. He releases it again and steps back, shaking both hands at his sides like he's flicking away water. "It's crazy, Lucy. This is *crazy*."

She steps toward him, but he takes another step back, needing space to breathe. He feels like the air is being sucked from his lungs when she's so close. As if reading his mind, she pulls her hands into the sleeves of her shirt.

But after a long moment, curiosity takes over. Reaching

forward, he tugs at her sleeve, pulling her hand out and toward him. His fingertips run over her palm before he turns her hand and presses it to his. Snapping, crackling energy followed by a delicious warmth and the relief of a strange, deep ache. The shape of her is obvious, but he can't close his hand over hers. When he presses too hard, her energy almost seems to repel his touch.

Is it really his mind doing this?

"Wild," he breathes. She seems to pull back, as if his touch borders on painful for her. "Are you okay?"

"Yeah," she says. "It's a lot to take. Your skin feels hot and so . . . alive? It's a little overwhelming for me."

Colin winces, looking away as he drops her hand and mumbles an apology.

"It's like I didn't exist, and then suddenly I was there on the trail," she says, explaining. "And that dress I was wearing? The thin flowery one? The little-girl sandals?" She grows quiet, and he looks up at her, waiting. "I think that's what I was buried in."

She's afraid, he realizes. Her eyes are this rich, grinding violet, flecked with metallic red. Hope and fear, he thinks, but mostly fear. Colin squeezes his eyes shut. He can read her *mood* in her *eyes.*

"Colin, are you okay?"

He presses the heel of his palms against his brows and

grunts, not a yes, not a no. He is most definitely *not* okay.

She steps closer. "After I saw you, I mean, I felt like I was supposed to find you, and I realize how that sounds. It sounds *creepy*. It's why I ran away."

"I almost went after you," he mumbles, but immediately wishes he hadn't. This conversation feels the same as barreling headlong into a sharp turn in the dark, on a new trail. He doesn't know how to navigate it.

"After that first day, I felt drawn to the school. I would sit outside and . . ." Out of the corner of his eye, he sees her look up at him. "You know when you hold your breath and everything gets tight and full and you wonder what's causing your chest to burn? I mean, it's only oxygen and carbon dioxide not being let in and out of your lungs, but it burns, you know?"

His eyes widen and he nods, barely. He knows exactly what she means.

"Seeing you was like being able to exhale and then inhale again." She searches his expression. "I know it sounds lame, but when I'm with you—even though nothing else makes sense—I'm glad I'm back."

She's said too much, and Colin doesn't know how to tell her that it's impossible she's dead, and this entire conversation is a figment of his imagination. But then again, if this is all in his head, should he even feel embarrassed for her that what she says can't possibly be true? How does one fight the spiral into insanity? His mother certainly didn't.

Rather, she fell into a depression so deep after his sister died that she wouldn't eat or move for days at a time. Finally, she insisted she saw her dead daughter walking around campus, lost her mind, and drove the living members of her family off a bridge.

He stares at her, feeling as if he's about to throw up. Her eyes are liquid metal infused with color. Her hair is white-blond only to him. She tells him she's returned from the grave, that she's here for *him*. "I . . . I need—"

"This sounds insane. You think I'm insane. I tota—"

"I'm sorry. I have to—"

"Please, Colin, believe me. I would never—"

He stands as she's midsentence, turning woodenly and walking as fast as he can back to the dorm.

Chapter 9 · HER

SHE WATCHES COLIN WALK AWAY AND CAN almost feel the frenzy of his reaction. The air seems to cool with every step he puts between them, but the imprint of his palm burns against hers. The conversation went both better and much worse than she expected. Better, because she was actually able to explain. Worse, because he left the way he did, looking as if he thought she was making it all up.

Standing, Lucy wraps herself in Colin's hoodie. She closes her eyes as she takes in his scent on the cotton. What else can she do but wait? She can't blame him for his panic and for the fear she saw so plainly on his face. The only way she can earn his trust is to let him see that all she wants is to be near him. She has time. She may even have forever.

With one final look, she begins the long walk back to her shed.

• • •

She sits by the statue of Saint Osanna the next morning with her arms wrapped around her legs pulled tight to her chest. She's grown used to the statue's strangeness; it's the only thing that feels as out of place in this living world as she does. The earliest risers shuffle past in the chilly air, talking, laughing, eating. Barely awake or focused. One with bright, flushed cheeks, one with wild red hair, and one with smooth, ebony skin. Despite this, Lucy is struck by how little there is to differentiate them. The space around each student feels dull and hollow.

Lucy thinks Colin must hate this weather, so drizzly and wet. Would he ride in this, hopping his bike from log to log, defying gravity on such simple engineering even in the rain? She wants to watch him like that—lost in something he loves.

Just as the sun finally reaches the tops of the buildings, Colin appears. He steps around the corner headed to work the morning shift in Ethan Hall, long legs, long strides, wild hair still too long. He pushes it off his brow and glances at his watch before starting to jog. Lucy ducks back into the shadows, pulling the hood of his hoodie up and over her head. Unlike every other student at Saint Osanna's, the space near Colin seems so full; the air is heavy with him. It distorts as if heated, swirling inward, wanting to be as close to him as she does.

"Good morning," she says into the cold, hoping it will pass along the message.

Chapter 10 · H IM

HAVE I TOLD YOU LATELY HOW AWESOME you are, Dot?" Jay asks, his mouth full and his second plate of French toast in front of him. They're sitting at the secret table in the kitchen, watching Dot and the other cooks prepare breakfast for hundreds of students about to pour in through the doors. Back here, they can eat in peace and steal extra bacon.

But this morning, Colin picks at his breakfast.

"If I'm so awesome, then why do I always have to take your dishes to the sink?" she asks over her shoulder.

Jay immediately changes the subject: "You going out after work?"

Dot steps up behind Colin, setting a carton of orange juice on the table before turning back to the giant range and flipping about seventeen pieces of French toast in ten seconds.

"Yep. I'm going to the poker tournament in Spokane. I pulled a royal flush right out of the gate last time. First deal of the night." She smiles and does a little dance as she begins slicing oranges.

"Dot, I'm not sure I like you driving all the way down there," Jay says.

"Oh please," she scoffs. "My eyesight is better than yours, kid. I've seen some of the girls you date." She makes exaggerated air quotes around the word "date."

"You wouldn't rather hang out with us than a bunch of old ladies? I'm hurt, Dot. If I were ten years older . . ." Jay trails off, wiggling his eyebrows at her.

"Jay, you are so creepy." Colin doesn't need any help feeling nauseous this morning. He got zero sleep. He barely wants to look up, for fear of seeing something new that confirms he's lost his mind.

He's a disaster.

Dot fills Jay's plate again and wipes her hands on her DON'T FRY BACON NAKED apron. "You know I'd go nuts if I never got away from this place."

Everyone grows silent, and Colin can feel them both watching him, waiting for his reaction to Dot's casual words. Colin: the orphan who has no idea what comes next and will probably never leave this tiny town.

To change the subject, he asks the first thing that comes

to mind—"Dot, you ever see a Walker?"—and immediately regrets it.

She stops slicing, knife hovering in the air. Colin can hear the rhythm of footsteps through the kitchen wall as students stomp their way into the dining hall. Finally, she shrugs. "I sure hope not, but sometimes . . . I'm not so sure."

It takes a few seconds for her words to make it from Colin's ears to the part of his brain that makes sense of them. "You think they exist, though?"

She turns and points the spatula at him. "Is this about your mom again? You know I loved her like a daughter."

Jay grows silent, his interest in his French toast suddenly renewed. He knows practically everything there is to know about Colin. He definitely knows the story surrounding how his family died, and more than that, he knows how much Colin hates to talk about it.

"I just want to know," Colin mumbles.

Turning back around, she flips more French toast in lingering silence before saying, "Sometimes I think they're with us and maybe we don't want to see."

Jay laughs as if Dot is joking. But Colin doesn't.

"I'm a crazy old lady about most things, but I think I'm right about this."

"What do you mean?" Colin begins tearing the edge of a campus newspaper into narrow strips, trying to look like this is just casual conversation. Like he's not hanging on her every word. "You believe the stories?"

"I don't know. We've all heard about the army man on the bench and the girl disappearing in the woods." She squints, considering. "Newspapers love to talk about how this place is different. Built on land where kids were buried. The fire that first week the school opened. We all know people have seen things, and more than a few. Some a bit clearer than others," she adds quietly. "Who even knows what's real anymore?"

Colin pokes at his food. "So you think they're all over, then? Ghosts and spirits and stuff? Not only here at Saint O's?"

"Maybe not 'all over,' but I bet there's always a few around. Least, that's what people say." Colin wonders if he's imagining the way she looks out the window, off into the direction of the lake.

"If you haven't seen them, how do you know?" Jay asks, joining in. "Some of the stuff I've heard—it's pretty crazy. You'd have to be nu—" He stops, glancing quickly in Colin's direction before stuffing his mouth full of French toast again.

"If you think this world isn't full of things you don't understand, Jay, you're too dumb to use a fork unsupervised." Dot's quiet laugh softens her words.

Colin feels sort of wobbly all of a sudden, like his insides have liquefied. He's not sure which scenario would be worse:

that he's lost his mind, or that the stories he's dismissed his entire life could be true. That Lucy could be dead.

"Why are they here, do you think?" he asks, quieter now.

She pauses, looking over her shoulder and raising an eyebrow. "You're taking this pretty seriously, kiddo." Turning back, she doesn't answer right away and begins chopping a large pile of dried cranberries. The sharp, fresh scent fills the space. "Who knows? Maybe to watch over us," she says, shrugging a shoulder. "Or to meet us so that we'll know someone when we're gone." She drops the entire pile into the mixer. "Or maybe they're just stuck here. Maybe they need closure."

"Closure like they want *revenge*?" Colin asks.

"Well, if they're bad, I reckon it's pretty easy to tell. I've always figured anyone from the other side is undiluted—good or bad. Life is all gray. Dying has to be pretty black or white."

She pulls the dough out and begins forming rolls as Colin watches, just as he has hundreds of mornings in his lifetime. Somehow every movement she makes feels more substantial, like he never noticed how much her experience weighs until now.

"Thanks, Dot."

"For what? Waxing poetic about dead folks?"

"I mean, when you're not talking about the hot barista at the coffee shop or the benefits of pineapple for your sex life, you're all right."

"I try." She points to the cabinet above the counter. "Grab my baking sheets."

Even after the familiar routine of helping Dot bake, Colin doesn't feel much better. If anything, he feels worse. He can count on one hand the number of times in the past ten years he's felt this mopey, but the things Dot said were the same kind of things he's heard his whole life: vague slogans about the afterlife and how Walkers probably exist and maybe his mother wasn't insane. It's the kind of reassurance that's easy to give because, ultimately, it doesn't matter anymore whether she was. She's gone.

She's gone, and his father is gone, and his sister, Caroline, has been gone even longer. Now Colin might be losing it too. It's the first time since his parents died that Colin is faced so baldly with the knowledge that he's completely alone in this world. No matter how much they care, Dot and Joe and Jay can't help him with this one.

Dot finds him sitting on the back step, drawing in the lacy ground frost with a long stick in his good hand. She opens the door, and warm air blows against the back of his neck.

"What are you doing out here?"

"Thinking." He wipes his face and she catches it, moving to sit by him.

"Are you upset, baby?"

"I'm good."

"You're not," she says, putting a warm hand on his knee. "Don't lie to me. You're the boy who never stops smiling. It makes it easy to spot when something's off."

Colin turns to look at her, and her face softens when she sees his red-rimmed eyes. "I'm losing it, Dot. Like, I seriously wonder if I'm crazy."

He hates the way her face falls and how guilty she looks, as if she's responsible for the weight of his tragic life. "You're not."

"You don't even know why I think that."

"I can hazard a guess," she says quietly. "You want to talk about it?"

"Not really." He gives her a small smile. "But thanks."

"I've seen some crazy things in my day. And Lord knows you've got better reasons than the rest of us to have some wrinkles in your sanity, but will it help if I tell you I know for a fact you're as sane as they come?"

Colin laughs humorlessly. "But how could you know that?"

Her expression steadies. "Because I know."

"Maybe I'm imagining you saying that. It's okay, Dot. I'm okay."

She studies him for a beat before pinching him hard on the arm. He cries out, immediately rubbing the spot. Dot has a pretty mean pinch. "What the hell, Dot?"

"See?" she says with a quiet laugh. "You didn't imagine that. And for someone who's survived things that would have left anyone else in the ground *and* lives their days like there will never be any more, sure, you sometimes give me good reason to think you're nuts. But if you're crazy, then I'm young and ugly, and we know I'm neither."

Colin makes a quick trip to check in on Joe before heading to class and is relieved to see his godfather sitting up, enjoying an enormous plate of French toast and bacon.

"Dot delivery?" he asks.

Joe nods, pointing with his fork to the chair beside the bed. "You have time to sit?"

"A couple minutes."

Colin sits, and the warm silence fills the space between them. It's their familiar routine: quiet sitting, little conversation. Colin looks out the window, watching students trudge to class while Joe eats.

"Sleep good?" Joe asks around a bite.

"I should be asking you that."

"I slept like the dead," Joe says. "Maggie pumped me full of painkillers."

Nodding, Colin says, "Yeah, you were looped."

"Who's the girl?"

Once he processes the question, Colin's heart seems to

freeze, and then it explodes into a gallop. "Which girl?"

"The one who came to me on the porch. The brown-haired one. Wanted to help, but said she couldn't."

"She said that?"

Joe sips his coffee, eyeing Colin. "You're going to think I'm losing my mind, kid, but I've got to know: Is she beautiful or horrible?"

"What?" Colin moves closer.

Looking quickly up at the door to ensure they're alone, Joe whispers, "The girl. Is she beautiful or horrible?"

Colin whispers, "Beautiful."

"I thought . . . Her face melted right off and then she became the most amazing thing I'd ever seen."

Colin is caught by a head rush so powerful, he needs a few seconds before he can answer. "It's probably the pain meds," he says, swallowing. "They make you see crazy things."

"No, kiddo," Joe mumbles, eyes trained on Colin. "That was before I fell."

"I . . ." Colin feels like his entire world has closed in around him. "You must be remembering it wrong."

Joe doesn't respond, and Colin reluctantly continues. "Her name is Lucy."

Joe's eyes close, and he shakes his head. "Well, I'll be damned."

Bile rises, thick in Colin's throat. "Joe?"

"Lucy was . . . the name of a girl who was killed here. Ugly time for this place, must be some ten years ago now. Looks just like her. I'm sure that's why my mind went off." He laughs, taking a bite of orange. "Must be the pain meds after all."

Colin ducks into a computer lab, leaving the lights off to remain hidden.

He remembers the first time he did this—high and drunk with Jay after a bonfire and ghost stories on the edge of the woods—sneaking in to see if any of the gruesome stories could actually be true. There were more hits than he would have imagined for something most people wrote off as folklore. Stories of a place where students seemed to die at a higher rate than any other boarding school in the country. But how many schools have such harsh winters and enormous, wild grounds? Colin never understood why it was a surprise that kids died or disappeared more frequently here than other places from things like exposure, pneumonia, and suicide. Even stoned he didn't believe any of the legends.

He has a vague memory of seeing the one Joe mentioned, about the girl who died. Most websites have information about the murderer and his subsequent trials and execution; because the murder happened a decade ago, there are only two news stories online from the time of the killing. Colin clicks a link with a photo, and covers his mouth with a cupped hand to keep from crying out when he sees her face.

Her hair is brown, her features less glasslike, but it's her. Beneath the photo is a story from the *Coeur D'Alene Press*.

Monday's arraignment of accused serial murderer Herb August Miller, who is being held for the killing of seventeen-year-old Lucia Rain Gray as well as seven other teens over the past eight years has been continued to June 1.

Prosecutors allege the 42-year-old former headmaster of Saint Osanna's boarding school outside of Coeur D'Alene stalked Lucia for several weeks prior to the murder. The murder of a teen at his school indicates Miller, who previously only selected victims far from his home state, was growing increasingly confident in his ability to evade law enforcement. Miller allegedly invited her to his cabin, drugged her, and took her to the woods, where he slit her throat before cutting open her chest. In what is now believed to be his gruesome trademark, Miller then removed her heart.

Police found Miller attempting to bury the body on a trail beside the school after a young boy saw him carrying a struggling girl into the woods. The boy alerted a staff member, who called 911.

"This is a killer we've been hunting for eight years and who has caused unspeakable heartache to many families across the country. It's possible he would have simply carried on at the school if it hadn't been for the bravery of the young boy in finding help," Coeur D'Alene sheriff Mo Rockford said at a press conference early Friday. "The capture of Herb Miller is a huge weight off the minds of national law enforcement, and this community owes a debt of gratitude to the boy and the staff for making the prompt call."

Miller has been indicted on seven counts of first-degree murder. The state is seeking the death penalty in light of the gruesome aggravating torture and mutilation factors. Seventeen-year-old Gray was the youngest victim of Miller's killing spree.

This isn't the first round of tragedy for the school, which was built on a burial site for settlers moving west and which lost two young children in a fire two days after the school opened in 1814. Saint Osanna's has been struck by tragedy regularly over the years, with its proximity to the woods, glacial lakes, and harsh elements resulting in a number of student and visitor deaths.

Colin stops, closing the window on the screen before anyone sees what he's reading. "Lucia Rain Gray," he says aloud. He lets his heart take over every sensation in his body, pounding relentlessly in his chest and throat and ears. Lucy was telling the truth.

Colin doesn't see her all day. She doesn't show up for history, and she's not outside at lunch. He doesn't find her anywhere on campus, and he grows more frantic as he circles buildings and checks every classroom. He tells himself he'll stop looking after this preliminary search but gives that up after gym, dressing quickly so he can scout the woods bordering school before seventh period.

Days go by, and Jay tells him that she's stopped coming to his English class, too. The desk she sat in that first day stays empty. Colin doesn't understand why that feels like a punch to the stomach. If this situation is as crazy as he keeps telling himself, then why does he even care? Why does he keep rubbing his palm, trying to remember what it felt like to touch her? Why does he want to do it again?

He wants to remember: Her skin was warmer than air, but not by much. Her eyes change, like ripples in a pond. She's never cold, even with the strongest wind outside. Except for a pencil on that first day, he's never really seen her touch anything. And even that looked hard, like she had to work at keeping it between her fingers. Her eyes, when she asked about Joe, changed colors as he watched, from deep gray to an aching, honest blue.

He considers leaving campus to try and find her but has no idea where she even goes when she isn't here. Does she vanish into thin air?

By Friday night, Colin has the same feeling he gets when he doesn't ride his bike for a long stretch—antsy and like something is growing inside him and pushing his vital organs into a tiny corner in his chest. He's worried that Lucy has left, but he's even more worried that she's simply evaporated. That she reached out to him and his rejection somehow sent her away. He takes his bike to the woods, riding the narrow trails along the rickety boards he and Jay propped there years ago. He hops boulders and streams, crashes down hills. He beats himself up until he's bruised and sore. He does everything he can to clear his mind, but nothing works. He eats dinner and tastes nothing. The heat in his dorm room feels claustrophobic, oppressive.

Sitting on his bed, he thumbs through a bike magazine before tossing it to the floor and flopping backward, fists to his eyes.

Across the room, Jay pauses his repetitive bouncing of a tennis ball against the wall. "Do you have any idea where she is?"

"No. The last place I saw her was . . ." His words fade away as he registers that maybe it doesn't matter where he saw her last. Maybe what matters is where this started for her.

"Colin?"

"I think I might know. I'll catch you later."

Jay glances out the darkening window, concerned, but keeps any objections to himself. "Just be careful, man."

Colin takes off down the path toward the park, headed for the strip of chain-link fence that he and Jay busted when they were freshmen, which probably hasn't even been discovered by the groundskeepers. It leads directly to where he thinks Lucy awoke by the lake.

The trail is only about a mile long, but he's practically frozen by the time he gets there. Now that he knows at least *some* of the legends might be true, Colin feels an instinctive shudder of fear as he nears the water. Once the sound of his sneakers on the gravel quiets, it's eerily silent. The idea that Lucy could be sitting out here alone makes his hands shake in a way that has nothing to do with the cold. Or maybe it's because he's afraid she's not here at all.

He looks around, hunching forward against the wind. The sky looms heavy and dull overhead, the clouds so thick it's impossible to tell where one stops and the next begins.

There's an old dock not far from where the trail ends.

It's missing a lot of planks, and the wood that remains is waterlogged and decomposing, but despite this whole area being off-limits, the most daring kids still occasionally horse around on it in the summer. Now, though, it's covered in a light dusting of snow, and for some reason, Colin isn't surprised when he sees Lucy sitting at the end of it, perched on an uneven outcropping of broken and rotting boards. Long, blond strands fall almost to her waist, and the wind lifts them, tangling them in the breeze that whips across the lake.

The wood creaks beneath the weight of his careful steps. She's changed her clothes, though her signature boots sit unlaced on the dock just behind her. The hoodie he left for her rests in her lap.

Now that he's here, he realizes he's spent more time trying to figure out how to find her than how to talk to her. Staring at her back, he files through appropriate openers. He needs to say that he's sorry, that he's a clueless boy who has no idea what to do with a living girl, never mind one who isn't. Maybe he should tell her that he's an orphan and probably needs an anchor as badly as she does.

Slowly, he walks toward her. "Lucy?" he says, and hesitates, taking in the scene in front of him. Her skirt is pulled up above her knees and her skin is pale and perfect in the retreating light, not a scar or a freckle anywhere.

"It's not cold," she says, looking down to where her legs

dangle in the water below. It has to be thirty degrees out, and the lake has that syrupy look, where the algae is gone and the water looks like it's hovering between liquid and solid. Colin's limbs ache watching the icy water lap against her skin. "I mean, intellectually, I know it's cold," she continues, "but it doesn't feel that way. I can feel the sensation of the cold water, but the temperature doesn't bother me like it should. Isn't that strange?"

The wind seems to have stolen his words, and he's not sure how to respond. So instead, he reaches out, placing a hand on her shoulder. Her eyes widen at the contact, but she doesn't say anything.

"I didn't know where you were," he says finally. "Are you okay?"

"I'm okay," she whispers.

He looks at his hands in amazement. He can feel the weight of her hair as it moves over his fingers, the texture of the skin on her neck, but where there should be warmth, there's only the tingling sensation of movement, a stirring breeze. It's as if whatever is keeping her here—keeping her body upright, her limbs moving forward—is pulsing beneath his fingertips.

They stare at each other for a long stretch, and he finally whispers, "I'm sorry."

A smile twitches at the corners of her lips, dimple poking

sweetly into her cheek, before the grin spreads across her face. Her eyes morph from dark to pale yellow in the light of the bright, full moon. "Don't be."

He's not sure how to reply because whether she needs an apology or not, he feels like a jerk for disappearing that night.

"Do you want to go for a walk?" she asks.

He smiles and moves back as she pulls her feet from the water, and he uses the hoodie to dry her legs. They feel like ice against his fingertips. Her eyes drop, and *holy shit*, he thinks she's looking at his mouth. Suddenly, his head is full of other possibilities: What would it be like to kiss her? Does her skin feel the same everywhere? What does it taste like?

"When did you do that?" she asks, pulling on her boots.

He struggles to rein in his thoughts. Reflexively, he licks his lips and realizes she means his piercing. "My lip?"

"Yeah."

"Last summer."

She pauses, and it gives him a minute to watch the breeze whip her hair all over the place, like it weighs less than the air. She takes a while to say anything else, though, so he watches her lace up her boots while she thinks. "The school doesn't have rules about that?"

"The rules are so old that piercings never made it into the book, but I dare you to try and wear short pantaloons to class. Dot and Joe say I can look like a 'no-good punk' as long as I act like a gentleman. You don't like it?"

"No, I do. It's just—"

"You sound surprised that you do." He laughs, watching her stand.

"I don't think many boys did that when I was in high school. At least not boys like you."

"'Boys like me?'"

"Nice boys. Burnout boys would be inked and pierced and rowdy."

"Oh, I'm definitely rowdy."

Her lips curve in a half smile. "I don't doubt that."

"And how do you know I'm nice? Maybe I'm a burnout with a ghost fetish."

She gapes at him, surprised, and he wants to grab a rock and crack himself over the head with it. But then she throws her head back and laughs this ridiculous loud, snorting laugh.

Colin exhales a shaky breath. Apparently ghost jokes are okay.

She grins up at him. "You *are* nice. I can see it all over your face. You can't hide a thing."

He watches her eyes shift from green to silver in the light, and her lips skew into his favorite playful smile. He considers her hair, her eyes, the way she fades into the background for everyone but him. "Neither can you."

"Really?"

"At least, not from me."

Her smile leaves her lips but stays in her eyes, even when she blinks away. "Good."

Something flaps in a cluster of reeds next to the trail, and the last forgotten leaves crunch beneath their shoes as they walk deeper into the woods. Their steps are evenly paced, but Lucy's seem lighter than his, quieter somehow.

And now that he's starting to let himself believe, he sees other differences: Her cheeks aren't flushed from the cold. While each of his breaths seems to float like small puffs of smoke in the air in front of him, the space in front of Lucy's lips is noticeably empty.

Beside him, she looks around as if she can see every detail in the light of the moon, and it makes him wonder, is she like a cat? Does she have amazing night vision? Although it seems strange that there would be any off-limit topics now that they've both acknowledged that she is dead and he isn't, he feels like it would be strange to ask her what it's like.

"So you believe me?" she asks.

He considers telling her what Joe said, but opts instead for the simpler answer: "I looked up your story. Saw your picture. You were killed by the former headmaster, out by this lake."

She nods, staring out at the water, and seems largely

uninterested in what he's told her. "I wonder why I like being out here, then. That's sort of morbid."

"Is it weird to not remember everything?"

She picks up a leaf and examines it. "I guess. The weird thing is it's all or nothing, and about the strangest things. I remember with crazy detail a bouquet of flowers my dad bought me for a holiday, but I can't remember his face."

"Wow." Colin feels lame but, really, what can he say to that?

"The other night I was thinking about it. You know those game shows where someone stands in a phone booth and money shoots up from the floor and the person gets to grab as much as they can in a minute?"

He has no idea what she's talking about but goes with it. "Sure."

"Well, some of the bills are twenties, maybe a few hundreds but most of them are ones. So it looks like it's a ton of money blowing around, but it's not. And no matter what you end up with, you're happy because you have money in your hands."

She glides around a boulder in the middle of the trail, and he hops on it and then leapfrogs onto a long, rotting log. He can feel her watching him out of the corner of her eye.

"Anyway, I feel like at some point after I died, I must have had a minute in a booth with my memories and I grabbed a couple of fives, but mostly ones."

"So, in other words, you're happy to have something—"

"But what I ended up remembering was pretty useless," she finishes, smiling wryly.

"Not enough green to buy much, eh? Like who you were or why you're here?"

She laughs, her eyes glowing with relief. "Exactly."

It's the relief that kills him because he's starting to believe that if one person was supposed to understand her from the start, it was him. "I'm sorry I was a dick."

"You weren't a *dick*." She snorts. "God, I forgot how much I love that word used like that. And 'douche.'"

"That one applies too. You were all, 'Hey, I died,' and I was like, 'Wow, that sucks. I gotta jet.'"

She laughs again, and this time it's loud enough to echo off the tree trunks around them. He loves hearing it, loves how someone so finespun could make such a big sound. "Well, how were you supposed to react? Actually, I think I'd have been more worried if you'd been totally calm about it. I would have probably thought, 'Maybe this guy is a burn-out with a ghost fetish.'"

It's Colin's turn to laugh, but it quickly fades away. "My mom started seeing things. It's how she . . ." He pauses, stopping to face her. "See, a few weeks after we moved here, my older sister, Caroline, was hit by a delivery truck heading into school. She was on her bike. Never saw it coming, I guess.

Mom kind of lost it, went off the deep end. Then, after about a month, she started saying she saw Caroline on the road a few times. One night, she got us in the car, told us we were going out for ice cream in town, and then drove the car off a bridge."

"Colin," Lucy whispers, horrified, "that's awful."

"My parents died. I survived. So, when you told me you thought you were dead, I guess you understand why I flipped out."

"God, yeah." She pulls her hair off her face, exposing every inch of smooth, pale skin. She's so beautiful; he wants to feel his cheek against hers. "I'm so sorry."

He waves her off, hating to linger on this. "Where did you go the last few days?"

"I don't really remember what I did, but I'm sure I was around. Here, or in the field. I can't leave campus grounds."

"You mean, at all?"

She shakes her head and watches him a minute longer before dropping her leaf on the path. It disappears almost immediately into the mud. It's his turn to stare, watching her profile as she looks out across the water.

"Lucy?"

She turns to him with a smile. "I like it when you say my name."

Colin smiles back, but it turns down at the corners after a beat. "*Do* you know why you're back here?"

She shakes her head. "Are you scared of me?"

"No." He should be, absolutely. And he wants to say more, to talk about the school and the stories that surround it, about the Walkers and how maybe that's what she is, and are they *all* trapped by the gate? He definitely *should* be scared. But now that he's with her, close enough to touch, he can feel only relief and that strange, intoxicating longing.

Suddenly walking side by side isn't enough anymore.

"Hold my hand?" he asks.

She coils her long fingers around his, both cool and warm, solid but retreating. He can feel points of contact against his skin, but never in the same place for very long. When he squeezes, a current runs through his fingers, making his muscles relax. She's like a constellation, alive against his hand.

When he looks up, her eyes are closed, her teeth biting down on her lower lip.

"What's wrong?" he asks. "Does this hurt you?"

Her eyes open, and hunger and joy swirl green and auburn inside. "Have you ever been in a pool and you hop out and jump right into a hot tub?"

He laughs. He knows exactly the feeling she means, flushing hot and amazing, but also such an intense change it feels like every nerve ending is firing. "Yeah. And how it settles into soothing hot instead of that intense oh-my-god-yes hot."

She nods. "I keep waiting for the settling." Her eyes fall closed again. "It never comes. When you're touching me, it's like the first moment of submersion, always. It's a relief so overwhelming it almost takes my breath away."

Colin's heart beats heavily inside his chest. Tentatively, she reaches up and brushes a trembling finger along the ring in his lip. "Did it hurt?"

"A little."

"The metal must be cold," she whispers, and he feels himself leaning toward her. "What does it feel like?"

"For me or for you?" he asks, grinning.

Chapter 11 · Her

F OR ME," SHE ANSWERS, REACHING TO PRESS A
fingertip against the cool metal.

*"Wrap your hand around the pipes," the teacher said.
"The cold and the warm together feel scorching."*

*Lucy released the pipes with a surprised hiss, looking up at the
teacher in shock.*

*"Some skin receptors sense cold, some heat. Both are sent to the
brain, but the brain hears these mixed signals as powerful heat. It's
a form of perception we call paradoxical warmth."*

Lucy gasps at the perfect memory and the intensity of the
touch, pulling her finger back in surprise.

Colin's lip ring was cold from the wind and his skin
was warm with blood, and like the pipes, the feeling of his
lip pressed to her fingertip was scorching. And although
she understands the science behind the pipes experiment,

there can't be any explanation in the world for what happened between them just now. For the brief contact—a few seconds—the air incinerated.

Colin swallows, his eyes never leaving her mouth. He blinks a few times. Is he going to kiss her? Her skin warms at the thought, and the closer he leans, the more flooded she becomes with a strange, intoxicating relief. It overwhelms her like a head rush.

Lucy knows now that she's been kissed before—even that she's not innocent—but it felt nothing like this. Memories of those monochromatic touches pale next to the vibrancy of Colin's skin. But this reaction turns sour in her thoughts, unsettling her. If the simple touch of his lip on her fingertip felt so intense, what would it feel like to actually kiss him? She's afraid she'd be unable to process so much sensation. And so she turns back to the trail, eyes closed for a moment as she savors the feel of the cold metal ring, the heat of his breath as he exhaled against her fingertip.

She's taken a few steps before she hears Colin move to catch up with her. If he's surprised by her reaction, he doesn't show it, and they continue to walk in silence. Every few steps, Colin's hand brushes against hers. Eventually, he gives up pretense and wraps his fingers around hers again. So carefully, just like the first time.

He bends to meet her eyes. "Still okay?" he asks adorably,

somehow managing to look both confident and completely unsure of himself. She can only nod, overwhelmed by his simple touch. His skin feels hot and alive, as if with each of his heartbeats she can sense the surge of blood in his veins.

He smiles widely. "So, if you can't ever leave campus, where do you live?"

Lucy takes him to her little home and is impressed when he doesn't look shocked to find her living in an abandoned shed beside the school. She lights the small gas lamp in the corner before stretching out her arms, almost touching the wall on either side. "This is home sweet home."

He folds his long frame on an old crate and she sits on another and tells him everything she remembers. The fragmented pieces from her human life are random and meaningless, but he listens like each piece is a part of a larger, greater story. When she starts to tell him everything she remembers since waking on the trail, she sees a shadow flicker on his face for a brief moment, as if he's sad that the story of her first life adds up to so little. But her memories from this life are so numerous in comparison, she treats them like gems. He watches and listens as he leans back against the dilapidated wall of the shed.

She tells him about sitting outside the school and watching students in their everyday routine and how she didn't feel even a single moment of envy; she simply felt as if she was waiting. She tells him that she didn't feel the need to find her parents even though they might still be alive and how that lack of compulsion worries her somehow. Wouldn't a girl want to join her peers? Wouldn't she go straight to her family?

She brings him up to the present moment with a simple, "I told you I died. You freaked. I wandered around and forced myself to stay away from the school and then . . . you came and found me. The end."

He laughs. "I had no idea you could talk so much."

"I haven't wanted to talk to anyone else."

His smile fades, and he looks around, like he's seeing the shed for the first time since he arrived. "Don't you want to be in a more comfortable place?" he asks. "It's kind of weird that you're alone out here."

"I like it. It feels like mine now, and it's clean and quiet and no one has ever come over here."

He hesitates and then glances down at his phone. "I should go." She watches him brush the leaves and pine needles from his pants. When he looks up, he tilts his head, wincing. "I can't leave you here."

"I've been here for almost three weeks now."

"Come with me, just tonight." He senses her hesitation and pushes on. "Just until we scare up some blankets and make this whole place less . . ."

"Rustic?" she offers.

"I was going to say creepy. We should *aim* for rustic."

We.

She follows him down the trail, unable even in her weightlessness to match his grace over logs and through the marshy bits. All of their talking seems to have emptied them of words, and they move through the moonlight in an easy silence until the hulking gray buildings of Saint Osanna's appear above the tips of the trees. The idea of a dorm room, of a comforter, a rug, and walls that keep the elements at bay seems almost decadent.

Colin's room screams "boy." Muted earth tones, bike magazines, dirty laundry. Greasy bolts on his desk, a soda can, a row of trophies. She can see, beneath the layers, strong architectural bones: dark wood windowpanes, polished hardwood. The shelves built deep into the walls are now cluttered with papers and bike parts and small stacks of photographs.

"Quite a man lair," she says. Colin flops down on his bed and groans a relaxed-happy noise, but Lucy doesn't want to sit down. She wants to go through his stuff. She has two school uniforms, a pair of boots, and a shed. She's fascinated with all of his *things*.

"A brown comforter? How understated." She smiles and runs her hand along the edge of his mattress.

"I like to imagine I'm sleeping in the dirt," he jokes. She

feels him watching her while she studies a pile of clothing near the closet door. He throws an arm over his face and mumbles beneath it, "Jay and I . . . we're not so skilled with the cleaning."

"Yeah . . ." She pushes aside a pair of socks on a shelf so she can read what books he has stacked there.

"At least my sheets are clean." He immediately clears his throat, and she continues to stare at his books. Awkward settles like a thick gel into the room. "I didn't mean that. Yes, I mean, my sheets *are* clean but . . . for sleeping. Oh my God, never mind."

Lucy is already laughing. "I don't sleep."

"Right. Right." He's quiet for several beats before asking, "Won't you get bored?"

"It's nice to be near someone. I promise I won't draw a mustache on you in your sleep."

He yawns suddenly, widely. "Well, if you do, give me a Fu Manchu. Go big or go home." He stretches as he stands, and a strip of bare stomach is exposed beneath his shirt. Heat pulses through her, and she wonders if it's possible for him to notice the way her entire body seemed to ripple. Hooking a thumb over his shoulder, he says he's going to go brush his teeth.

Without Colin's eyes on her, she feels free to look around a little. Not to dig in his drawers or look under his mattress, but to take a closer look at the pictures on his desk, the trophies on his shelves.

He's won races and stunt contests. He snowboards, and from the looks of it, he used to play hockey. Ribbons and plaques line two shelves, and there are so many, she quickly stops trying to read each one.

On his desk there's a picture of a small boy with a man who looks like she imagines Colin will in his thirties—thick, wild, dark hair and bright eyes. Scattered on his desk are papers and Post-its and a few pay stubs from what she assumes is the dining hall. Tucked under his keyboard and sticky with spilled soda is a picture of Colin at a school dance with a short brunette. His hands are on her hips. She's leaning back into him, and they're not just smiling tight, staged smiles. They're laughing together.

A tight ball forms in her chest and expands into her throat. The way his hands rest on her hips is mesmerizing, as if she is firm and his and *there*. Lucy doesn't know how his touch will ever feel normal to her and whether she'll ever be able to be close to him the way she imagines this girl was.

The skin on the back of her neck burns warm when she feels him return to the room, and she quickly puts the picture back where it was. She thinks he notices, but he doesn't say anything and neither does she. It's too soon for the conversation of what they are, let alone who that girl was. Even so, Lucy can't quite stop the jealous fire that licks at her insides at the image of Colin with someone else.

"I realize this is lame," he says, "but I'm actually really tired."

The clock reads two a.m. "God. Of course you are. Sorry . . ."

With a small smile, he climbs under the covers and pats the mattress next to him. Lucy climbs onto the foot of the bed, careful to stay on top of the comforter, and sits cross-legged facing him.

"You're going to watch me?"

"Until you're asleep and I can sneak a permanent marker from your desk."

He smiles and curls onto his side. "Okay. 'Night, Lucy."

Questions pulse in her mind in the blackness of the room, begging for answers. About her, about him. About why the universe sent her back here and why he seems to be the only thing that matters. "'Night, Colin."

"Hey there, new girl." Jay grins, pulling out a chair next to his and patting the seat.

Colin ignores this, pulling a chair out for Lucy across the table from his friend. "Lucy, Jay. Her name is Lucy."

"Lucy is a sweet name, but New Girl is better. It's mysterious. You can be whoever you want to be." Leaning forward, Jay gives Lucy his best smoldering smile. "Who do you want to be, New Girl?"

Lucy shrugs, thinking. She'd never considered this aspect

of being new, and untethered, and unknown. Everything she's done has been on instinct. She looks through the open doorway to the dining hall, where most students eat. All of the girls bleed together into a single, boring uniform.

"I play bass in an all-female band called the Raging Hussies, have a math fetish, and open beer bottles with my teeth." She grins at him. "One of those is true."

Jay's eyes narrow. "Please tell me it's the band one."

"My vote is teeth," Colin says.

"Sorry," she says with mock sympathy. "Math."

Jay shrugs, taking a bite of bacon. "That's also hot. I mean, whether or not you play the bass with a bunch of hussies, you like the lake. *That* makes you interesting."

"What's interesting about liking the lake?" Lucy turns and searches Colin's face for explanation, as if trying to decipher if he's told Jay her secret. "What's not to like about it?"

"I love the lake," Colin says with an easy smile, apparently enjoying the interaction. "Tons of bike trails, and no one else ever goes out there." With a wink, he adds, "I'm not afraid of what's out at the lake."

"I don't care about the stories," Jay says. "It just *looks* creepy. In the summer, it gets so hot and muggy that everything in the air warps. In the winter, the glacial lake freezes and everything turns blue." Jay spears a forkful of eggs and points them in Lucy's direction. "You've heard about the Walkers, right?"

Lucy shakes her head, cold spreading from her fingertips up her arm. Instinctively, she shifts closer to Colin.

"People say Saint O's is haunted. And *no* one goes to the lake; some people around here claim they've seen a girl walking around under the water. Hell, this whole place is supposed to be haunted."

Lucy shivers, but only Colin notices. He puts a gentle hand on her thigh below the table.

"But if you want to know what I think," Jay begins, and the eggs fall back onto his plate with a quiet smack. "People don't like walking all the way down there because they're a bunch of lazy asses who'd rather sit in their rooms and open beer bottles with their teeth."

"I see," Lucy says. Jay watches her, expression unreadable.

"Jay and I aren't scared of ghosts," Colin says.

Jay laughs and shoves his plate away. "No, dude. I don't *believe* in ghosts."

When Lucy looks over at Colin, he's watching her, grinning with their secret in his eyes.

Lucy creates a schedule built of classes with teachers who never take roll. Only one class is with Colin—history—but it's in the middle of the day when she needs to see his reassuring half smile, his fingers tapping out an impatient rhythm on his desk, the fingers that she knows want to touch her.

It's harder than she'd have imagined to be, well, nothing. She watches everyone constantly, wondering if some phrase, some small mannerism, will spark a memory or a hint of what she was and of how she can stay earthbound and leave the school someday with Colin.

She finds herself thinking back on what Jay said about the Walkers and the stories that surround the school. She knows she should have asked more questions, should ask them still, but the instinctual tug she feels to be near Colin builds like static in her ears, blocking everything else out. Her questions, her doubts, her *purpose,* seem secondary to the corporeal buzzing she feels beneath her skin in his presence. She's as physically drawn toward Colin as she is repelled by the gate.

"Lucy?" Her head snaps up at the sound of her name, all thoughts of Walkers gone. It takes a minute to remember where she is—French class, with Madame Barbare, who Lucy doesn't think has ever noticed her before. Like most teachers at Saint Osanna's, Madame Barbare assumes that if you've made it past the security gates and are wearing a uniform, you obviously belong in her class even if you're not on her roll.

Her voice echoes in Lucy's ears, reverberating up into her skull, where it bounces around uncomfortably. It's the first time in days someone other than Colin has said her name. "Y-yes?" Only when Lucy looks up does the teacher's attention move to her, and Lucy can tell she's called a name whose owner was a mystery to her.

"I have a slip here telling me to send you to the counselor's office?" She phrases it like a question, and it feels like she's asking Lucy to confirm. She stands, painfully aware of the attention of the entire class, and takes the slip.

Send Lucy to Miss Proctor's office.

Clearly someone has noticed the girl with the stolen uniform.

Lucy has seen Miss Proctor in the halls, speaking casually with students or calling out to wild, wrestling boys down the hall. She's young and pretty, and the boys stare at her backside when she walks past. But the woman sitting in the counselor's office isn't Miss Proctor.

This woman is short and squat, settled in a chair to the side of the desk, her eyes focused on a stack of papers in front of her. Her blue suit is the color of the springtime sky of Lucy's memory, and it feels incongruous with the dark, shadowed office and the woman's bulky, shapeless form.

The woman looks up, watching Lucy walk from the door to the chair.

"Hi," she says finally. "I'm Lucy?"

"I'm Adelaide Baldwin." The woman's voice is softer and more sultry than her appearance would ever suggest.

"Hi," Lucy says again.

"I'm the head of counseling services at Saint Osanna's." Ms. Baldwin sets some papers on the desk beside her and clasps her hands in her lap. "You've flown under the radar here, it seems." She pauses. When Lucy offers no explanation, she continues. "I like to check in with the faculty every month or two, to find out if we have anyone . . . anything different on campus. This morning Ms. Polzweski mentioned that she'd seen a girl around school who she didn't believe was enrolled. We generally like to handle these issues internally before bringing in any authorities."

Lucy feels as if a brick has caught in her throat. "Oh," she whispers.

"Where are your parents?"

Lucy doesn't have an answer. She can feel Ms. Baldwin's eyes on her as she fidgets with a magnetic paper clip bowl on the desk in front of her. It's strange to be alone with someone other than Colin and be the object of such careful scrutiny.

"Lucy, look at me." Lucy looks up at the woman, meeting eyes filled with concern. "Oh, honey."

Something like hope unfurls inside Lucy when she registers that there are no secrets between them and that somehow Adelaide Baldwin knows Lucy isn't any ordinary student walking into this office. Lucy plays with the hem of her sleeve, asking, "You know who I am?" She suspects that with this question, she has irrevocably shifted the conversation away from something official and related to enrolling her, to something unofficial and related to keeping her hidden.

"You were a local star heading to Harvard before you were killed."

Lucy has to swallow her fear of the answer in order to push the question out: "If you know I died, why aren't you surprised to see me?"

Instead of answering, Mrs. Baldwin asks, "When did you come back to Saint Osanna's?"

"A few weeks ago." Lucy looks past her, at the kids leaving the building and walking toward the quad, or dorms, or dining hall. "I found classes where the teachers don't seem to notice me. Why is that?" she asks. "Why is it that nobody sees me?"

"Because they aren't looking. They don't need to see you, Lucy."

"Need to see me? I don't understand," Lucy says. Does Colin *need* to see her? And for what? "So there are others? Here, at the school? Jay said something about Walkers?"

"That's what some people call them, yes. They walk around the grounds, tied to this place for one reason or another and unable to leave. It's different for each of them." Ms. Baldwin begins placing files and stacks of paperwork back into her bag. Apparently their conversation is over.

Panic begins to fill Lucy like a rising tide. "I don't know

why I'm here," she says quickly. Will Ms. Baldwin report her to the authorities she mentioned? Are there some sort of ghost hunters that will send her back? "It felt right to come here."

"I know."

"Do *you* know why I'm here?" Lucy asks.

"No," she says. "You're not the first I've seen in my day."

"Where are the others? The Walkers? Is that what I am?"

Ms. Baldwin doesn't answer, simply gives a little shake of her head. It's as if she's already resigned to the reality that there's nothing to be done about the problem of Lucy.

"Can I stay here? At Saint Osanna's?"

The social worker nods. "I don't think we have a choice. Exorcisms don't work. *Nothing* seems to work. We just have to wait for you to vanish." She blinks away, dropping a pen into her bag and mumbling, "Thankfully, most do."

Lucy's chest seizes and she turns to the window, staring out the filmy glass. *Vanish?* Where would she go? How can she stop it?

Ms. Baldwin pulls her out of her thoughts. "Do you have money?"

Lucy hasn't had a need for it yet, being confined to the campus and lucky enough to not need food or water. No one in the laundry facilities noticed a ghost girl sneaking out boots and socks and old uniforms. "No."

Ms. Baldwin reaches for her bag, pulls out an envelope, and removes several twenties. "I doubt anyone would notice, but I don't want you getting caught taking something. Where are you staying?"

Lucy takes the money and curls it into her fist. It feels warm from the purse and scratchy against her skin. "In a shed."

Ms. Baldwin nods again as if this is satisfactory. "Does anyone else know about you?"

"A boy."

The woman laughs and closes her eyes, but it isn't a happy laugh. It's an of-course-a-boy-knows laugh. A why-did-I-even-bother-asking laugh.

Ms. Baldwin nods resolutely as she stands. "Take care, honey." She hitches her purse up and over her round shoulder.

"Thanks."

Adelaide Baldwin faces her and smiles a little before turning to the door. With her hand on the knob, she pauses, facing away so Lucy can't see her expression as she says, "The other kids who are like you? They seem to want to take someone with them. Try not to, Lucy."

Chapter 12 · HIM

T HIS GIRL, *THIS GIRL.* SHE HUMS TUNELESSLY
along with songs she says she doesn't remember.
She does the craziest things with her hair and uniform, weaving leaves and ribbons into her long braid. She
laughs loudly at his jokes when they walk down the hall
together and doesn't seem to care that no one ever notices
her. Colin wonders why that is. Jay sees her. A few of the
teachers. But that's it. It's as if, for them, her face blends into
the background. Plain. Generic.

But Colin notices *everything.*

And these small details—her simple confidence, flirty
smile, and infectious laugh—make it impossible for him to
stop obsessing about touching her the way he wants to. She's
easy with her affection: a hand on his arm, leaning into his
side on a bench. But he's so fascinated with her, with her

thoughts and lips and hands, the easy touches make him increasingly hungry, feeling too small in his skin.

She asks him to walk her around campus and the woods and tell her about growing up in a small town where the prestigious boarding school employs practically everyone.

"People assume I had this traumatic childhood—which I guess I did—but it was mostly me being a crazy townie and doing wild tricks wherever I could. There were so many people here taking care of me, it was impossible to ever feel lost or lonely."

She smiles up at him, but her eyes are a provocative, sympathetic indigo. He drags his frantic gaze across her face, cataloging every expression. This kind of longing makes him want to roar, to hurl logs and stones, to *claim* her somehow.

"So, were you always the Kid Whose Parents Died?" she asks.

He laughs at her instinctive recollection of how everyone in this small town has an unofficial title. "I think I used to be. Now I'm the Kid Who Jumped Fifteen Feet to Flat in the Quarry and Didn't Die. Even Dot heard about that one."

Shaking her head, she says, "You were *crazy* to do that," but her eyes have gone metallic brown, swirling.

"Not you too!"

"Colin. Objectively, that was an insane move."

"It's not insane," he says. "It's about fear. Everyone has

the same abilities *physically*, at least they can. The difference is I'm not afraid to try." Colin can remember that stunt better than almost anything: He pulled his bike to the ledge, took a deep breath, and balanced—eyes focused and muscles taut—before jerking the frame up in a hop over the lip. The bike cut a razor path straight down to the boulder, slicing cleanly through the air. Both wheels glanced off the stone in unison before rolling a rocky path down to the base of the quarry. He landed at the bottom next to it. Body: bruised. Arm: broken. "I met you the next day," he adds. He'd still felt nearly high from the jump, and then she was there: the most gorgeous thing he'd ever seen. This second memory, just as clear.

She hums, brushes her fingers against his, and the tickling current travels up his arm before evaporating. He wants more. He practically aches for her touch. It's more than hormones. It's like he's physically drawn into her space, has to force himself to keep any sort of acceptable distance. He pulls away slowly, forming a fist.

"Wonder what your title was," he says, distracting himself from the sudden urge he has to drag her down on the trail and cover her body with his. "The Girl with the Snorting Laugh?"

She snorts, and then smacks his arm as if it were his fault. "Maybe."

"The Girl with the Wicked Eyes?"

"Only to you." Her dimple makes a cameo appearance.

"Right," he says, laughing. "The Girl Who Kicked All the Boys' Asses in Chemistry?"

She starts to answer, grinning, her jaw already pushed out in pride, but she looks at his hands, formed into tight fists at his hips, and her expression straightens. "What's wrong?"

He shakes out his hands, laughs nervously. "Nothing."

"Are you upset?"

Colin begins walking again, tilting his head for her to join him. He doesn't know how to do this, how he'll ever do this. He *likes* her. He wants Lucy to be his girlfriend in every way that matters, including the ways that mean he can touch her. The urge to kiss her is becoming suffocating.

"Colin?"

Stopping, he turns back to face her. "What?"

She laughs at his stalling, walking toward him. "What's wrong?"

"I like you," he blurts. "A lot." His heart clenches and then begins pounding manically, and he half wants to turn and run down the trail. Instead, he stands and watches her expression shift from surprise to elation.

"Yeah?"

"Yeah. And it's hard to be so close all the time and not touching," he admits quietly.

"For me too." Stretching onto her tiptoes, she whispers, "But I want to try."

His tongue slips out, sliding over his piercing.

"I think about it," she says, her breath smelling like rain and petals. "I want to kiss you until you're dizzy with wanting too."

It takes Colin four tries to get a sound past his lips. "You mean you're dizzy with wanting me?"

She lifts herself up again, and he feels a sensation like lips against his cheek. He turns to her and is met not with her mouth but with her quickly ducked head. Just before he can step back, a little embarrassed and a lot confused, her hand presses against the front of his shirt.

"Wait," she says. "Just go slow."

First with his cheek, then with his nose barely touching her lips, he moves closer, hoping that the way she shakes is from anticipation and not something far less pleasant. She tilts her head just enough for him to brush his mouth over hers, and his fists curl in restraint at his sides. It's different; her skin there *feels* different. Still buzzing energy and the sense that if he pressed too hard she would evaporate, but lips nonetheless: full and smiling and now wet from his. When he comes back again and tastes her, she makes a tiny sound of relief. It's a sound of lust, of air and fire, and Colin nearly loses himself: grasping, fingers digging. But instead, he pulls back, breaths choppy as he looks down at her.

"Okay, that was a good start."

"A good start?" she says with a small laugh. "My mind is a giant sieve, but I'm pretty sure that was the best first kiss in the history of this town."

He gently touches her elbow, carefully urging her to start walking again. The kiss was an enormous step in the right direction but still only a fraction of what he needed from her. Inside his chest, a rope coils tightly, fraying at the knots.

Colin's cast came off two days ago, and he doesn't think he's ever been so grateful to be able to wash dishes. He and Dane finished cleaning the kitchen, and Colin lingers around to keep Dot company. She's been quiet tonight. No whistling while she cooks, no smacking them with the spatula. Just thoughtful, quiet Dot, and it weirds him out.

"Long day?" he asks.

She shrugs. "You know how it is when a storm is on its way."

"Your barometric knees acting up?"

She scowls at him over her shoulder. "Very funny, smart guy." When she turns back to the sink, he can see her reflection as she looks out the wide window overlooking the back side of the quad. She looks worried. "It's sort of like that," she begins, searching for words. "Something feels off. I'm not sure what."

Colin swallows hard and busies himself by stacking plates. "Hey, Dot, do you remember a girl named Lucy Gray?"

She pauses as she unties her apron. "Of course. Everyone around here remembers that name."

"Yeah." Colin struggles for breath. "So were you on campus when . . . when it all happened to her?"

"Why're you asking about something like that?"

He shrugs, taking a heavy sack of flour from her arms and placing it on the counter. "No reason. Some kids were down at the lake, started talking about it at lunch."

She pins him with a serious expression. "I better not catch you down there."

"Of course not," he says. It's a lie, and as a general rule, he doesn't lie to Dot. But Colin is always at the lake and figures since it's the same lie he's told over and over throughout his life, it counts as only one.

"She was killed," Dot says finally, watching as he begins sorting clean silverware. Out of the corner of his eye, he can tell she's got her fist planted on her hip and he can almost hear the ticking sound as her brain works something out. "Do you remember any of it?" she finally asks.

He points a handful of forks at his chest. "Me?"

She nods.

"What? No."

"She was killed when you were six."

He lived on campus and had just lost his parents. He remembers so little about that time other than the strange, constant desire to dissolve and float away. "I don't remember anything about it."

She nods and turns back around, bracing her hands and looking back out the window. "No, I guess you wouldn't. You had so much going on around then. It was brutal, Col. Just . . ." Her head drops and she shakes it. "Just awful."

He doesn't want to hear her version of the story, but a sick part of him wants to know everything.

"Your parents had died, and you were living at Joe's. I don't think you could sleep that night, and Joe was at a meeting with the other dorm heads. You were out on the porch playing alone with your little army men." She turns to look at him and smiles sadly. "You saw him carrying a girl into the woods. You ran and found me. It didn't save her, but because of *you* this guy was caught. We had no idea that monster was living right alongside us. And he had killed . . . God, I think he had killed seven other kids."

Colin stands and bolts from the kitchen, feeling his dinner coming back up.

Chapter 13 · HIM

XCEPT FOR THE BLURRED-EDGE MEMORIES OF
their funeral, Colin has few solid recollections of his
parents or the car crash that left them dead on impact
and Colin strangely unharmed. Their caskets had been posi-
tioned side by side at the front of the church, and the smell of
lilies was so strong, it turned his stomach. His dad's chest had
been crushed by the dashboard and the funeral home was
forced to reconstruct it: replacing muscle and bone with metal
rods and wax. Colin remembers only an angry purple bruise
peeking out from beneath the cuff of his dad's starched white
shirt. His mother's arm had been torn from her body by the
seat belt—something he didn't learn about until years later—
and the sleeve of her favorite pink dress was just empty. Like
they thought nobody would even notice.

He wondered why anyone would want to see someone

they loved like that, skin the wrong color and eyes that would never open again.

That's not how he wants to remember.

He wants to open his brain, to tear out the ugly pages and replace them with new, happier ones. Ones where moms and dads don't die and monsters don't carry girls into the woods in the middle of the night.

He hadn't felt sick like that again until Lucy. He thought knowing more of her story would be a relief, another missing piece of the puzzle fit perfectly into place. Instead, knowing he was the last person to see her alive has taken blank pages and inked them with horror and gore.

But she's here now, alive or not, standing across the threshold when he opens his door. Her smile makes the other stuff easier to forget. At least for a few hours. It's been three days since Dot revealed his role in the events surrounding Lucy's murder. Each night, whenever he started to tell her, his throat felt like it was closing shut.

Like always, Lucy pulls off her boots and heads straight for his window, reaching out to push back the curtains. It's been trying to snow all day, and a few small flakes flutter beneath the lamppost to fall slowly to the ground. Even though it's dark out, the sky is bright, practically glowing, and full of clouds that seem lit from behind.

"No stars tonight."

"It's a snow sky," Lucy says, her nose pressed to the glass. There's no smudge from where her skin touches the window, no cloud of condensation. "My grandma used to say it looks like someone left the TV on in heaven." She laughs and then pauses, turning to him. "How did I remember that?"

"I don't know. Maybe it's like amnesia victims. Certain things trigger specific memories."

"Yeah, maybe."

She turns back to the sky, and he closes his eyes, trying to shut out the pictures that are burned there forever. He wants to tell her more about her death and about his role in it all. But there's something else, a voice inside his head that repeats itself over and over, telling him it's a bad idea.

Dot said ghosts come here because they have unfinished business. Maybe that's why Lucy is here. He knows that should mean something to him, a warning to take this more seriously. He doubts anyone would come back from the dead because they lost a library book or missed sitting in school all day. It would have to be big. To settle a score? Revenge? He shakes that off; Lucy would never hurt him. He *knows* that. But if anyone has unfinished business, it's definitely Lucy. What could be more unfinished than having your heart carved out of your chest by a man your parents trusted to keep you safe?

He shivers as Lucy turns to face him.

"Cold?" she asks.

"Nah, just twitchy."

Lucy closes the distance between them, stopping only when the toes of her socks touch the toes of his. He struggles against what feels like every element in his body conspiring to shift him closer to her. He wants to kiss her again.

It's so quiet, so hard to believe that there are rooms full of people on the floors both above and below them, on the other sides of these walls. And Lucy is so silent. She doesn't fidget or cough or seem to constantly be adjusting things the way other girls do. He thinks he can almost hear the snow beginning to fall outside.

But in the absence of all those distractions, there's something else, something that hangs in the air between them and makes every single one of his senses somehow supernatural. When she reaches up to touch his bottom lip, tracing along the silver ring, it's as if all the air around them moves with her.

He's frantic with what he wants from her. Her eyes melt into deep amber. "Kiss me," she says. "It's okay."

He bends to kiss her, barely touching her lips with his. Each kiss is short, careful, punctuated by glances and the quiet murmurings of, "Okay?" and her reply, "Yes." If he focuses too hard, he starts to wonder whether he's even touching her. Physically, her kiss is so much less than every kiss he's had before, but inside, he's close to erupting. His hands find her waist, her hips, pull her closer.

She shivers, wincing. It's too much. "Shit. Sorry," he says.

But she tugs on his shirt and gives him a look of such determination that he bends, laughing a little, and just barely kisses her mouth.

He doesn't want to be that guy, the one who pushes for more and more and more, because he knows every touch overwhelms her, but he's dying to know how her skin feels, to see how her hips fit against his. He feels greedy. "I want you to stay." His eyes hover on her mouth before nervously meeting her gaze.

"Can I?" she asks. "Is Jay gone for the night?"

"I think so."

She lies back on his bed, and he bends over her, tracing an invisible line from her throat, past her collarbone, before unbuttoning the top three buttons of her shirt. No scar is visible on her skin. No heart beats beneath his fingertips, but something else seems to hum in its place.

Her short kisses melt like sugar against his tongue, and like a gust of wind, she rolls him to his back. He feels the weight of her over his thighs, how her shape pushes against his. Warm, but also somehow not. It's the most beautiful torture: the shadow of sensation, gone before he even has a chance to process it.

It's like he's dreaming. All of the imagery, no actual relief from the way he aches for her.

"Colin . . ."

"Yeah?"

"Take off your shirt."

He stares at her, seeing no trace of hesitation, and reaches behind his head. His shirt is gone in an instant. Her hands, and the illusion of her weight, press down on his chest; a teasing sensation brings goose bumps to his skin.

But every feeling is gone too fast as he sits beneath her, hesitant to touch for fear of flooding her with too much at once.

She whispers, pressing words against his neck, his ears, his jaw. "I like the taste of your skin. You smell like soap and grass and the ocean." Her teeth tease at biting, pulling on the ring in his lip; her hands are everywhere.

His own hands grow desperate then, pulling her shirt from her shoulders, touching her stomach, her chest, grasping and wanting to memorize every curve.

"Too rough," she says, gasping. He's afraid she's trying to hide that he's hurt her.

"Sorry, sorry," he says, pushing his hands into his hair. He closes his eyes and pulls, grateful for the solid shape of this known sensation. He hasn't ridden his bike in days, hasn't run, hasn't done *anything,* and he suddenly feels like a bear trying to carry a crystal; his muscles are going to burst from his skin and take off with this tension. He wonders if this is what people mean when they say almost having something is worse than never having it at all.

Her palm moves along his cheek, vibrating. "Look at me."

He looks up into eyes the colors of blood and night and sky. Deep reds and blues, streaking indigo.

"You should . . . touch yourself if . . ." She doesn't even blink. Doesn't do a single one of those timid-girl things, like fiddling with her hair or covering her face. She just waits, watching.

"You mean . . . ?" He can feel his eyebrows crawling to his hairline. *"Myself?"*

"Yeah." And then she smiles. It's the sweet, dimpled smile that does him in, the way she seems both vulnerable and demanding. It makes the absurdity of it, the ingrained need for covertness, disappear.

He does what she asks, roughly shoving his pants down his hips and closing his eyes only when she whispers his name. It's quick and familiar, and heat rolls along his skin as he tries to catch his breath. But it wasn't really what he wanted. She's watching him, her turbulent eyes never leaving his body. And although they blaze with fascination, he can tell it's not what she wanted, either.

Colin urges her down into the blankets with him, curling

to the side and pulling her back to his front. Her weight shifts between heavy and nothing, pressing and retreating like wind against a pane of glass.

They say good night, and then again, unwilling to let go.

She breathes, he realizes. Her short breaths match the rhythm of his own, and he settles into the comforting pattern. A bittersweet ache pulses deep in his chest. And as sleep begins to drag him under, he can't fight the fear that the more he needs her, the more impossible it will be for her to stay.

His eyes grow heavy, his muscles grow lax, and he feels himself slip away.

Colin dreams of Lucy in her flower dress and white sandals, her hands clasped on her stomach and lilies all around her.

Chapter 14 · HER

SHE'S TRYING TO STAY PERFECTLY STILL AS HE falls asleep, listening to the pattern of his breathing. Colin hasn't biked in days, hasn't beaten himself up and worn himself out like he used to. Lucy is used to seeing him always moving, almost vibrating with his barely contained vitality. But now, as he approaches sleep, he seems oddly quiet. It gives her the tiniest twinge of unease, even as his arms are tight and strong and his broad chest presses to the curve of her spine.

Colin inhales and mumbles something before his body seems to deflate, growing easy and tired and even warmer somehow. She misses that release, the physical letting go of sleep.

Lucy has been back here for more than two months. Sixty-five sunsets, and tonight is the first time she feels the sensation of drifting to darkness. She assumes people who love to sleep mean that they love this part of it most: the peaceful disengagement.

As she relaxes, she feels like she's back on the trail, but this time it's only in her mind and it's different somehow. She's underwater. Bubbles rise from her lips as she exhales, and when she looks up, they turn into silvery stars in a violet sky. Reeds become branches, stretching to touch each tiny spot of light. Ahead of her is the same dusty trail, but in the darkness it is a soft brown-black. The surface seems covered in a strange mixture of the lake bottom and tree bark from the earth outside.

The trail doesn't go on forever as trails sometimes do in dreams. It ends straight ahead, where there is no turn or hill; there is only nothing. A soft blackness. In this world, where ghost girls can walk and touch and laugh, black isn't a terrifying chasm. It's just the other side of white.

She keeps walking until she's not walking anymore; she's simply moving. Turning left, then right, then left again until she's back at her trail, waiting. Instinctively, she feels her body curve and press back against Colin one more time just before she lets herself fall into the black.

Chapter 15 · HIM

HE'S NEVER STAYED OVERNIGHT AT A GIRL'S place, so maybe there's a strange sense of intruding that he hasn't yet experienced. But Colin has had girls sneak in and sleep over, and never in any of those nights did they ever up and leave while he slept.

Lucy is gone when he wakes up, and even though it's probably because she was bored to tears, he still feels a little ditched.

From his window, he can see that it snowed sometime during the night. A lot. The sky is heavy and gray, and it's almost impossible to tell where it ends and the ground begins. He groans when he sees Dot's garden. He broke his arm the day before he was supposed to clean it out. There are still a few pumpkins scattered around, and the tomato plants are brown and brittle, nearly bowed to the ground beneath the bulk of the snow. Their forgotten fruit stands out in gruesome contrast to the frost-covered vines, like little shriveled hearts draped over a blanket of white.

He goes downstairs to help shovel and salt the walks behind the kitchens, wondering the entire time if Lucy went back to her shed. He has no idea how someone so slight walks in the thick, wet snow. He tries to not think about her stuck somewhere, locked in a step that went too deep, unable to pull her weight out of the drift. For about the millionth time, he wishes he understood what the hell she *is*. By now he's sweating, but his fingers feel like ice. The very thing he's been avoiding—the fear that Lucy could be gone as quickly as she came into his life—presses in on him.

"Hey, stranger," Dot says.

"Hey," he answers absently.

"You okay this morning, hon?" she asks as he stomps the snow from his boots. She's buried in one of the lower cabinets, digging out a couple of large stockpots.

"Sure." Inside the kitchen, Colin opens cupboard doors and closes them again. He feels like he's shorted out somehow, and nervous energy courses through his limbs. He's not scheduled to work today, but somehow being surrounded by the hustle of morning chaos and grumbling employees is more comforting than the silence of his room.

"You seem a little anxious."

"I'm fine."

She eyes him skeptically.

Turning away, he starts putting bread into the huge industrial toaster. "Just wondering if I should put out some more salt." He motions out the window, where white blankets the grass and walkways, drapes every shrub and tree.

"Let the groundskeepers do that stuff." Dot steps up behind him and pats his shoulder to soften her words. "You're a sweet kid, you know that?" she says, attempting to smooth his hair. "And you're so much calmer lately. Haven't seen you in the infirmary in more than a month."

"Har-har." He sits, takes a bite out of his toast. He hadn't realized it had been that long.

"So either your bike, skateboard, and kayak are all broken, or you've found a new girl." She hovers for a moment before stepping away, but Colin doesn't bother answering. Now that she knows the truth, he wonders how Dot would react if she saw him with Lucy.

As she continues her morning routine, he listens to the familiar squeak of her shoes on the tile floors and pushes his food around the plate. If he didn't have breakfast, Dot would bring in the cavalry. But each bite feels like hardened glue settling in his gut.

The minute he's done, thoughts of doing anything but finding Lucy are out the window. Maybe it's true that she came here for him, but it's also now true that he feels a strange shift in the fabric of the sky, as if a weightless girl pulls the entire atmosphere with her when she leaves his room in the middle of the night.

The first thing Colin notices when he reaches Lucy's field is that the snow is undisturbed. He tells himself it's fine. He doesn't even know if Lucy would leave footprints, but somehow he knows she hasn't been back.

He's panting by the time he gets to the shed and bursts through the door. The blankets on the old air mattress are smooth and untouched. Lucy's book sits, undisturbed, on the table, a dried piece of lavender marking the page.

He's running on adrenaline, and before he realizes it, he's gripping the handrail and climbing the steps of Ethan Hall. The bell has rung, the halls are empty, and a strange sense of déjà vu washes over him.

He looks in every classroom on the first floor before heading upstairs. In the library, he checks the little alcove near the storage closet where she likes to sneak away and wait for him to finish work.

She's not there.

Colin checks the bathrooms on the second floor, peeks into each classroom that he passes, the dining hall, and even the janitor's closet. Nothing.

He texts Jay to meet him near the auditorium. Jay comes whistling down the hall, but the moment he sees Colin, his expression sobers. "Whoa. What's wrong?"

"Have you seen Lucy?"

"Not since yesterday."

Colin presses his forehead against the window.

"Col, what—"

"She's gone." His voice sounds so hollow and strange, like it belongs to someone else, and his breath fogs up the glass in front of him. "She was with me last night, and when I woke up . . . she was gone."

"Relax. She's probably just with—"

"She doesn't have anyone else." He meets Jay's eyes, waiting, wanting him to understand what he's saying without actually having to say it.

"I think we're having a moment here," Jay says, trying to ease Colin's suffering. It works, and he almost smiles. Then, serious again, Jay adds, "She's kind of a quirky girl, isn't she?"

"Uh, yeah."

"All right, man. Let's find your Lucy."

But they don't find her.

When they trudge out to the trail, Jay doesn't say a word. When they circle the entire lake, he follows in Colin's wake. When they cut across the snow-covered field and step inside the little shed to find it empty, he doesn't ask Colin any questions.

Lucy doesn't come back that night.

And when Colin skips school the next morning to wait for her in the shed, she doesn't show up then, either.

For ten days, he looks. He goes to class, he works when he has to, he finds his way to the trail where she woke up, hoping she'll be there again. Maybe she'll walk toward him, wearing her ass-kicking boots and a stolen uniform that's too big.

He considers telling someone that she's missing, but then realizes there's nobody to tell. No one even notices that the pretty girl with the unsettling eyes and snow-colored hair is gone.

Finally, he can't take the dorm, the school, the shed, any of it. Every single wall is imprinted with her shape, her willowy shadow. He bursts from the grounds on his single speed, blowing powdered snow and slush over the sidewalk as he takes off.

Legs pumping, heart racing, blood so hot so hot so hot in his legs, his chest, his grip so tight he can feel electric pulses of pain up and down his newly healed arm.

He jumps from curbs and trucks, train cars and the cables between. He rides over an icy rope bridge he's never been able to balance on before, along a narrow train track, and slips only twice. The sound of the train as it roars down the track, closer and closer, only makes him see more clearly, breathe freer. Feel *alive*. He does backflips he shouldn't. He rides until his outsides feel as battered as his insides.

He tries to pretend that he's not looking in every shadow for her. He decides it doesn't matter. Nothing matters. Death lingers in cars, in quiet school buildings, and beneath the freezing earth. Death is everywhere, but his ghost is gone.

When he makes it back to his room in the thick of the night, he's bruised and covered in scrapes. He suspects one of his ribs is cracked, but he's alive and Lucy is only a memory.

Chapter 16 · HER

LUCY HOVERS ON THE EDGE OF A DREAM WHEN the air seems to change around her. Behind her eyes it's been wonderfully dark, but it's so simple to lift her lids, let in the dull sunrise that creeps into the room. Colin is there, sleeping and warm. Somehow in the night they've changed places. She's behind him with arms wrapped around his ribs.

"Are you working breakfast?" She glances at the clock. It's already seven. "You're going to be late."

He rolls over so fast it's jarring, his eyes full of terror and relief. And fury.

"Lucy."

Fury?

He grabs her, pulling her to him so fast that she gasps as he presses his face into her neck. She closes her eyes, and the rapid beat of his heart moves through him and into her, vibrating her silent chest, and she feels so full, almost carbonated. He makes a sound of frustration, almost a howl, as if he can't hold her tight enough, can't wrap enough of himself around her. She laughs and urges him onto his back, but when she looks down, she realizes he's not laughing.

"What's wrong? And what happened to you?" She reaches for a scrape on his forehead, an angry bruise on his chin. Those weren't there before.

He sits up abruptly, and she slides from his lap onto the foot of the bed, landing a few feet away from him. His fury is bigger now. There's more fire than affection in his hazel eyes.

"Where have you been?"

"What are you talking about?" she asks, reaching for him again. "You've been asleep. Last night was . . ." She stops, terrified now that what they did was only a strange, dark dream. "Last night you touched me and . . . I thought . . ."

"Last night? Last *night*, Lucy? Last night you weren't here. You've been gone for almost two weeks."

Cold fingers slip up inside her chest and curl around where her heart used to beat. "What?"

We just have to wait for you to vanish.

Thankfully, most do.

"Where have you been?"

She can see it now, the subtle changes that happen to the

living in only a few short days: His hair is the tiniest bit longer. A cut on his knuckle has healed over, and new ones surround the fading mark. "I didn't know I was gone!"

He yanks at his hair before standing and walking to his closet. He's in a different pair of boxers and begins pulling on clothing as if he doesn't want to be seen. A wrinkled dress shirt and blazer. His school tie left open around the very neck she finally kissed. Layer upon layer that separates him from her. "Luce, I last saw you ten days ago. It was December seventh, today is the *seventeenth*."

Her stomach drops into an abyss. "I don't understand," she says.

"I looked for you—at school, the trail, the shed—" He stops and presses his knuckles into his chest roughly, as if it hurts the same way hers does. "One minute you were here and then you were just *gone*. Where did you *go*?"

He steps closer and then away, making a fist. He seems torn between wanting to come to her and wanting to punch the wall.

"You fell asleep. And for the first time, I was able to close my eyes and dream. . . . It didn't even seem that long. I . . . saw this dark trail underwater. I walked to the end, where it was dark and . . . calm. And then I woke up just now."

"Well," he says, picking something up from the corner of the room and placing it on the bed. Her clothes, from that night. She hadn't even realized she was wearing nothing but underwear. She crosses her arms over her bare chest, suddenly self-conscious. She sees him wince, but he says, "I'm glad you felt supercalm on the black underwater supertrail. I was freaking out, thinking I'd never see you again."

"Colin, I'm so—"

"I have class."

The walk across campus is excruciating. He won't talk; he won't look at her. Worse, he won't touch her.

She reaches over, tentatively putting her hand on his, and he pulls back, like he's surprised all over again by how it feels. She'd hoped her touch would be familiar, comforting even. But maybe the quiet buzz of sensation only reminds him how impermanent she is.

"I had no idea I would disappear." Her steps slow, then falter, widening the space between them.

He exhales slowly before stopping, turning to face her. "I know."

Is this how break-ups happen? Someone disappears— literally or metaphorically—and the rhythm is forever ruined? "I would have been a mess if the situation were reversed."

He reaches for her but then shoves his hand into his hair.

"I'm not trying to be a dick. I seriously thought you were gone for good. I'm just really freaked."

Apparently, there will be no comforting touch in this reconciliation, and this thought leaves her overwhelmingly sad. She hates having no answers. She died, she's back, and she wants to be near him with every particle of her strange body. And still, there is absolutely no meaning to any of it. "I'm here," she says lamely.

His eyebrows pull together and his eyes darken a shade. "For how long? I mean, how can we know?"

Shrugging, she looks past him at the trees rooted so firmly in the frozen ground, at the buildings that have been there for more than a century. Ghosts have haunted the world since the beginning of time, and suddenly, she's plagued with the desire to know how to do it right.

Chapter 17 · HIM

"SO SHE WAS JUST . . . BACK? LIKE, WITH NO EXPLA-nation of where she'd been?" Jay's stretched out on his bed, thumbing through an old magazine he found under his pillow. Colin doesn't look too closely.

"Yeah. It's sort of—" His eyes move to the ceiling. "Complicated."

"Complicated. Dude, you're talking to the guy who took two chicks to the formal and managed to get away with it. I think I can keep up."

"Jay, this isn't a joke."

With a bored sigh, Jay sits up, throws his feet over the side of the bed, and assesses Colin. "Look, I know this isn't a joke, okay? And I get that Lucy's . . . *different* from other girls. I've never seen you dive this deep into anything," he says, lifting a single brow for emphasis. "I just want to know that you're okay."

"I am," Colin says. It sounds like a lie, even to him. If he were okay, he would have told Lucy everything, including his role in her murderer being caught. Including the fact that he was the last person to see her alive and couldn't save her. The superstitious fraction of him feels like he needs to hold some detail back, as if the entire truth would untie the balloon from the cart and he'd be left to watch it drift away.

"What if she . . . like, what if she went on a bender?"

"She didn't."

"Or, I don't know, Col. Like, back to a boyfriend in Portland for a week. I wasn't kidding when I called her mysterious. Literally no one around here knows her, except you and me. If I said, 'Lucy who hangs with Colin,' it'd take anyone else five minutes to remember what she even looks like."

Colin stares at him, hoping to burn a hole in Jay's forehead. "I can handle this."

"Are you sure? Because when she was gone, you were flipping out. I know you've lost your entire family, but I've never seen you like that before. You didn't talk to me, or Dot, or even Joe. When was the last time you talked to Joe?" When Colin doesn't answer, Jay presses on. "And I—what if it happens again? You gonna be okay then, too?"

Colin pushes away from the desk and scrubs his face with his hands. The answer to that is a big, unequivocal NO, but there's no way he can tell Jay that. "We're working it out. It won't happen again. We're good."

This is one of those moments that define why they're friends. Jay knows Colin is lying his ass off, but he also knows it's the only way he's holding it together.

"See, this is why I don't *do* relationships." Jay makes little quotation marks with his fingers, and Colin rolls his eyes.

"Sure it is."

"All right, then," Jay says. "Where is the magic elusive spirit girl, anyway?"

Colin's head snaps up, and he gapes at him—Jay's hit awfully close to home—but he's smacking his gum and flipping through his magazine again. Clueless.

"She'll be here any minute." Colin closes his math book and glances at the clock, trying not to appear as restless as he feels.

Jay stands and adjusts his baseball cap, walks to the window and back, before resuming his seat on the edge of his bed. He's as anxious to get out there as Colin is. "We seriously can't leave until she gets here? I'm bored."

Colin shakes his head. "I want her to come along."

The night before Lucy came back, the night he almost rode himself into the ground, was the first time Colin felt sane in days, like he'd beaten his anxiety into submission. Some of the stuff he and Jay have done is a bit crazy and a lot dangerous, but it's always been the case that, on his bike or board, everything blurs at the edges until he's focused on one thought: *breathe*. The wilder he is, the safer he feels. It's a paradox he can live with. It's just that now he wants Lucy to stay close.

"It's a good thing Lucy's cool or I'd have no choice but to kick your ass," Jay says. "So where are we going? They put in this killer jump at the track, but last week it was full of Xavier posers, so that's out."

Colin fiddles with the straps on his biking shoes, remembering the night with Lucy at the lake, her legs dangling to the knees in the frozen water. Other than the section near the oak tree, she seems to like water—the pond, the lake, her crazy dream about underwater blackness. "I think the lake's frozen over. No way will anyone else be down there. You up for some tricks?"

Jay agrees and heads down to mess around with his bike while Colin searches through the piles of clean laundry for something warmer to wear.

Lucy materializes at the door, wearing a new stolen uniform. This version has the ugly navy slacks, which is probably why it was easy for her to find and snag: Hardly any of the girls wear them. But her black boots lace almost to her knees, and her hair is piled in a messy heap on top of her head and bound with a bright red ribbon. He has no idea where she found it, but she looks like punk rock trying to go straight. He still can't get over how relieved he is to see her. The weirdness of having a girlfriend he can barely kiss seems so unimportant compared to the relief he feels at having her back.

"Not exactly standard attire," he says, tugging on her white oxford where she's knotted it just beneath her ribs, mocking the cold air around her.

Her mouth curls up into a teasing smile. "The administration is free to notice and unofficially expel me."

He laughs. Lucy's been lurking around campus for more than two months—minus the ten days of unexpected vanish—and no teacher really bothers to question her presence, let alone her decidedly non-dress-code boots.

She glances at his bike shoes hanging from his free hand. "Where are we headed?"

"Your favorite place: the lake."

"Sure. To . . . ride?" She looks skeptical.

Grinning, he pulls her with him as he turns to leave. "Trust me; it'll be fun."

Chapter 18 · HER

LUCY HASN'T BEEN BACK TO THE LAKE FOR weeks, not since the day Colin walked with her around the entire lakeside trail and she discovered what she now knows is the site of her murder.

So while Colin and Jay prep their bikes, she wanders off, taking the time to actually look around. Winter has dug its claws into this part of the world, and everything looks at once more barren and also softer. Snow blankets everything, tree branches are softened with white and blue reflected from the glacial water. In her memory, the autumn leaves are flames and her disorienting awakening is a hell long since past.

She finds where she landed and for some reason is surprised that no traces remain. There's no girl-shaped bruise in the earth, no chalk outline of a body. She fell, she's here, and it's time to carry on.

Heading back to the lake, she sees Jay and Colin on the ice, zipping around.

"Wait," she says. "You're riding *on* the lake?"

"Yeah. It's frozen," Colin says, hopping up and down on his bike. The tires squeak against the ice as if in agreement. "Solid."

"Are you *crazy*?"

"Absolutely," Jay calls.

Before she can respond, Colin has his hands up, placating. "No, no, honestly, it's safe. It's at least three inches thick, and we do it all the time."

He clearly expects her to be horrified—anyone hearing this *should* be horrified—but Lucy isn't. She's only curious. Three inches thick doesn't sound like a lot, and she gives in to the strange high that suddenly tears through her. She almost believes if she looked down at her arms she would see red blood surging through newly solid veins. Sitting on a snowbank at the lakeshore, Lucy watches the two boys trace snakes of tire prints in the thin layer of crunchy snow on the surface.

She's never seen Colin like this before. She loves how loose he is, how he lets the bike be hard while he prefers flexibility, molding to its movements, sliding over the pedals and leaning into the force of every sharp turn. He spells her name in the layer of snow over ice, and he hops on his front tire from a soft embankment, landing in a crouch on the pedals.

"Wanna try?" he calls.

Shaking her head quickly, she answers, "No."

He laughs and pedals over, carefully kissing her cheek. He looks down at her, as if surprised. It feels different here, where it's snowing and the air is heavy with water on the verge of solidifying. She presses her fingers to her skin when he leaves, pushing the memory of the sensation farther inside.

Jay spends a while packing snow into a ramp, and they take turns launching from it. The ice creaks when they land where the tire tracks have patterned the lake, and they instinctively shift the angle of their jumps to avoid the spot.

Despite their care and obvious skill, she looks down, suddenly unable to watch. Instead, she focuses on the way her skin swirls in the strange blue light. Tiny ice crystals land on her arm and then sink in, becoming part of her. Colin bikes over and kisses her again, releasing a puff of steam against her face. It disappears into her cheek.

"Jump's ready," Jay yells from the middle of the lake.

Colin pedals away from her before turning and taking off hard down the hill and onto the ramp. He flies through the air, his torso twists and arches, and for only a moment, she can see his eyes close in euphoria, can imagine what it would be like to see him make that face closer to her own. His arms flex and his hands squeeze the grips as he recovers and lands. Releasing a loud "Whoop!" he circles back as Jay takes off. Over and over they ride the ramp, and each turn their jumps are more daring, their lands are more solid, and their cheeks glow redder in the frigid air.

"I'm starving," Jay yells as he bikes to the lake's edge and pulls his phone from his pocket to check the time.

"You're always starving. Ten more minutes." Colin pedals to Lucy. "Are you bored?"

As soon as she shakes her head, he's off again. But this time, what has to be his twentieth jump, Lucy can tell immediately that he's crooked—too far to the right—and when he lands, the ice splits open with a deafening crack.

Water, blue and sharp, bubbles up and across the surface. Colin slips under as if he's melted into the lake; there's not even a moment when he gripped anything but his bike handles. It all happens so fast, but the yawning pause after he disappears feels like it lasts a year, and never has the world been more silent.

He's gone. Beneath the snow and thick ice. Lucy is screaming and Jay is screaming, digging his arms into the water, reaching wildly for Colin. The first thought hits her like a dark shadow: When he's dead, will he be able to find her?

"Colin!" Jay yells, lying flat on the ice and leaning over the jagged hole. He shoves his arms in again and again, feeling for any trace of a body. The ice where he leans groans and cracks, and he scrambles back as Colin appears and punches at the solid surface. Jay tries to grab his hand, but he can't reach him.

"GET HIM!" Lucy screams, scrambling closer to the edge. "Jay, get him out. Get him out. Get him out!"

Jay lunges, but Colin is too far away, now moving beneath the ice in the wrong direction. Lucy shoves him aside and dives in without thought, but the water pushes her up, bobbing her uselessly against the ice. She has no strength against the weight of water that presses into her. Colin falls unconscious, his face eerily blue as he begins to slip away. It makes him look already preserved.

With a surge of wild strength, she ducks under to grab his sinking hand, pulling his arm close enough that Jay can grab him. He's screaming so many words at her as he pulls Colin out, but she doesn't hear any of them because she's already out and up, running for help.

She charges down the trail, screaming her head off and intent on heading straight for the kitchen or Joe's or somewhere where someone can help. She falls in the snow and gets up again, clothes leaden with water that's quickly turning to ice, and limbs propelled by terror.

"Luce?"

It has to be a hallucination. In his voice she hears relief.

But it's impossible because she just left him unconscious and frozen and dying on the lake.

"Luce, *stop!*"

Whipping around, she sees Colin behind her on the trail. Somehow he manages to both smile and apologize with his eyes. "Stop," he says. "Please."

She can't see through him, can't blink him away. He's there, saying her name one more time and waiting for her to respond, hands curled into fists at his sides.

Relief floods her so rapidly that she's choking on words, unable to speak. All she can do is turn and run, throw her entire body against his. He catches her, and where he has always been hard and too solid, now he's simply warm and perfect. His forearms wrap around her back, pulling her to him, and he presses his face into her neck. Not too hot, not too much. Just Colin and the contours of eyes and lips and nose and chin against her skin. She feels him kissing her, feels his mouth open on her throat, his lips tasting her skin before he whispers, "Hi."

Strange, but perfect. They feel the *same.*

She wants to scream words of relief into the air. Her question, "How did you get out?" comes out shrill, her voice disappearing in a rasp at the end.

Colin silently bends and kisses where her neck dips into her shoulder. "Where are we?" he whispers, voice heavy with awe. "Is this how it always looks to you?"

"Where is Jay?" she asks, looking behind him down the trail. Muffled shouting drifts from the lake, and Lucy registers with a leaden clarity that Jay is there, panicking.

But Colin is here. And *dry*.

Understanding seeps into her, slow and thick. His skin is like her skin and it's warm and soft and familiar. His skin isn't freezing. Looking back down the trail again and behind Jay's crouched body, Lucy can see the top of Colin's soaking-wet hair and a single unmoving hand against the ice.

Panic and confusion flood her. "Hey," she says, tugging at his hair so that he meets her eyes. And it's then that she finally sees what he sees when he looks at her: His irises swirl, flames licking. Where his used to be amber-dark, honey flecked with gold, now they are molten. He's afraid, excited, and hopeful.

And she can see, too, that he knows something is wrong. He knows and he doesn't care.

"Just touch me." He shakes his head, looking around as if caught inside a wholly different world. "Just pretend it's okay."

She nods, lifting herself on her tiptoes to kiss him. Lips press, tongues touch, and then it deepens, finally. The warmth and wet of a real kiss, the vibrating taste of his sounds, and the pressing hunger of Colin finally able to take more. He grows frantic, and a spreading tingle engulfs her skin, flames down her neck and across her chest. She feels the heat in ten pulses in her fingers, ten pulses in her toes. And yet, while his eyes fall closed, hers cannot. She's simply fascinated with what's happening. He exhales through his nose and lets out a sound of longing that is so strained and tight, she digs her fingers into his hair, wraps everything that she can around him.

But it isn't enough; she's not strong enough to keep him yet.

Somehow, in the split second before it happens, she feels it. A small jerk to the back of his ribs, the impact of life being forced back into him. Or of him being forced back to life. And then he's gone, hurled backward through the air, gasping and choking, propelled by an invisible band around his chest. Lucy is left alone on the trail where, for an achingly perfect moment, he was just like her.

Chapter 19 · HIM

THE CHANGE IS SLOW AT FIRST: SILENCE IS broken by a rhythmic beep. Darkness gives way to light. Numbness bleeds into pain.

He's somewhere between awake and asleep. Or, maybe, alive and dead.

Colin always thought that dying would be the hard part. But feeling life seep back into his body is pain unlike anything he's ever known.

It burns. His fingertips feel capped with lead weights, red with heat. Every inch of his skin pricks and pulses; the pain is so intense he can hear it, as if he's on fire and the flames lick and tick near his ears.

Is he dreaming? Only a dream could whisk you from heaven to hell in moments and leave you willing to give up anything to do it over again. Wasn't it only seconds ago that he was somewhere else? Somewhere both too bright and too dark, a world made of prisms of color warping rhythmically, as if everything around him pulsed with energy. For a flash, he remembers his skin prickling all over with the most intense anticipation he'd ever felt.

A face floats in the hollow space between his memories. Cool lips grow warm against his, and color swirls in irises that tell a story he wants to remember. He finally got to touch her.

If he sleeps again, maybe he'll go back. Maybe she'll be there too.

Voices seep into the quiet, and he opens his eyes, blinking against the dim light. Stark walls surround him, and the nauseating traces of antiseptic and coffee hang in the stale air. Everything around him seems lifeless.

The infirmary.

He flexes his hands, but they move in jerks. His fingers are stiff and numb, like rusty cogs. Colin tries to sit but quickly realizes it's a bad idea. The room shifts and bends in front of him, and he collapses back into a pillow that's too soft, hitting his head on the bed frame. Tubes and wires wrap around his arms, and each breath hurts more than the last. It feels like he's inhaling propane, exhaling fire, yet he's shivering.

A girl outside the room is asking to see him. He recognizes his name and turns his head toward her familiar voice. His lips know the shape of her name, but when he tries to say it, there's no sound.

"I promise I won't stay more than a few minutes," she says.

"I told you, I can't let you in there." The other woman's voice is familiar, but where he's used to hearing soft honey, he now hears only edge.

"I'm not leaving," the girl says flatly. "Please, tell him Lucy is here."

Lucy. Blond hair and swirling eyes. The lake. The ice. Cold like he's never known. The fear that he would die and then those fleeting moments when he didn't care.

"Do you think I don't know what you are?" The voices are closer now, quieter. "No way am I letting you get to that sweet boy."

The silence outside his room stretches, making the air around him feel even more stagnant and stale. He opens his mouth and exhales Lucy's name, but it's too quiet for anyone to hear.

"You know about the others? Where are they?" she asks.

"If there's even one more here, that's one too many. You're going to break that boy's heart. Or worse."

Maggie. Colin remembers her name, and everything comes back in a cluster of images and sounds: How many times he's been in this bed, how many times Maggie has set

his dislocated shoulder, stitched his cheek, given him everything from aspirin to morphine.

"Please," Lucy says. "Just one minute. I promise I won't
stay long. . . ."

"Listen," Maggie says more gently. "There's nothing good
that can come out of this. Leave that boy alone. Go take your
haunting somewhere else."

Haunting.

The door swings open, and Maggie enters alone. Her tall
shadow slants across the far wall as she moves to the bed.
Behind her, Lucy lingers in the hallway, catching his eye.

"Hi." She waves.

He lifts his arm a few inches off the bed to wave back.
Lucy's skin is pale and almost glows beneath the artificial
light. She doesn't look real. The monitor registers the blip
in his heart rate when he realizes that for the first time ever,
Lucy looks like *exactly* what she is.

With one more apologetic smile, she disappears down
the hall.

"Well, look who's awake."

Colin turns his attention to Maggie as she begins adjusting
his tubes, checking the monitors. He wants to ask her what
happened with Lucy, how she knows that Lucy is a ghost,
and what she meant by "haunting." He wants to ask her if he
hallucinated the world of light and shadow, silver fire from

Lucy's touch. His heart squeezes painfully at the thought that it wasn't real. But when he meets Maggie's eyes, he realizes she's waiting for him to say something.

"Sorry, what?" he asks.

"I asked you how your pain is, honey."

He stretches his arms. They hurt. His head hurts. His legs hurt. "I'm a little rough," he manages.

"Can you give me a number?" She points to a series of cartoon faces on a poster, ranging from smiling to crying, with a score below each.

"Um . . . I'd say eight?" His skin screams *ten*. It feels like it's peeling away, from his fingertips to his torso.

Nodding, she pushes the contents of a syringe into his IV. "That's what I thought."

Colin watches the clear fluid disappear into his arm. He remembers the burning cold, the colors, the girl. "What did you give me?" he asks. Whatever it was, he wants more.

"Don't worry, sweetness. It's fentanyl. You were screaming when you came in. Should have taken you to the hospital."

"Can you let me see her? Lucy?"

Colin wonders if he's imagining the way she seems to stiffen. "You need to rest now, sweet boy. Joe went to get some dinner and will be back soon."

He doesn't stay awake long enough to see Maggie leave the room.

• • •

Opening his eyes feels more challenging than lifting a car. The weight of sleep is unbelievable, and it's only the sound of Joe walking into the room with Maggie that convinces Colin to struggle against the pull to return to sleep and memories of Lucy and her luminous world.

Joe tells him what Colin has already remembered: He fell into the lake, and the low temperature caused his heart to slow. Luckily, the exposure was minimal, and being young and fit enough means there should be no lasting effects.

Apparently, word of the accident has spread across campus, and some of the braver students have begun venturing out on the ice to see the scene of the crime for themselves. Joe's rambling fades out when Dot walks in, all business, and she wordlessly takes in the scene: Colin in bed with cuts and bruises that cover pretty much everything not hidden by the cotton gown. Joe trying to avoid yelling by chatting incessantly. The beeping monitors on a cart near the bed.

"Colin," is all she says.

"Hey, boss."

"Dot's going to stay until you're asleep for the night. All right?" Joe's forehead pinches into about a hundred wrinkles, and for the first time ever, it occurs to Colin that the man who took his first sick day when he fell through his porch might actually be done in by a punk kid giving him a heart attack. "I need to go back and make sure the students are off the lake."

Colin's stomach cramps with guilt. "Okay," he mumbles.

In an uncharacteristic gesture of physical affection, Joe bends and kisses his forehead. "I'm glad you're okay."

He turns and leaves, his old blue coat folded neatly over his arm. Colin looks to Dot the second Joe's out the door. "Where's my bike?" he asks, but his voice turns to air on the last two words.

"Lost in the lake is my guess," she answers, patting his arm gently. Anyone else might be full of I told you so's, but instead, he can see the apology all over her face. He's in the infirmary, suffering from the effects of hypothermia because he was horsing around on a lake in December—somewhere he shouldn't have even been. He won't be able to work for who knows how long. And Dot gets that it kills him that his favorite bike is gone.

"I know we haven't talked in a couple weeks, but you'd tell me if something was going on, right? Something driving you to do crazy stunts on a frozen lake?"

He can tell that she's barely suppressing the need to chew him out, and he nods, smile tight.

Her face registers that he hasn't really answered. "Think you're up for another visitor?"

Almost as soon as Colin nods, Jay walks in, stands at the

foot of the bed, and looks at Colin like he's seen a ghost. "You scared the crap out of me, Col. I didn't think you were going to make it."

"Thanks for pulling me out."

"Lucy pulled you out," he says, and Colin feels his eyes go wide. *Lucy?* The girl who can barely handle his kiss pulled his unconscious body from a lake? Jay's already nodding, a grin pulling at the edge of his mouth as if they're both imagining Lucy opening that beer bottle with her teeth. "Right? It was awesome. I basically punched the hell out of your chest to get you breathing." His eyes narrow, and Colin can see the traces of another smile. It's a struggle for Jay to stay serious for long, but for Dot's sake, he works to keep it somber.

Colin knows Dot is probably putting the pieces together, but he can't think about that right now. She's unable to look at either of them, her wide eyes trained on the shape of Colin's legs under the pile of blankets.

"That explains the bruises on my sternum," Colin says.

"Really?" Jay sounds kind of impressed.

Colin pulls open the top of his hospital gown to show him the blue fist marks blooming across his chest. Jay laughs and turns it into a cough when Dot shoots him a sharp look. There are some Dot moods even Jay's charm can't penetrate, and one of those is Protective Dot. "Hey, do you know where Lucy is?"

Jay's eyes slide to Dot again, probably sensing the tense set to her shoulders, and then back to Colin before mouthing the word, "Here."

She stayed.

When the moon fills the window and spills across the floor, Colin actually starts to feel awake. Dot has left, and the far side of the room is empty but for the vaguely geometric shadows of medical equipment. Everything around him looks oddly . . . *plain*. Even the shadows here lack the dimension of those hovering alongside the strange trail.

Maggie pads into the room for another check of his vitals. "Feeling okay?"

He shrugs and gives her a pain score when she points to the faces on the wall. "It's about a six."

She pulls a packet of pills from her pocket and offers a cup with water. "Will she try to come back?"

He looks up at her. Maggie's eyes are shadowed in the dark room, and she's making a note on his chart, but he knows she's not asking about Dot.

"Probably. Why wouldn't you let her in?"

She sighs and straightens the blankets over his legs. "I'll tell you the same thing I told her: Nothing good can come of this."

"How did you know what she is?"

"How did *you*?"

"She told me," he says. "But she didn't have to tell you. You just knew."

Maggie nods and meets his eyes. "She was killed just after I started here. I never knew her, but her face was plastered all over the news." She pauses, studying him as her eyes fill with pain. "But that's not what you're asking, is it? Yes, I've seen her kind before around here."

Colin swallows, but the question he wants to ask isn't forming quickly enough.

"Tell me," Maggie says. "When she told you she was dead, did you decide it didn't matter how strange she was, didn't matter that when you kiss her she doesn't feel like any other girl?" She leans closer, resting her hand on the side of the bed. "Did she feel like she was put back on this planet just for you?"

It feels too intimate, what she's saying. It feels like she's looking underneath his skin. And he hates the echo of her words: *You're going to break that boy's heart. Or worse.* He tugs the blankets up around his shoulders.

"Well." Maggie sighs, picking up her clipboard and tucking it under her arm. "I've been in your shoes, Colin. That girl needs something, and nothin's gonna stop her from taking it. You think about that." She turns to leave, stopping in front of the door. "And maybe she *was* put here just for you. You'll give and give until you hollow yourself out. But when that girl disappears without warning, without a trace, you ask yourself how long she can be gone before you break."

The shift change at work is silent outside his door, and the only indication that time has passed is the appearance of an unfamiliar gray-haired nurse materializing at his side and recording his vitals.

She runs her hand along the IV tubing, checking for kinks. "I'm Linda. I do hospice in town, and came in to give Maggie a break. How's your pain?"

"Better. Around a three." Colin stretches, reaching to push the button at the side of the bed that helps him sit up.

"That your girlfriend in the hallway? The brunette? Tall as a tree, but skinny?"

Colin's monitor picks up, and the nurse glances at it. *Brunette.* "Yes," he says. "Can I see her?"

She smiles over the top of her clipboard. "I was told you were to rest."

He stares at her, trying as hard as he can to silently communicate that she should let Lucy in. That he won't tell anyone.

She starts to leave and then pauses at the door, looking back over her shoulder. "Thirty minutes."

"Thirty," he repeats in a burst. "I promise. Thank you."

Pale yellow light bleeds into the room as she slips out, and he counts to eighty-three before the door opens again and Lucy steps in.

"Colin?" she whispers.

He scoots over to make room for her on the bed. "I'm awake."

The air stirs as she moves next to him, and the mattress dips surprisingly under her added weight. They sit side by side, stiff and silent. Colin has no idea where to start asking about the world he saw, what he felt, whether any of it was real.

"Are you okay?" she asks finally.

"I think so. Are you?"

She nods. "Do you want to talk about what happened?"

"Was it real?"

She studies him, but doesn't seem to need him to explain more. "I think so."

Colin can feel his fingers grow clammy. It would be so much easier to explain if it happened only in his mind. "The world didn't look like anything I'd ever seen before. It was bright, and . . . like there were more layers to everything. I know that doesn't make sense, but I'd never seen color like that. And you . . ." He glances up to her quickly. "I felt you, Luce. I mean, we were the same."

The memories fill his thoughts slowly, slithering in:

icicles hanging from silvery branches, leaves greener than a December day has ever seen, a shimmering crystal-blue sky wrapping through it all. It's a world worthy of a dream.

Her eyes darken, mocha swirling into burgundy. "What was it like to go in?" she asks hesitantly.

Only a few fragments before he fell in are clear. "I noticed a puddle of water on the ice right before it cracked," he says. "But it was already too late. How is any of it possible, Lucy? Did I die?"

She reaches for his hand, and it surprises him how strong she feels. "I don't know."

She doesn't say anything else, and he leans back, closing his eyes. Colin feels tired and sore, but mostly he feels like he does after a really long ride with a couple hard falls. The idea of falling in a frozen lake used to seem so extreme; it makes him wonder why he's not in rougher shape.

They don't talk about what it was like to finally feel each other for the first time. He doesn't tell her about Maggie's warning, and he doesn't tell her that even when he realized what was happening, it never occurred to him to worry he might die.

He certainly doesn't tell her how badly he wants to go back under.

Chapter 20 · HER

COLIN IS HELD IN THE INFIRMARY THE NEXT day, and Lucy walks back through campus, feeling increasingly untethered with each passing step.

Warnings haunt her. Two people now have seen Lucy and reacted as if she were anything but good.

They always take someone with them. Try not to, Lucy.

Go take your haunting somewhere else.

The words, delivered with such certainty, taste all wrong in Lucy's thoughts. Where would she take Colin even if she could? How could she possibly take her "haunting" somewhere else when she can't even manage to pass through the school's iron gates?

She walks away from the buildings, down the long gravel road leading toward the majestic stone buildings. Even out of her sight, they feel just as imposing. Her anchor is this school, these grounds, and—most of all—that boy lying bruised and broken in the infirmary.

Lucy presses her hand to the cold iron gates and then leans forward, resting her forehead there too. Objectively, it's cold. The cold takes over every inch of her skin, and yet it's completely without discomfort. No sensation in the world registers above the memory of feeling Colin the day before.

Warm skin, the wet of his lips, and the ache for more in every one of his sounds. Being with Colin like that was how she always hoped it would feel. Being with him in his human body and her ghost one felt like trying to mix fire and ice.

It's about more than feeling him, though. It's about the depth of her wanting. She *wants* him. There's a small, hollow void, even when she's right beside him, and it's because they truly know *nothing*: not why she's there, how long she'll be back, or even why she disappeared two weeks ago. How much time do they have together? Weeks? Months? A year? Is she here only to be near him and enjoy him, or is she here to make up for some sin in her human life?

Footsteps crunch on the gravel on the other side of the gate, and Lucy opens her eyes, taking a surprised step backward when she sees Maggie heading in to work.

"Trying to leave?" Maggie asks, eyes narrowed.

Lucy's ingrained manners battle with her frustration. She remembers the way the world seemed to snap like a rubber band when she'd tried to walk through the gate and how she ended up right back where she'd started. "I'm guessing you know I can't."

Maggie's laugh comes out sharp. "I was hoping it would be different for you." She studies Lucy for a beat. "What are you doing out here, girl?"

"I'm *thinking*," Lucy answers, defensive. "I'm out for a walk. I'm worried for Colin, and I'm confused."

"I'm sure you are. Can't find it in me to be sympathetic, though."

Lucy feels a bit like an amnesia victim who has woken to discover she's committed some great, secret crime. She'd happily avoid being horrible if only someone would tell her *how*. "Why weren't you surprised to see me? Everyone else who works here, I mean those who even bother to *really* look at me, act like I'm something to fear. You basically shooed me out with a broom."

"I suppose fear is how most people react to seeing a ghost." Maggie's answer is so matter of fact that Lucy feels her exasperation boil up inside. But Maggie holds up a hand to keep her from responding. "I was new here when you died. It wasn't that long ago, girl. Dot, Joe, all of them knew you as a student and still aren't sure if they believe you're the same girl. I tried to tell them the first time that ghosts come back to this place, but until you, no one seemed to want to believe me."

"What ghost was here before?"

"No way," Maggie says, shaking her head. "I'm not going down that road with you."

Lucy watches her, seeing a trace of vulnerability beneath the stern surface. "Then at least tell me why we come back."

This time, Maggie laughs. "I suspect you're here for that boy. He's like a magnet for you."

"Why is that a bad thing?"

Narrowing her eyes, Maggie says, "Don't know exactly why it's *him* you need. I wish I did, Lucy. But you think long and hard about how you felt when you saw Colin lying in the hospital bed. Were you relieved he was safe? Or disappointed you didn't kill him?"

It's too much. The nurse has crossed a line, and no matter how much Lucy wants to understand, horror and rage course through her so quickly that she turns, walking toward campus without another word. She doesn't look back to see, but she's almost certain she hears the rattling of the gate behind her.

Kill him? How could Maggie even suggest it? Lucy is the one who pulled Colin from the water, who ran to find help. Maggie herself admitted that she didn't know everything, but even knowing *something* is a lot farther along than where Lucy is. She only knows that she is falling for Colin and will do anything to not disappear again.

• • •

Obviously there have been others who've come back. Jay talked about the Walkers. Maggie clearly has stories of her own. And Lucy remembers something Ms. Baldwin said, that people don't *look*. That most people don't *need* to see. Could it be that simple? Lucy's spent countless hours watching the students around her—looking for a memory or something familiar—but maybe she's looking for the wrong thing. Maybe it's not a thing she should be watching for, but a *who*.

Without a destination in mind, she continues on, turning this way and that, moving from sidewalk to snow-covered lawn to gravel path and then sidewalk again. Following nothing but the instinctual map that seems to be unfolding in her mind.

She finds herself beside the statue, running her fingertips down the smooth, extended arm of Saint Osanna. The marble hums beneath her fingers, and Lucy curls her grip more firmly around it, feeling it warm. Somehow she knows there's life there—of one form or another, even if it's life in the way she is. If Lucy can return and form a makeshift body out of the elements, why can't the statue possess a spirit just the same?

Feet crunch through the snow, and she turns, catching Jay as he almost passes her by without noticing.

"Jay."

He stops, looks over at her vacantly before blinking into awareness. "Hey, rocker chick."

He walks to her, eyeing the statue skeptically before sitting beside her. Empty seconds tick by before either of them speaks. Finally, Jay asks, "How was he when you left?"

"He seemed fine," Lucy says, and then reaches up, tucking her hair behind her ears. "I can't stop thinking about how he could have died."

Jay is already shaking his head. "You don't know Colin like I do. Colin is the guy who never questions whether he can or should do something. He just does it. The stuff you saw him doing at the lake was nothing. Last summer, we went skydiving with my dad, and Colin pulled his chute at the last minute and landed easier than any of us. As crazy as it sounds, Colin doesn't know what dying even means."

Lucy curls her hands into fists, wanting to ask Jay about every single time Colin has dared to put his life in danger. But she suspects they would be here talking for hours.

"He's a good guy," Jay says, turning his face up into the biting wind.

Lucy swears she can feel blood pounding through her veins just thinking about him. "He seems like the *best* guy."

Smiling, Jay looks over at her. "Yeah, I guess that's what I meant." He pulls his jacket collar up, wincing at the cold. "What are you doing out here?"

She shrugs, shying away from answering and lying to Jay. "Waiting for someone."

He stands, shoving his hands deep into his pockets and tilting his head toward the dorm. "Clearly you're a badass, but I'm freezing. I'm going to head back to the room." He frowns a little, thoughtfully. "Do you live on campus?"

Lucy nods, noncommittal. "I'll let you know if I hear anything about Colin."

"Same."

She watches him walk away, shoulders up and head down, his short strides like tiny stabs aimed at the icy walkways. Lucy feels like there should be more there with Jay, some acknowledgment of the miracle of what happened or reliving of the trauma, but he's so matter of fact about it all.

She can tell it's cold out from the way students hunch over into their middles, grip their bags, lean into each other. At the entrance to every building, they rush in toward the warmth of the halls, but Lucy stands out in the wind, fascinated with how it no longer seems to fight her. Instead, she closes her eyes and presses back, determined to stay earthbound. Determined not to disappear or take Colin anywhere. Determined to find another like her.

Darkness is threatening and it's started to snow when Lucy looks past the trees and sees two figures pressed into the growing shadows of Ethan Hall. The boys huddle over something held between them. One laughs, and the other reaches up to touch his shoulder.

Lucy freezes.

The way the boy touches his friend is familiar. It's exactly the way Colin touches her, gently, preceded by a slow approach, as if he's afraid to startle her with the contact. Narrowing her eyes, she takes in their features. The careful one is tall and broad, athletic in build. His hair blows across a tanned forehead, skin that sees sun every month of the year. Even from this distance, she can see that the other boy, the one he touched, has smooth, unblemished, skin that resembles porcelain in its clarity. Like Lucy, he lacks the small scars and imperfections that are the hallmarks of the living.

He's like her.

Her mind turns wild at the realization, reaching for the opportunity to understand. She pushes herself forward, walking to them in only a few strides, calling out, "Excuse me!"

When they look up, terrified, and step apart immediately, Lucy realizes her mistake. They are lovers, hiding in the shadows for the privacy of an intimate conversation. Their silence is heavy with the panic of being discovered, and the living boy presses his hands to his face.

But the ghost stares at Lucy, eyes slowly widening. Stepping away from the wall, he moves toward her, wearing a smile.

She stares, unable to look away. He looks completely

inhuman, unreal. But she knows she's never noticed him before. "I didn't—" she stammers, holding up a shaky hand.

"I'm Henry Moss." He reaches forward and takes her hand, and it stills in his grip. "You okay there?"

His fingers are warm and feel like smooth glass. Releasing them, Lucy stumbles back a few steps before turning and falling back at the feet of her favorite statue. Her mind reels, wondering how she didn't think to look before—that there could be another like her, here *now*.

After a pause, the boys follow to sit on either side of her, and Lucy can feel them exchanging a look over the top of her head, though she can't begin to imagine what they're thinking, given the whirlwind of her own thoughts. For a second, she wonders if they can see the surface of her skin rippling with the impact of this discovery.

"This has been the most insane twenty-four hours of my . . . life," she says, laughing.

"Let's start with your name," Henry says, bumping his shoulder gently against hers.

"Lucy." She looks over at him, searching his face for any sign of life, and can't see it. There's no pulse in his throat, no freckles, no scars. Nothing but perfection. He simply looks like he's been drawn here. "You *are* like me, aren't you?"

Henry smiles so widely that his bright blue eyes crinkle at the corners. "I think so."

"Are there others like us here at Saint Osanna's?" She hesitates. "Walkers?"

Shaking his head, he murmurs, "I haven't seen any lately. Never really used that word to describe myself before."

"Lately? How long have you been here?" She wants to apologize for her rapid-fire questions, but Henry seems entirely unsurprised by her hunger to know these things. She wonders if it's possible that she's seen Henry a hundred times in the past few months without having noticed.

"I don't know. Sometimes I feel like I've been here forever. I only really remember being here for the past year and a half."

"But you've heard of the Walkers?"

"I've heard stories, sure," he says, shrugging. "It's why students are told not to go down to the lake, why this place has such a creepy reputation and Halloween is this huge deal." He presses a hand to his chest, giving her an indulgent smile. "I just assumed we were *misunderstood*."

Lucy allows a small smile to escape before she remembers her biggest fear, and the question comes bubbling up abruptly: "Have you ever vanished?"

He winces sympathetically. "Happened to me a couple of times when I first got here. That was the scariest. But it hasn't happened again for a while now." He looks to the boy beside him, confirming, "Maybe a year, Alex?"

"At least a year," Alex agrees.

"Really?" she asks, curiosity and vibrant hope making her voice come out thick.

Shrugging, Henry says, "I assumed it was kind of an adjustment thing."

Relief floods her so rapidly that for a pulse she feels unsteady. Her gaze drifts back to Alex. There's something oddly fascinating about the living boy. Henry doesn't look quite human to her, but there's something strange about Alex, too. She feels an eerie pull toward him. It's different from Colin, of course, but the air around Alex isn't empty like it is around the other students. Instead, it has almost a hypnotic hum to it.

His skin is sun-kissed, but now that she's closer, she sees the circles beneath his eyes. And there's something underneath, an exhaustion in the way he holds himself, bruising that pushes up beneath his skin, stiffness in his movements. It's almost like Lucy can see through him, to a part that lies deep inside, draining him.

"Lucy, where is your Protected?" Henry asks. Lucy jerks herself back to the conversation. His eyes move over her face as she tries to understand his question.

"My 'Protected'?"

He grins. "Sorry. It's how I think of Alex. I mean, where's the person you came back for?"

"You mean Colin?"

Laughing, he straightens and wipes his hands on his jeans. "I need to start at the beginning with you, don't I?"

She presses her hands to her cheeks in what she knows to be reflexive movement, a leftover from the long-forgotten days when she would have blushed. "I'm sorry. I'm having a hard time processing some of this. I knew there had been others at one point or another. I just didn't think I would *meet* any."

"Well, partly that's because you're here for Colin. I don't think it's natural for Guardians to think that much about anyone other than our Protected. But I suspect we're all over. We're the kids no one ever remembers. We're the ones no one misses at the reunion. Even I haven't noticed you before."

Because he wasn't looking, she thinks.

Alex and Henry continue to watch her with the same small and patient smiles while his words hover in the air. She laughs briefly, a soft exhale. "You think we're *Guardians*?"

"I do," Henry says. "And there's no one here to tell me I'm wrong. I didn't know anything when I got here. I walked around, aimless. But when I found Alex, being near him didn't just feel right; it felt critical. As in, when I left him alone, I felt I was doing something *wrong*."

"Yes," Lucy whispers, tingling down to her fingertips.

"I don't know why he needs me, if it's because he was sick

and I make him healthy, or something else. But in the year since I found him, I feel like I finally have purpose, and lately, I feel stronger every day. Just look at him; he looks so much better, too. Something in his eyes . . . I know I'm doing what I'm here to do."

Lucy looks to Alex again. Is that what she sees, his illness? She wonders if Henry sees it too. When she looks at Alex, she doesn't feel quite as hopeful about his condition. She also doesn't see anything different about his eyes. They're blue, in the same way that hers are brown. *Except* to Colin.

"You're sick?" she asks.

"Acute lymphocytic leukemia," he says matter-of-factly. "Henry found me the week I was diagnosed." He glances at Henry before adding, "I'm in remission now."

"I'm so glad," Lucy says. "But—*who*? Who sent us back? Why us? Why Colin and Alex?"

Henry stills her with a hand on her knee. "You're wasting your time asking questions. I asked them every day for a year, and trust me, no one will drift down from the clouds and give you the welcome pamphlet."

Lucy envies Henry's certainty, and maybe the only way she'll get it is with more time. The thought is both a relief and mildly depressing. "How much do you remember about your life before?"

"Not much," Henry admits. "I know my name. I know

I loved sports because I have brief memories of playing, or watching. But other than a flash here and there—a face, a feeling—it's pretty blank. Nothing around here looks familiar."

Lucy remembers waking on the trail and the instinctive way she knew where to find someone. "So you weren't a student here?"

"I don't think so, no."

"We've gone through the yearbooks," Alex offers. "Nothing."

"Huh." Lucy pulls at her lip, thinking.

"What's 'huh'?" Henry asks, leaning forward to catch her gaze.

"I was a Saint Osanna's student. I died here. According to an article Colin found, I was killed at the lake. That's where I woke up. I figured that we had this connection, which explained why I was here for him."

"Oh. Wow," Henry says. "I'm so sorry, Lucy."

"But then what *is* the connection? Why are we both here? And why can't we leave?"

Henry and Alex look at each other, each of them shaking their heads. It doesn't add up. Lucy pulls her sleeves over her hands. She's not cold, exactly, but a strange creeping sensation spreads up her arms. "How are you so sure about the Guardian thing? Don't you ever worry you're . . . bad?"

Henry's roaring laugh is so surprising, Lucy actually scoots back when it bursts from him. "You think you'd come back to hurt him? Can you even imagine?"

She can't. She shakes her head, exhaling a slow, anxious breath as she aches to let go of Maggie's horrible suggestion. "But you're here and Alex is still sick." Before Henry can protest, she adds, "And yesterday, Colin fell into a frozen lake and almost died. It's hard to feel like it's a coincidence that it was the first time I went along with him. I sort of feel like a bad omen."

Henry's expression straightens. "First, Alex might have been sick, but he's getting better. And that kid who fell in the lake is your Protected?"

She nods. "Yeah, he fell in and . . ." She starts to tell them about the trail, about being able to touch Colin as if they were made of the same thing, but for some reason, she stops. It feels too complicit somehow, as if the accident benefited her too greatly. "And I thought he was going to die," she says instead.

"But *did* he?" Henry asks, smiling a secret smile that makes Lucy uneasy, as if the location of the missing puzzle piece is obvious to everyone but her.

"Well, no, but he could have."

"I've heard of him," Alex says. "We don't hang out with the same group, but he's known to be pretty crazy. Hasn't he broken, like, practically every bone in his body?" He laughs. "No wonder he has you."

"Well, yes, but—"

"Lucy, stop," Alex says gently. His hand barely hovers over her arm, a practiced touch. "Colin's here; he's safe. Has it occurred to you that maybe you're the reason he *didn't* die?"

Chapter 21 · HER

THIS TIME, WHEN LUCY WALKS BACK ACROSS
campus, she barely registers that the howling
wind no longer throws her across the path. Long
strands of her hair whip around her face, and she pulls it back
absently, lost in Alex and Henry's words.

Guardian.

He almost died.

But did he?

She doesn't think Colin has any idea how big a story
this has been around school, and when Mr. Velasquez's car
pulls up in front of the dorm, it seems like the entire student
body is camped outside. Colin looks pale and weak when
he climbs out and walks to the front door, the headmaster
pushing back the surge of whispering bodies to create a path
forward. Lucy backs away from where she's standing near

the pond and sits on the bench where she first told Colin she died. She wishes she had even one drop of Henry's certainty, because if she chooses not to believe him, then she's every bit as lost as she was before.

Lucy's grateful for the short days of winter. Sunset is at 6:08, and at 6:30 Colin is opening the dormitory door to silently let her in.

"Did you eat?" she asks once they're in his room, door closed, music playing in the background. Jay has come in and left again, letting Lucy and Colin reconnect in relative peace.

He nods, studying her as he sometimes does, as if he can unlock her secrets with the pressure of his attention. "Dot brought me about five meals."

Only now does it occur to Lucy that Colin could be sick, like Alex, that maybe that's what they have in common and why each of them has attracted a ghost. But though Colin looks and feels different to her than other people, she doesn't see the same underlying exhaustion she saw in Alex. There's no illness draining the life from him right before her eyes. If anything, even in his weakened state, Colin seems more resilient. The air around him pulses with life. "Are you tired?" she asks, fidgeting.

"No. I feel like I've slept the last two days away." He sits down on the edge of his mattress, pulling the heavy brown comforter up and over his shoulders. "And I can't stop think-ing about the lake."

"I keep seeing you falling through. And then on the trail . . ." She tries to temper the longing in her voice, but her skin hums with the memory of what came after.

He blinks away and looks out the window. Fat snowflakes gather on his windowsill. "If I didn't die, but I could touch you, then you must be somewhere in between too."

"I have no idea." She moves closer but keeps some space between them when he shivers slightly. "I don't think I'm the only one like me at Saint Osanna's."

Colin turns to look at her, his face shadowed in the dark room. Bluish marks sweep heavily under his eyes, but she can see interest bloom across his expression. His lips curl into a half smile. She tells him about looking for others and finally finding Henry and Alex.

"They're like us. Henry died too, and is back."

Colin's brow furrows, and a hundred reactions cross his fea-tures before he says simply, "And the other guy, Alex, is . . . *me* in this scenario?"

"Yeah, they're together."

"Alex Broderick? Tall, blond kid?" Colin asks, and Lucy nods. "He's gay?"

"Do you know him?" she asks.

"Well, I don't *know* him know him, but I've seen him

around. He used to play lacrosse and stuff before he got sick. Cancer, I think."

"Leukemia. I guess that's when he found Henry, right after he was diagnosed."

Colin shifts under the blankets, eyes growing heavy.

"So I've wondered, if I'm a ghost, then how do I move things, wear clothes, touch you? But if I'm mostly solid, how do I know I'm not some form of demon instead? Who sent me here?"

Colin nods beside her.

She tells him about how long Henry has been here, about how with Alex being sick, Henry is sure that he was sent back for him. "I've always felt like my heart was taken from my body, but it somehow ended up in you. I think Henry kind of feels the same way, like he's keeping Alex safe."

"I'm glad," he says, leaning to kiss her cheek. "I've always felt safe with you. I wonder if ghosts like you are everywhere, protecting people."

"You're not surprised?"

"Why would I be?" he mumbles, already drifting off.

Lucy turns and looks out the window, for the first time realizing that she is the only one who is surprised by any of this.

In the middle of the night, Colin pushes the heating pads off his chest and legs and climbs out of bed. He wraps himself in about four sweaters, twitching with constant shivering. His desk chair creaks as he sits down and begins typing. It's 2:14 in the morning.

"What are you doing?"

"Looking stuff up," he mumbles.

"What stuff?"

"Spirit stuff. Dying."

"Do you want to talk about it?"

He scratches the back of his neck and throws her an apologetic glance over his shoulder. "Not yet. Sorry."

She lies back to stare at his ceiling, at the tiny solar system she likes to imagine Colin meticulously sticking in place everywhere he's lived. "You okay?"

He grunts in affirmation, and she rolls over, wishing he would come closer. She's had a taste of what he must have felt when she was gone, and here in the dark, with him so far away, she feels a strange itch to talk some more about what he felt on the trail and what he thinks happened. It feels like a tight spring has been lodged in her chest, uncoiling slowly upward.

"Do you know how many people have had near-death experiences?" he asks, oblivious to her anxiety.

"How many?"

"Thousands. More than thousands. Most of the stuff written about it is religious. But not all. Some people think that near-death experiences are a form of hallucination, but since I know you felt everything too, we know I wasn't hallucinating."

She rolls back over, forcing a lighter tone. "Are you cruising around NearDeath.org?"

"No," he says without humor. "Seriously, Luce. So many people have almost died or *actually* died, and seen things or experienced things like I did, and these people are fine. There's even a *Journal of Near-Death Studies*. There's a Near Death Experience Research Organization. Like, *science*."

"Pseudoscience."

"Lucy, that makes *you* pseudoscience."

"I'm not near dead, Colin. I'm dead dead."

He ignores her, and she listens to the sound of his fingers on the keyboard. They don't seem to be cooperating, and he swears repeatedly under his breath. "You're neither dead nor alive," he counters. "You've been sent back. Or, maybe your mind has separated from your original body and has figured out a way to come back as my Guardian. And I can be like you; we know that now."

"Not easily," she says, growing strangely full of excited energy. She stands, feeling like she wants to take off running. "And probably not again."

"I *felt* you, Luce. You felt me, too. And not in a maddening too-much-too-little way." His tone makes the vibrations inside her grow. There's a steely determination there she hasn't heard before. "Are you telling me you didn't like it?"

She's silent, unable to speak past the strange humming in her chest. She did feel him, and he felt better than anything.

"This one guy had the same thing happen," he continues. "Fell in a lake, hypothermia, saw the world in a way he'd never seen it before. The whole thing."

"Huh."

"Yeah, and he's on this message board saying he did it again, because he wanted to know that what he saw was real."

"You need to *recover*," she says. "You're not seriously thinking about this as a good thing, are you?"

The answering silence fills the room like rushing water. She walks closer and leans over him, reading the message board posts over his shoulder. There are thousands of entries. He follows a link and creates a user name and password.

She bends and kisses his jaw, his neck, hoping to distract him, but she can feel him grow tense under her touch.

"You need to sleep."

"In a minute. I want to join this site."

"I think this goes against Guardian protocol." She tries to keep her voice light, but the words come out stiff and formal. She doesn't want to police Colin's activity. Even more, she doesn't understand this strange hyperactivity that has overtaken her. "This website creeps me out," she says instead.

He laughs at this, at the ghost girl being afraid of ghosts. "This one guy sees hypothermia almost like an extreme sport. Because of the way your cellular activity slows, brain death is the very last thing. This guy on here, ColdSport, thinks it can be done in a way that challenges the system, like biking up a big hill or running a marathon."

He's serious. She looks at the forum he's logged into. There are three user names that take up most of the posts. Three crazy people out there preaching to their own tiny crazy choir. She slips her hands inside his sweaters, along his skin. "Colin, stop."

His skin is fever hot, and he shivers beneath her palms. Standing, he reluctantly follows her back to his bed, but her mind is reeling. When he finally falls asleep, she slips over to his desk, hovers on his chair, and focuses intently on pressing each key on his keyboard to enter her search.

She finds hundreds of stories, but shuts down the computer when she registers that none of them sound like what happened at the lake.

Chapter 22 · HIM

THE SILENCE IS LIKE A THICK CURTAIN BETWEEN them. Colin washes dishes as best he can and hands them, through the invisible film of discomfort, to Dot, who dries and puts them away.

"You're awfully quiet," he says, digging his hands into the warm, sudsy water. They're better today: fingers less stiff, his grip steadier.

"So are you," she shoots back.

He drops the baking sheet he was scrubbing and turns to look at her. "Christ, Dot. Just say whatever it is that you're thinking."

"Are you going to tell me about this Lucy?"

Colin groans, turning away and looking out the window. He's been expecting this ever since Dot heard the name "Lucy" at the hospital. Dot remembers Lucy's murder as clearly as if it happened yesterday, but as far as he knows, Dot's never seen him with her. For all she knows, it's just another girl.

"She's a girl in my class," he says, returning to the dishes.

"I've seen her, you know. She looks a lot like a girl named Lucy who went here years ago. In fact," Dot says, stepping closer, "she looks a lot like the dead girl you asked about a few weeks back."

Colin stares at his hands in the water. They're shaking now, but it has nothing to do with having gone into the lake.

"I told you, I always heard the stories," Dot whispers, her voice trembling. "Different people insisting they'd seen a girl at the lake, the man in uniform sitting on a bench, or a man walking around campus, sweeping the walkway. Maggie swore up and down for years that this place was haunted. But, Lucy . . . being such a part of your world . . ."

Colin turns to her, eyes pleading. "Dot, do you remember when you told me and Jay that there are things we don't understand in this world?"

Dot nods, eyes wide.

"And do you remember when you promised me I wasn't crazy? Do you believe what you told me?"

She laughs, reaching up to put a soft hand on his cheek. "I do."

"So can you trust me?"

Shaking her head the tiniest bit, she whispers, "I don't know. It just doesn't feel right."

"It doesn't feel right because you don't understand it, not because it's wrong," he says. "For the first time in my life, I feel like I know what I want." Looking back and forth between her eyes, Colin can see that Dot is going to give him more leash than she's ever given him before.

Her eyes fill with tears, and she offers him a half smile. "Just feels like I never see you anymore."

Colin shifts where he stands, his eyes boring into the soapy water. "Been busier than normal. School . . . friends," he says, swallowing down the guilt that blooms in his chest.

The silence stretches on before Dot sets her towel aside, reaching over to place her hand on his forearm. "Promise me you won't do anything dangerous."

When he nods, Colin realizes he's made a promise he has no intention of keeping.

Colin is accustomed to being the center of attention. He's competed in bike races and trials competitions practically since he could walk. He's crazy tall; he's never been shy. And when his parents died, no one gave him a minute alone for years.

But the attention he's getting today is all wrong. Two news vans are parked on campus, and the reporters camped inside try to ask him questions before Joe calls security. His classmates are hysterical; some are insisting it was the ghost of the lake that made him fall in. Others eye him like he's some kind of mythical creature. Everyone wants to touch him. Teachers seem shaken, and there's a mandatory assembly on winter safety in the gym. He feels the pressure of every pair of eyes, watching to make sure he's okay, that his arms work, his gait is steady, that he's making sense. The words "tragedy," "close call," and "fences" are being thrown around.

Here's the thing: It wasn't a tragedy. It wasn't a close call. If they build a fence around that lake, he'll tear the motherfucker down. He wants to go back. He wants to know that what he saw was real, that the way Lucy felt wasn't his imagination. The minutes with Lucy in that world felt better than any crazy trick, more visceral than anything else happening around him. His body might have been dying, but he felt alive. Really alive.

He knows that should scare him, but it doesn't.

"Oh. My. *God.* Colin!" a voice screeches behind him, and reflexively, he ducks his head, anticipating the set of claws that will run up his neck and into his hair.

Amanda grips his head and digs in her nails as she pulls him into a hug. "I heard you died for like an *hour!*"

"I didn't die."

"I have been *freaking out*, Colin. Freaking. Out."

"Sorry," he says, extracting himself from her clutches. Of course, Lucy chooses this exact moment to drift down the hall and settle beside him. She glances at Colin, then at Amanda, but where he expects raised eyebrows, he gets only an amused smirk.

"Hey," she says.

"Hey." He smiles at her, eyes lingering on her lips until she smiles outright. "That's better."

Amanda ignores Lucy. "Shelby called me last night and told me what happened. And, oh my God, I totally flipped out. Like, what if you had died? What if you had *died*, Colin? We would have been completely fli—"

"Amanda, have you met Lucy?" He interrupts, hoping she comes up for air. He's embarrassed both for Amanda's lack of manners and the Past-Colin who actually had sex with this girl.

Amanda regards Lucy as if she's never seen her before. "Hey," she says, uninterested, before turning back to Colin. "Did it hurt? Did you get all hot? And undress?"

He lifts an eyebrow in the way that Lucy likes and feels her slide closer.

"I didn't undress," he says.

Amanda has the gall to look disappointed. "Oh, good. I hear a lot of people do that when they're hyperthermic."

"Hypo," he mutters.

"I was getting there," Lucy says, grinning up at him. "Just didn't have enough time."

Colin feigns shock, pressing his fingertips to his rounded lips. Out of the corner of his eye, he can see Amanda working up to something. She fills with an inhale, pulling together irritation and outrage and trying to coat it in indifference. "You were there?"

Lucy nods mildly at Amanda and stretches to kiss his jaw. "See you later."

He waves, cursing Lucy under his breath for leaving him alone with his ex-girlfriend, though he can't exactly blame her for not wanting to stay. With perfect timing, Amanda's roommate approaches, wearing a sympathetic smile.

"Hey, Colin," she says. "How are you?"

"I'm fine," he answers, for the thousandth time today. But this time, he doesn't mind as much. He's always liked Liz. He owes her big-time for the damage control she managed after his breakup with Amanda. "How are you?"

"Good," she says simply. And right when Colin expects her to move on, she adds, "I had a cousin who fell through the ice. Up in Newfoundland."

He nods, disappointed and already disengaged. He's heard a variation of this story about half as many times today as he's answered the obligatory "How are you?" What follows will be the predictable: *You're lucky you made it out alive. He was never the same again. She lost her left thumb, had permanent nerve damage in her face.*

But he should have known Liz would break the mold. "He was unconscious on the ice for hours and lived."

"What?" Amanda forgotten, he steps closer to Liz, surprising her so much she steps back into the wall.

"He fell in and managed to climb out, but it was four hours before he was found with no detectable pulse. At least, that's what they guessed."

"And he's a vegetable?"

"No, that's the weirdest part," she says, smiling in a strange way that makes his skin hum. "He's totally fine."

By the end of the day, Colin is practically vibrating to talk to Lucy. It's only when he sees her headed toward him and away from a mass of students walking to the trail, bundled up in holiday-themed scarves and hats, that he remembers tonight is the Winter Social.

"Where is everyone going?" Lucy asks once she reaches him, turning to watch the migration.

"The upperclassmen have this evil thing called Winter Social every year before the holiday. Everyone except us townies gets nostalgic and weepy over being separated for two whole weeks. The seniors decorate the overlook above the lake and—"

"*Our* lake?"

He looks down at her and smiles at the possessive bite to her voice. "Yeah. But don't worry. They don't venture down to the lake itself. Nobody does," he adds, hoping she hears the same in his. "They decorate the area on the hill above it and play horrible pop music, and everyone makes out with everyone else, and then people start fighting because they've snuck in alcohol, so it turns into a giant drama."

Lucy grins. "Sounds fun."

"It's a social at a boarding school. So, basically, you hang out with the same people, just half a mile away from where you usually hang out."

Ignoring him, she says, "And it's about time you took me on a date."

"Trust me, Lucy. It's not your thing."

"How would you know?" Her grin turns seductive. "Being near the lake and kissing you sounds like my thing."

He finds himself unable to argue with that reasoning.

A long path of battery-operated lights line the way to the overlook, and thousands more hang from every possible tree branch, illuminating the dozens of bodies that wave in swarms to the music blaring from four speakers flanking the area. The overlook is outlined with propped-up wreaths of holly, and everything in the surrounding area looks icy blue in the moonlight.

It's hard to believe how close he is to where it happened, and Colin finds himself looking off into the distance, down the hill to the other side of the lake, where the ice opens up to the blackness below. There's no way he'll be able to see it from here, but he imagines the jagged hole surrounded by warning tape, the signs telling everyone to stay away. He wonders what it says about him that he's not afraid, and rather than fear or dread at the memory of being plunged into the darkness, he feels longing and anticipation, the tease of adrenaline trickling through his veins.

Jay walks up beside them and stretches. "The lake looks so much smaller from up here."

It feels like the world around them falls silent for a beat before Jay coughs, breaking the tension. Colin turns his attention back to the other students.

"Kiss me, Lucy. We're under the mistletoe." Jay makes exaggerated smooching sounds at her, pointing over his head to one of the many branches laden with plastic mistletoe.

Lucy pretends to stretch to kiss Jay's face, but then runs away, feigning disgust. Colin watches, fascinated, as Jay chases her off down a small hill and she ducks behind a tree, laughing and shrieking when he tries to touch her. Colin has no idea how Jay would react if he felt Lucy's skin against his, and even more, has no idea how she would react if he managed to actually grab her, but for the moment, she doesn't seem concerned about it. It's the first time Colin has ever seen Lucy act her age.

"Having fun?" he says when she returns. He can't be imagining the pink flush to her cheeks, or the way she seems almost breathless with happiness. He can't be imagining how substantial she feels when she presses against him, as if a solid girl is forming beneath the fog of her skin.

"The most. I have yet to see any flasks, kissing, or drama, though."

Colin watches as Lucy bends to tie a loose shoelace on her boots. The boots are black, but tonight, under the lights and snow, they look iridescent. He wonders if everything becomes somewhat unearthly as soon as she puts it on.

"Ready to dance?" she asks.

"Not even a little." He follows her anyway.

As Lucy dances, Colin wonders how she doesn't stick out like a lit flare among the other, less graceful, students. Her hands move rhythmically over her head. Her feet glide, almost disconnected from the earth. She's weightless as she playfully dances circles around him, lighting up with laughter. He's never seen her like this, and it makes it easier for him to resist the pull he feels down the hill, toward the lake.

And then her smile fades for a beat, and her eyes move past him to the edge of the overlook, the tipping point, sloping downhill. The lake feels like a throbbing beacon in the blackness. Her eyes turn the same warm amber they do when they lie side by side, and he can think about nothing but how badly he wants to kiss her. As he stares, she blinks up to him, caught.

"I was remembering what it was like," she says, guilt draining her eyes to a soft gray, adding, "I'm so glad you're okay."

For whatever reason, her voice sounds fainter when she says this last part, and he knows exactly why. If she feels what he feels, she wants to walk downhill, into the shadows, if only to just look at the sharp cracks and cold, silent water beneath.

Chapter 23 · HER

S HE'S STRADDLING HIS WAIST, BUTTONING AND unbuttoning the first half of his shirt, over and over, fascinated with how much concentration it takes. She's seen him do this with one hand in only a few seconds.

But after he fell in the lake, it took him a week to be able to button his shirt easily.

She watches her fingers move along his chest and down across the toned lines of his stomach. Her flesh flickers between ivory and peachy opaque. She has no scars, no freckles, no bruises. Aside from the way her skin seems to glow and dim, there's nothing that differentiates her from an airbrushed photograph. Colin's hands are rough and damaged. He has a small birthmark on the back of his left wrist, scars across two knuckles on his right hand. He's so obviously human, and she is so obviously not. She wonders for a flash what it's like for him to see these differences now, after the lake and the snow, and their skin that felt the same.

"What do you think I'm made of?" she asks.

"I think you're made of awesome."

"I mean, you're mostly carbon. Nitrogen. Oxygen. Hydrogen. Some other stuff."

"Probably a *lot* of other stuff." He laughs. "I eat a lot of junk food."

"But what am *I*?" She presses her hand to his chest again, brushes a curl off his forehead. Even when she's trying as hard as she can to be still, she swears she can feel the collisions of thousands of molecules inside her. "I feel like my body is solid mass but . . . so different. Like I'm made up of the elements that happen to be hanging out in the air at any given moment."

He slowly peeks up at her and smiles. "You're definitely here, and you're definitely different. I think I like your theory." His eyes sparkle. "So I guess we should be glad you weren't brought back somewhere near Chernobyl. You'd be even hotter."

She laughs and he grins at his own cleverness, but their smiles fade as they stare at each other.

"When I kissed your cheek at the lake, before I went in, you were more solid," he says.

She felt it too. Felt stronger, more present. "Maybe it's the water in the air. It's drier here in your room with the heater on. If there's more moisture in the air, there's simply more content for my body to steal and use."

He makes a sound in the back of his throat that sounds like agreement.

The question bubbles up, escapes. "What were you thinking when you found me on the trail but you were still in the lake . . . ?"

He blinks away, looking out the window. "I didn't feel cold or hot or scared. I only wanted to find you."

"Why don't you seem to want to talk about this?"

He pushes his hands behind his head. "Because I want to do it again."

The sentence, finally and so plainly spoken aloud, echoes in his room, hanging like a thick, plastic curtain between them and coating the moment with a strange, leaden shadow. Her immediate reaction to his words is a paradoxical relief, so her response comes out thickly, like it's fighting to stay on her tongue. "Colin, that is insane."

"What do you mean?" he asks, sitting up so she's forced to move off his lap. "I ended up on that trail, beneath your tree, Luce. There was something different about that world, something perfect. And you were there. It isn't insane."

She tucks her legs under her and stares at him. Part of her—the part that is dark and tiny and dangerous—feels a thick, curling love for what he's saying. He's right; it *wasn't* insane. For those few minutes, she could touch him, kiss him. He was hers. On the trail, he was just like her.

And then she remembers that she's supposed to be his Guardian, and a sharp spike of guilt shoots through her.

"It was easy to find you," he says. "Like we were meant to be there together."

"Colin, I know what Henry says about me protecting you, but . . . I mean, you could have frozen to death. You could have drowned."

He leans forward, carefully kissing her bare shoulder next to the strap of her top. He pushes it aside and kisses the spot where her heart should beat. What feels like pure white electricity shoots through her. She wants to put her hands in his hair and hold him there.

"I don't think so," he says. Lucy opens her mouth to argue the obvious, but when no words come out right away, Colin shakes his head. "Just listen. Okay?"

She nods, unable to protest convincingly. She has no idea how much time she has with him. It lends a certain urgency to every minute. She wants him in the water, on the trail, in the underwater starry sky, with her.

"What if I could go into the lake again and have an hour with you every now and then? Just us, curled up together in the snow. Luce, the world was crazy there. It was silver and light and, like, *alive*." When he pauses, she can't find words, and in her silence he barrels on, encouraged. "I have to see it again. Jay could come with us and pull me out fast. . . ."

She remembers feeling his skin and his lips and his laughter. She remembers tasting his sounds and feeling how they fit. He kissed her like he was discovering a new vibrant color. And while she remembers other kisses, smiles pressed tightly to hers, she knows it was never like this. Still, the temptation tastes wrong somehow, a vinegar-dipped sugar cube.

"I don't know if he would be up for that. . . ." She trails off shakily.

"After you walked away in the hall, this girl Liz came up. She said her cousin fell into this lake in Newfoundland. He got out, but was unconscious on the ice for four hours."

Her eyes snap to his. "What?"

"Four," he confirms, grinning at her reaction, as if she's already signed on to this.

She stands, moving to fiddle with a cup full of pens on his desk. She lifts it easily, as if it weighs nothing. Before she has a chance to marvel at the achievement, he stands and walks over to her, buttoning his shirt.

"I read about the story, Luce. It's true. It was all over the local news. And it's happened before. Apparently, there's at least one story about it every winter. The reporter is one of the guys on the forums now. He's totally obsessed with it." He puts a hot hand on her shoulder and squeezes gently, but this time she barely registers it. She wants more information. "I think if we're careful, we can make it work. Plus," he says, quieter now, "that kid didn't even have a Guardian."

"If I let you do this, I'm not a Guardian," she says, stepping out of his grip. "I'm something bad." She tries to keep her voice light, but the truth keeps the words stark, blown bare like a smooth tree trunk.

"You're definitely not *bad*," he says with the kind of conviction that she's certain she'll never have. "Do you know how I know?"

She looks up and melts. In the dark room, his eyes are deep amber, his lashes long and his blink so slow and patient. "How?"

"Because I've lost everyone I loved. Instead, I got you. The universe might have taken the others away, but it sent you back."

"But don't you ever wonder why you need a Guardian, and why it's *me*?"

"I used to." He glances out the window and then down at his shoes, kicking at something on the floor.

She watches him closely. With a small tug of anxiety beneath her ribs, she realizes he's kept something from her. "What changed?"

He looks up again and meets her eyes. "I think we're connected because I was the kid who saw your murderer take you into the woods. I told Dot, and she called the police."

Lucy stills, her hands bracing on the desk chair behind her. "Why didn't you tell me this?"

Colin speaks over her, apologizing immediately. "I was afraid that if you had closure, if you knew all the details, that you'd go away." He reaches out, touches her arm as if to convince himself that she is, indeed, still here.

"So they caught this guy because of you?"

He shrugs. "I think so. That's what the article said, anyway."

She feels her smile form on her face and spread down into her chest, where she never feels hollow when she's with him. "I may have only a pocketful of memories about anything useful, but I do know one thing."

"What's that?"

"You were my Guardian first, then."

His grin matches hers, but it has a distinctly cocky twist to it. "I like to think so."

Chapter 24 · HIM

COLIN IS POSITIVE THAT LUCY IS INTO THE idea of returning to the lake. Her eyes are this crazy orange, as if her entire brain is on fire with the possibilities, and the light passes back through her irises like a telegraph to him: Do this. *Do it.*

"This can only end badly." But her voice wavers a bit, and he wonders if it's something she's thought about before today too.

Days turn into weeks, and the snow keeps falling, blanketing everything that doesn't move. Colin doesn't push, doesn't talk to Lucy about going into the lake anymore. Instead, their conversations slowly grow heavy with everything left unsaid.

One morning she asks him what he's thinking about and

his starkly honest answer, "How you felt on the trail," makes her turn and walk away, arms crossed over her middle as if holding herself together.

But she finds him later, after class, a small apology in her eyes and in her smile.

He says his aloud. "Sorry. I know you don't like the idea." And holds her face between his palms, repeating it against her lips.

They walk together, hands entwined, back to his dorm. She reads on his bed while he does homework, lying on her stomach, her legs bent, feet slowly kicking back and forth. Colin gives up pretending to read for outright staring at her, remembering the trail, her hungry kisses, her solid weight. There was nothing insubstantial or unsatisfying about the kiss on the trail. He felt her laughter.

"Lucy."

She hesitates before looking up, as if sensing something particular in his tone. "Mmm?"

He watches her fingertips stroking her collarbone while she stares at his hands. Her eyes flash warm and deep amber when she catches him looking at her throat, at the spot he first parted his lips and tasted her skin. It was sweet and the tiniest bit salty. She tasted of girl and rain and relief. He doesn't say anything else, only looks at her, thinking, *Please. Please.*

"I can't," she says. "*You* can't."

"Why?"

"I wouldn't be able to live with myself if we did that."

He can't help it. He smiles when she says this, and her mouth twitches at the corners.

"Colin, I'm serious."

But he can't stand the thought that it won't happen again. His curiosity feels like an itch across every inch of his skin. "I need to know if what I saw was real."

Her eyes melt to the color of warm honey before she turns back to her book, her fingers making a tight fist around his comforter.

"There's nothing in the world as good as what happened on the trail," he says.

When she looks up, she looks so miserable. "I know."

"But we don't have that *here*," he whispers. "It isn't the same."

She squirms, pulling her hair over her shoulder and squinting at the words on the page in front of her. He ignores her feigned distraction, crawling toward her in a way that makes him feel like a predatory cat hunting prey.

"Lucy."

Her eyes remain trained on the page. "What?"

"Let me try this."

"Try what?"

He reaches for her, gently urging her to twist and lie on her back, easing her down onto his pillow.

It takes nothing to undress her. The slip of a button, a tug of a zipper. Soft fabric pulled over her head. He pinches a simple clasp and exposes a world of smooth, bare skin.

"I have an idea," he assures her, his hands slipping her pants down her legs. "Just trust me, okay?"

"Okay." She nods, watching him with eyes that churn a deep, coffee brown.

"I've given this some thought."

She laughs, and it's husky and low. "I bet you have."

He tastes the skin of her ankle, her knee. Thigh. He blows a breath across where leg meets hip. "Is this okay?"

She nods, eyes wider than he's ever seen them, and he simply exhales right where her legs are parted.

He doesn't even have to pretend to breathe fast. He's practically out of his mind with wanting this girl, watching her writhe below him. Her fingers find his hair and pull. Her back bows, and with one last puff of air across her skin, he hears a sound he's never heard a girl make before, something between a sob and a plea. But still, he sits up and kisses her afterward, and apologizes.

Curling into him, she apologizes too.

"I want to actually *touch* you next time," he says into the sweetness of her neck.

She presses her face into his shoulder, her second apology coming out only as air.

He does what she asks and stays away from the lake and the misty trails and the ice. It feels like the snow swallows him too. A heavy weight settles into his bones, like blocks of cement anchoring his feet to the ground. But his insides rage. Colin and Lucy go to school, he works when he's scheduled, and they spend long nights cocooned in his blankets and wrapped around each other so close that he can't tell where he ends and she begins. But it's not the same.

He tells her she's more than he ever hoped for.

He tells her that he's in love.

He asks her to never leave.

But she does.

When he opens his eyes in the blue-gray light of dawn, the air is unmoving. There's no soft hum next to him, no phantom weight pressed against his chest. He sits up slowly, runs his hand through his hair, and stands, dressing in the first clean clothes that he finds. He doesn't look back at the empty bed.

Eight hours of school stretch in front him, and he wonders how he'll make it through, carrying around the restless need to look for her, wrapped up in the knowledge that it's useless. He can't even think about how long she might be gone this time. Days? Weeks? Longer? Thinking of her is like pressing on a bruise: fascination, sick pleasure, and lingering pain.

On the walk to work, he remembers what he said as they fell asleep. *Stay.* He thinks he felt her slipping through his fingers even then, felt her grow lighter in his arms as she arched against his body like a feather caught in a breeze.

He's done everything she's asked, but it wasn't enough.

Colin talks Jay into skipping school the next day. They throw the bikes in the back of his truck and head out to the lake, hiking their way to where a few daring sledders have packed down the snow.

For a few hours, he's almost able to forget. They ride through the cold until he's sweating beneath layers of clothing, pushing himself harder than he has in ages. They tackle the trails, jump off ramps, and each wipe out at least a dozen times on an impromptu ramp they cut into the snow.

Colin is balancing on the back of the bench near the lake when Jay finally asks the question Colin knows has been gnawing at him.

"She's gone again, isn't she?"

Colin's tires land with a soft crunch, and he looks up at Jay, squinting against the brightness of the sky. "Yeah."

"Shit. Dude, do you think she's off using somewhere?"

"She isn't into drugs." Colin glares at Jay before looking down and flicking a leaf off his handlebar. The hills are silent, but the wind howls around them, catching the snow and spinning it before letting it fall back to the ground. "I think I need to tell you something."

Jay kicks the snow from his boots and waits.

"So, Lucy . . . Man, I don't even know how to say this." Colin laughs at the absurdity of this and feels a wave of sympathy for Lucy in hindsight, for his reaction the night she told him the truth. But, God, he *needs* to tell someone. He's not sure he can go another day shouldering the weight of her absence alone. "She's dead," he says simply, after all.

Jay's legs buckle, and he catches the back of the bench before slipping. "What the hell? How are you just telling me—"

"No! Not like that. I mean, she's *always* been dead, Jay. Well, not always. But at least as long as I've known her."

Eyes narrowed, Jay's expression pinches into irritation. "That's not funny."

Colin doesn't answer; he only stares down at the slush as it seeps into the sides of his shoes. "You *know* she's different."

"Yeah, *different.* Like with the boots and badass take on the frumpy uniform and how she doesn't look at anyone but you. Not dead."

"I know it sounds crazy—"

"You think?" Long moments of silence stretch between them before Jay adds, "You're serious about this."

Colin meets his eyes, gaze unwavering, and nods.

"So she's what? Like . . . a Walker?"

"Yeah, essentially."

"But I've helped her with her coat. I've . . ." Jay trails off, blinking.

"We don't understand everything. She met another ghost here at school, and he's convinced they're, like, guardian spirits or something."

"Okay?" Jay scratches his neck, looking completely confused.

"So, just stay with me here, okay?"

Jay nods, and Colin breaks a brittle twig from the tree beside him, poking deep holes in the snow near his rear tire.

"When I fell into the lake that day, I think I had some sort of out-of-body experience. I was standing behind you, watching you freak out. Then, I don't even know why, but I walked away, down the trail. Like, I wasn't even worried or scared. Lucy was running down the trail, and I yelled for her to stop. She thought I got out of the lake somehow. I mean, she could see me, even though my body was with you, on the ice. And, Jay, I could *feel* her." Colin can't tell if Jay believes any of this because his face doesn't register any reaction. But Colin pushes on. "Before I went in, and now . . . I can't really touch her. I *can*, but it overwhelms her. And when she touches me, it's never enough." Colin can feel the heat in his cheeks; he and Jay don't talk specifics. "Sorry, I know this is TMI, but I need to get it out."

"It's cool. I mean, I sort of owe you one. I'm pretty sure you were awake that one time Kelsey stayed over and—"

"I was," Colin says, waving away the awkward memory. "Lucy's touch makes me crazy because it's always almost enough to feel good, but then it stops short." Grabbing the back of his neck, he winces. "I mean, we can't . . . like, no way could we be together like that. And it's not even about that. It's *her* and the way everything looked when I went in . . . Seriously, Jay, it was the most incredible thing I've ever seen."

Jay blinks away, out toward the span of trees hiding the lake from their view. "This sounds crazy."

"I know."

"No, I mean, I'm legitimately worried that you have brain damage."

"I don't. I'm not crazy, Jay."

Jay looks back at him then. Colin can tell when his best friend believes him because his face falls, and he looks defeated, as if insanity or brain damage would be a far easier solution. Colin laughs, because he's had the same reaction.

"This is funny?" Jay asks, confusion bleeding into defensiveness.

"No, not even a little. It's that I know exactly what you're thinking. I *wish* I was crazy."

"I don't have a lot of experience with crazy people. I haven't ruled it out yet."

"Well, then, let me get everything out." He pauses, glancing up at Jay before dropping his gaze to the stick he's stabbed deep into the snow. "I think we could do it again."

"Do what again?" Jay asks slowly, enunciating every syllable.

"Go into the lake." Before Jay can get a word in, Colin barrels on. "I started researching hypothermia, and it takes a long time for the brain to shut down entirely. I mean, in between being cold and being dead, there's a lot of room."

"You are crazy."

"No, Jay, listen. I understand it. Metabolism slows. The body shuts down to preserve energy. But the mind is still active, and in that time, I'm somehow able to be *like* her. Before Lucy disappeared, I promised I wouldn't talk about it anymore, but staying out of the lake didn't keep her here."

Jay groans and rubs his face, and it's at this moment that Colin knows his best friend is going to help him. "So we do this now, or when she gets back?"

"When she gets back. I don't know if I can find her now. I don't know where she is."

"Are you sure about this? I mean, this isn't riding on chains and boards over the quarry, Colin. The day you went into the lake was fucking scary. I thought you died."

"I'm here and fine." Colin tells him about Liz's cousin,

how he fell through the ice and stayed out for four hours. How he's alive and walking around. He tells Jay about the forums, how the people there see hypothermia as the ultimate extreme sport. "You're the only one I'd trust."

"So how would this work? We'd like, plan it? Have supplies? A time limit?"

"Exactly." Colin's heart begins pounding in his chest; his veins are infused with a high better than any adrenaline rush. He lays out his plan: he'll strip down, submerge himself long enough for his pulse to slow and his core temp to drop, and then Jay will pull him out. "We'll time it right down to the second, and you'll resuscitate me. We can take some equipment from the campus infirmary. After what happened on the lake, no way is anyone going to risk needing the winter emergency kit. Lucy will stand on the trail where she was before, and we'll see if it works."

When he's done, Colin is shocked to see that Jay doesn't look all that horrified, even when he says, "See if it works as in *see if you don't die*?"

Colin smiles. "Jay, I'm not going to die."

Jay watches him, and Colin can feel the weight of every second as it passes. He doesn't want to force Jay into anything, but he can't lie to him either. "You don't have to," he says, hoping Jay can hear the apology in every one of his words. "But I'll do it without you. I have to."

Jay doesn't react, only nods like he's hearing something he already knew. "You know this will be the wildest thing we've ever done."

"Yeah."

Jay exhales deeply. "Okay, you crazy asshole. I'm in."

Chapter 25 · HER

COMING BACK THIS TIME IS JUST AS MILD. A blink. A tugging on her limbs. Darkness becomes light. But where she was warm and happy, waiting for the boy on the trail, she's now scorching hot. Colin's back is pressed to her front once again.

And this time she knows she's been gone, because she feels as if she's been woken up, and Lucy knows she doesn't sleep. She vanishes.

"Hi," she whispers into his back.

He stiffens. "Lucy?" His voice is thick with sleep.

"How long?"

His spine relaxes, pressing back into her. "Just two days."

"You okay?"

"No." His alarm goes off, and he swats the snooze button with his palm before rolling over to face her.

"I'm sorry."

"You don't need to be."

She pushes his hair back. "I am anyway. I tried not to get so relaxed again."

He kisses her so carefully, as if too much contact will cause her to evaporate. His tongue glances her lip, her tongue, the skin of her neck. His piercing is cold; his skin is hot. His hands pull her closer, shadow up and down her sides and over her curves. "Missed you," he whispers.

Last time, when she returned from being gone, he looked angry. This time, he seems resigned. She pulls back so she can see his face more clearly. His freckles have faded in the past month, and only now, with a couple of days away, does she notice. His eyes are dimmer in the dark room, but something fierce drums behind them, matching the rhythm of his pulse in his throat.

His Adam's apple bobs as he swallows thickly. "I told Jay."

"Told him what?"

"That you're a Walker."

She falls silent in the face of such a blunt admission.

"I was freaking out and worried I imagined everything. I needed someone else to hear it and believe it." He laughs dryly.

She nods, supposing she can't be upset with him any more than he can be with her for disappearing. "Okay." She draws out the word carefully. "How'd he take it?"

He rolls onto his back, staring at the ceiling. He's shirt-less. Lucy's eyes move instinctively to his bare skin, over the smooth lines of his chest, the definition of his stomach, and lower. "He didn't believe me at first. But we didn't talk about that for long. We talked about me going into the lake again."

Lucy's body pricks, each element drawn to the surface, making her feel like a brittle, spiked shell. "Colin."

"He's game, Lucy. He said he'll do it for me."

"And are you doing it for *me*?" she asks, hearing the bite in her words and feeling proud that they came out the way she intended. "Because no, thanks."

"I'm doing it for both of us. I know it will work." He gives her his trademark slow blink, filled with cocky confidence, but the gesture is wrong. He's doing this because she would never ask it of him even though he probably sees straight through her to her traitor glee.

"This is a bad time to talk about this," she says quietly. "I just got back, and I know you were scared when I vanished again. I feel like I can't say no to this, but I want to." The lie burns in her throat.

He sits up, facing away from her and bending to put his head in his hands. "We'll talk about it later, then."

Later turns out to be in the crowded dining hall, surrounded by four hundred other students. Later turns out to be with Jay.

"I told Lucy that you know," Colin says before taking a giant bite of pizza. Suddenly the drone of hundreds of students feels completely silent.

Jay and Lucy stare at him for a beat before looking at each other. "Yeah," Jay says. "He told me. Sorry about the . . . being dead."

Lucy smiles weakly, raises her hands and shakes them. "Ta-da . . ."

With the truth out between the three of them, Jay lets himself look. Really look. It's not like Lucy has never been inspected; Colin stares at her all the time, examining how she fits together or maybe trying to get his mind to believe what his eyes see and his heart feels. But other than Colin, no one *ever* looks at her. Not like this. Jay's attention is unnerving and unrelenting.

"Dude, she's not made of wax. You're making her twitchy."

Jay sits back in his chair, letting it teeter back on two legs. "I can't tell."

Colin leans forward. "What?"

"I mean, unless you look closely, she just looks like a chick."

"She *is* a chick," Lucy says, annoyed at the conversation that's happening as if she's not sitting right here.

"I mean, yeah, your skin is supersmooth, and you look kind of . . ." He waves his hands vaguely. "Glassy. But you look like a chick."

She scowls. "Maybe we can talk about this somewhere other than the middle of the dining hall during lunch."

"In case you haven't noticed, no one looks at you," Jay says, slapping his chair down with a loud clap and reaching for his apple. "So no one is watching us, either."

She exhales and looks away, out the window to where snow is falling in fluffy handfuls from the silver-blue sky. She listens to the sound of the boys digging into their lunches for several minutes before Jay speaks.

"Colin says you're not up for the lake again."

Her head snaps to Colin, and she narrows her eyes.

"I think he's right," Jay continues, leaning forward and catching her gaze. "I think it's like an extreme sport. He's healthy and young; my obsessive hunter father has ensured that I know CPR. The infirmary is full of supplies. And I got Colin back last time without anything."

"Which was lucky for everyone," she counters. "Were you this enthusiastic when he suggested it to you yesterday?"

"Nah," Jay says, grinning. "I thought all those hits to the skull had finally done him in. But I've come around."

Lucy shakes her head at this strange display of trust and loyalty. "Why are you invested in this?"

Jay takes a bite of apple and shrugs. "Colin's lost a lot of people. I like the idea that he'll chase you down and keep you from getting away."

Lucy looks at Colin, who is watching her with a painfully vulnerable, hopeful expression. He squints, analyzing her eyes, and then smiles. She doesn't know what color they are or what he's seen, but somehow he already knows she's going to say yes.

She'd pushed for a warmer day, but January in Boundary County has few of those to offer. With blankets and a duffel bag of pilfered equipment in Jay's backpack, the three of them head out to the lake.

Jay talks nonstop as they walk. Lucy can't tell if it's nervous energy or how he is when heading out to do any activity motivated by complete insanity. She and Colin hum in agreement or dissent whenever it seems called for, but she can tell Colin isn't listening either. His fingers are wrapped carefully around hers, and she grips them as tightly as she can manage. She can feel his skin squeeze between her fingers and meets his surprised eyes.

They crunch through the snow to the giant open gash in the ice and unload everything, the air humming with the strangely loud silence that comes in a moment perched on the edge of adventure.

While she waits, she takes a moment to look around. It's easy to see why the lake's gotten such a paranormal reputation. In the blue-gray light of the winter afternoon, it's downright eerie, and ribbons of fog seem to cling to its sur-face. It isn't hard to imagine ghosts walking aimlessly along the shore, or even a madman dragging a young girl to her death. Lucy stares at the icicles looping from the box elders, heavy and gaudy with splinters of sunshine slanting through. She looks at her tree towering above the two benches at the edge of the lake. She doesn't think she's ever taken the time to look at it before, but now that she does, a shiver runs through her that has nothing to do with the January wind tugging at the ends of her frozen hair. The branches arch upward, each spindly twig like fingers hoping to pluck a ghost from the sky. Jay blows loudly into his hands and she turns toward him, grateful for the distraction.

Lucy isn't sure what she expected—maybe Colin walking around the site of the cracked ice, inspecting, maybe psych-ing himself up to the act—but whatever it was, she certainly did not expect him to strip down to his boxers within min-utes of the supplies being set up and jump feetfirst through the original crack in the ice into the frigid water.

She barely has time to be gripped with panic, to feel every part of her shift to the middle and clench where her heart used to beat. His head dips underwater and he surfaces, gasping and cursing, his arms grabbing wildly for the tether they've attached to his wrist.

"Cold! Oh my God, it's cold!"

Jay bounces at the edge of the entry point, jittery and unsure. "You done? You want out?"

"No, no, no, no!" Colin yells. "Just . . . shit, it's cold." He shivers violently.

"Colin!" Lucy calls. Her chest grows with the sensation of hot, rushing water filling her empty heart. The heady sensation is disorienting, completely at odds with the panic her brain tells her to feel. "Get out!"

I'm done.

This is insanity.

I don't want this.

She reaches for him, but Jay bats her hands away. "I got this. Lucy, this is what he wants to do."

Teeth chattering, Colin nods and then dunks under the freezing water again, determined to soak his hair.

"This is wrong," Lucy whispers. "Jay, this is going to kill him."

"It won't," he says, voice steady. How can he be so sure when everything inside Lucy is colliding?

"I'm okay. I'm okay. I'm okay," Colin whispers over and over again. "I'm okay."

After what feels like an eternity filled with the sound of water lapping against ice, of Colin's huffing breaths, of Jay muttering reassurances over and over, "You can do this; you got this; you can hang, buddy, come on. A few more minutes and you get to touch your girl. You can do this," Colin shudders once, and then his eyes roll back as he turns and bobs in the water.

Jumping into action, Jay reaches for Colin's arm and pulls him out, dragging him on his side to a foil blanket spread out on the ice. He checks the time and then watches him lying there, unmoving.

"Revive him!" she screams, slapping his shoulder, hard. "Why aren't you reviving him?" She looks at her hand, at the flush of blood she can almost see pumping beneath her skin. Something hums in her ears—a heartbeat.

"Just give him a minute," Jay says with a level of calm she can't comprehend. "We've checked this all out. He's good for a while."

Colin's semilifeless body is blue and mostly naked, laid out on the foil blanket. He looks skinnier than she remembers; his muscles spasm sharply. As soon as Colin has coughed all of the water he inhaled out on the foil, Jay sits back and just watches him shiver.

Jay seems *calm*. He's totally onboard with this insanity, no nerves, no hesitation.

Just as she's on the verge of screaming her panic into the dull gray sky, she hears, "Luce. Turn around."

She swivels toward Colin's voice and her heart melts.

Chapter 26 · HIM

LUCY LAUNCHES HERSELF AT HIM, HEAVY AND warm and full; her lips find his neck, his jaw, his mouth. He could consume this girl, he thinks. He could bury himself in her and never come up for air.

With her neck exposed and her smile so big it reflects the sky above, Colin realizes he'd expected they would run off into the powdery snow and strip and just get down to it. But when she raises her head and looks at him, her eyes full of relief and excitement and fear and desire, the only thing he wants is to be here, like this. The world around him is so bright and full of detail, he finds it hard to even blink. It's exactly like he remembers.

She's taking his lead, her fingers wrapped around his arms, waiting for him to decide where he wants to go. All he knows is he doesn't want to watch Jay when he starts resuscitating him. Colin tugs her arm and leads her to a bench a few hundred feet down the trail.

Colin remembers his tenth-grade photography class and how exposure is measured in lux seconds—brightness over time. The sweet spot was always that point where everything was visible, but before the light bled through, erasing the details. Here, in this world, it seems that the amount of light that can exist is limitless, and all it does is show him more. More color, more detail. Each rare leaf has a tiny skeleton, visible from even ten feet away. The clouds are gone. The sky is blue, yes, but also green and yellow and even red. When he inhales, he thinks he can feel each molecule colliding inside his lungs.

They sit. They smile. This is the strangest thing that has ever happened in this universe; he's convinced of it. His body could be dying on the lake and whatever it is that makes him live—his spirit or soul—is beyond elated to just be here.

Lucy wraps a blanket around his shoulders. She climbs into his lap, facing him, wrapping them up so only their heads peek out the top.

"I'm not cold," he says.

"I know. But it's weird to see you like this, without a blanket." She smiles, bending to kiss his jaw. He lets his head fall back, feeling.

Her hands slip up his front,

solid

solid

solid touches. His skin rises to meet her fingertips.

She talks softly as she kisses around his neck, his face, his ears. "You okay?"

He nods. This place is the most intense thing he's ever seen, and Lucy feels better than anything, than everything, even than warm water running down cold skin or the first bloom of sugar on his tongue. Better than fast sex or a faster downhill ride.

"You're humming." She laughs.

"I'm in heaven."

She stills, fingers paused, splayed across his ribs. "You're not."

"I didn't mean that. Settle down, Trigger. I meant metaphorically."

She leans back and watches him.

"You think I'm insane, don't you? You think this is insane," he says, suddenly made uneasy by the intensity in her swirling gray-green eyes.

"Yes," she says, leaning back in. She sucks his ear. Tugs at his hair. "No." She moves closer, squirming over him. "There's very little about us that isn't absurd."

"Most of it's not *absurd*," he says, for some reason prickling at this. "We aren't absurd. It's that . . ." He searches for the right ending and gives up, laughing. "You're dead and I'm kind of in between right now."

"Oh, *that*," she says into his neck. "Not absurd at all."

His hands find waist, ribs, breasts. They grow wild and impatient, itching to feel every inch.

Although part of him realizes that Lucy simply feels like *girl*—soft curves, skin that responds to his fingers, and her half-word exhales—most of him thinks that Lucy feels like no other girl ever. She's softer; her sounds are the best sounds. He grabs her hips, squeezes. An embarrassing groan escapes his lips at the shape of her.

But it makes her smile. "You like to squeeze."

"What?" He lifts his head, trying to understand her meaning through her eyes. They're honey, hungry brown.

"In the picture with your ex-girlfriend?"

"The picture with Trinity from the winter formal?"

She nods. "You're gripping her hips. You're gripping them like you *knew* them."

He grins down at her. "That is such a chick thing to notice. 'Like I knew them.' What does that even mean?"

"Like you gripped them a *lot*."

"Let's not talk about my ex-girlfriend right now, please."

"I'm serious. Do you miss being with a girl you can grip?"

"No."

She's skeptical.

"I want that with you, it's true. But I don't want sex so much that it's worth getting it elsewhere."

She fights a smile, though Colin doesn't know why. "Let that smile out," he tells her. "I'm so crazy about you and your hips that I can't grip."

Lucy gives him a smile that could power a small town.

"You're so hot," he whispers.

To prove him wrong, she grabs a small handful of snow off the back of the bench and presses it to her chest. It stays there, crystalline and twinkling in the unearthly blue light. Slowly, her skin takes it in. He imagines their bodies like this must be such scavengers, needing to steal anything solid to take form. Now his girl is made of snow and beauty.

"Tell me a story," she says.

He stares at the giant sky for a beat before an image pops into his head. "My parents used to have this huge king-size bed. At the foot of it was a wood chest my grandma had sent from Tibet or Thailand or something. I was jumping on the bed and slipped and cracked my collarbone on the edge of the chest."

Lucy winces over him, a full-body-impact wince, and it makes him laugh because what on her could break?

"So my mom rushed me to the emergency room, and I got put in the world's most awkward cast. I was almost six and we called it the Rack. That was right before they died."

He's run out of words. It's not a very telling story or even that long. It was only the first of several times he's broken a collarbone. He fiddles with the ends of her hair, tying it in knots and watching it unravel.

"Do you miss your parents?"

"Sometimes. I only sort of remember them. Sometimes I wish I knew enough to miss them more." It feels right, somehow, that they would have the hardest conversations here, where they can reassure each other with actual contact. What he wants to tell her is how he gets his chosen family. He gets her.

"What do you remember?"

He can understand why Lucy seems fascinated with the possibility that a part of Colin's life is as fragmented as the entirety of hers. Colin has particles of memories of his parents, supported by pictures and stories from Dot and Joe. "I don't remember much. Most of it's been filled in for me. Dad was kind of dorky. I'm sure he would be the kind of dad that embarrasses the hell out of me now." He laughs. "But he was fun and would play on the floor. Carry me on his shoulders. Tell me way too many details about the animals at the zoo. That kind of dad. My mom was careful. Well, they both were, especially after Caroline died. And at least until she lost it, Mom was quiet and liked to read and write and overthought everything. Never wanted me to run or hurt myself. Dot says that's why I'm so crazy now. She says I'm like them but turned inside out. I keep my careful bits on the inside. She says it's why I'm so easy to be around but so hard to know."

Lucy is tracing something on his chest. A spiral or letters, or a shape. Finally he realizes she's drawing a heart. Not a heart like a valentine, but a *heart*. It calls his attention to his lack of pulse, to the hollow organless sensation he gets when he realizes he's not corporeal. Suddenly he feels like his chest is sinking inward, like a crumpling empty paper bag. He stills both of her hands between his.

"Did they have a good marriage?" she asks.

"I think so. I mean, they died when I was six, so . . ." He looks out at the crystal-blue lake in the distance. "Caroline died right after we moved here. I'm sure that didn't *help* their marriage."

Colin stares at a spot over her shoulder. "I've been thinking a lot lately. I wasn't very old, but I know my mom drank a little before we lost my sister. It got a lot worse after. And no one blamed her; I mean, her nine-year-old kid got hit by a delivery truck. I'm pretty sure everyone understood why she went off the deep end. But what if she wasn't crazy? What if she really did see Caroline? Is it possible she was really there?"

"It's possible," Lucy says. "*I'm* here."

"I'll never know, will I?"

"I don't know. But you'll see them again."

He pauses, looking up to where she's hovering above him. "You think so?"

She studies him for a beat, searching his expression. "Yeah, I do."

He kisses her for that. For being so convinced his family will find each other, for the possibility of a good life after death. For knowing it's what he needed to hear even if he didn't know it.

Her kisses are small and sweet, little sucking lollipop kisses on his lower lip, nibbling kisses, finally the aching deeper kisses he wants.

"I'm glad you're here," she says. She's glad he's *here*. Not that she's back there, in his human world of flesh and bone. He finds that he feels the same.

Every word sounds so much more intimate when it's accompanied by the sensation of flesh under fingers. Colin has never felt this close to anyone, not even in the infatuation stage, when he becomes a mindless walking erection. This feeling here is almost too intense, when he kisses her, this need to get beneath her skin with fingertips and lips and each hungry part of him.

Conversation falls away, and his touches grow desperate

because he can feel a strange rhythmic pressure on his chest and knows it's Jay, behind them, back at the lake, reviving Colin's body. He's warming from the inside out.

Colin rolls Lucy off the bench and onto the trail and starts to touch lower and lower, feeling her hip bones and hidden skin, beneath silky fabric, to where she melts into smooth, wet girl. Her hands dig down and wrap around him, constricting in this insane, perfect way, and in a flash he worries that they've wasted all this time talking, but then he looks down at her and she's grinning the happiest, goofiest smile, and it grows wider and wider even as he starts to dissolve out of her hands.

He's not ready to be gone, but he knows he gets to keep her anyway, and every second of today has been better than any second that came before. Colin vanishes with the vision of Lucy, rumpled and half undressed, her swirling eyes and ruby lips smiling out the word "bye."

Chapter 27 · HER

LUCY DOESN'T NEED TO REMEMBER HER ENTIRE life before to know she's never spent so much time staring at a boy's fingers.

They jerk as if attached to a metal cogwheel, ratcheting open and closed.

Colin flexes them again and again and then, catching her watching, curls them into a fist. "Luce."

She looks up at his scowl. "Mm?"

"I'm *fine*."

"Your hands are . . ." She makes jerky finger gestures, unwilling to say *broken*, or *stiff*, or, worst of all, *wrong*.

"Come here. I'll show you how fine they are."

Finally, a relieved giggle escapes from her throat in a sharp burst. It sounds edgy, like it might be too close to a sob to hold its shape. She can't believe he's here, and person-colored, and warm. And that, five hours after being in the frozen lake, the only thing that seems to be off is how slowly he bends his fingers.

"It wasn't that bad. Coming back, I mean," he whispers into the darkness of his dorm room. He's hidden beneath several layers of blankets, and the space seems exceptionally quiet now that Jay has worn out his postresurrection high and left for the night.

What he says is true. Jay insists that bringing Colin back was easy. But agreeing with Colin right now feels wrong, as if the universe is merely waiting for her to say that stiff fingers and a few bruises are a small price to pay, before snatching everything away at once.

It felt like they were together for days. Days of talking and touching and holding each other so closely there was no air left between them. In reality, it was only fifteen minutes. Jay said he started to freak when Colin was shivering so bad he almost jerked off the foil blanket. But time felt generous then, stretching every minute into what felt like twenty.

"Lucy, stop staring at my hands and come over here."

She slips in beside him, and he pulls her close, her big, warm spoon. She feels stronger and more present than she can ever remember feeling, and Colin mumbles something happy and content.

"What?"

"You," he says sleepily. "Just wondering if you feel different because you're different or because I'm feeling you differently."

"What do you mean?"

"You feel more solid. Stronger."

"Stronger how?" She wants to know if it feels the same to him, as if she's growing more permanent.

Instead of answering, he says simply, "I want to go in again."

If Lucy thought Jay and Colin were organized before, they're almost militaristic this time around. New rescue equipment and supplies are spread out on the carpet in front of them. They choose the best time of day based on the almanac and weather predictions. They pack and repack supplies, outlining every possible scenario down to the smallest detail.

It's reassuring . . . in a completely warped way. She knows that if she protests too much, Colin will hear the lie in her words. She doesn't want him to risk his life, but there's a part of her that strengthens and blooms every time he talks about this. Is it greed? She's not sure how to process what she's feeling, this fascination with watching someone she loves be so wholeheartedly reckless.

"Last time I held your core temp pretty steady at around ninety-two." Jay snickers and adds, "'Course, it'd be more accurate if I could measure rectally."

"How many times do I have to tell you you're never going there," Colin says.

Lucy stares as they cackle like twelve-year-olds before turning back to the notebook in her lap. She scribbles messy circles and squares, flowers and clouds, trying to remember her favorite words and how they come together under the pressure of her pencil.

Crystalline. Lattice. Momentum. Sublimate. Enthalpy.

The words burst into her thoughts, reminding her of a classroom, of traveling to the university to study in the humid summer months, of a scholarship that would have been hers. When she looks down at the paper, she's surprised to find each letter written in perfect script, no shaky or disappearing lines. She stares at them, reveling in these small pieces returning. She's never been able to hold a pencil for long, let alone put ideas to paper, so watching the words uncurl from the tip of her pencil is almost as fascinating as the guys' strange obsession with this new lake activity.

"Holy crap, Luce!" Colin shouts, and she immediately freezes, breaking the pencil lead against the paper.

"What?"

"You're *writing*." He's grinning as if she's a toddler and just took her first step.

Jay gives her a slow clap and whistles. Standing, Colin

leaves their giant sprawl of gadgets and books and blankets to come sit near her on the bed.

He reaches over, rubs her shoulder, and announces, "I think you're stronger lately. More solid."

She watches him. He's repeating himself, and his speech seems the slightest bit off, as if he has to build his thoughts one piece at a time. Before she can tell him that this is the same thing he said last night, a window blasts open, bringing a sharp funnel of freezing air inside and interrupting Colin's excitement. He forces the window closed, and when he returns, his hands are as cold as hers, but somehow the thrill it gives her—the hint of the cold to come—feels like fire.

She wonders if this is how a tiger feels when it catches the scent of prey on the breeze, or how a long-distance runner feels with his toes bordering the starting line. She feels like she might explode from her skin and vaporize into a million tiny glittering particles. Does this lightness, this exhilaration she feels as Colin strips down to his boxers, mean she might take flight?

Last time Colin stripped and jumped straight in, like if he thought about it too long, he wouldn't go through with it. This time, he stares at her, his grin building as slowly as his blinks are delivered. She steps back, and then again, turning to the trail before he's even submerged.

• • •

It's exactly what she expects it to be. They meet at the spot on the trail, and turn, laughing and running with the wind down the path to the shed, feet tripping over feet.

Jay said he thinks he can give them an hour.

An hour.

Even with the bright white-blue of morning outside, it feels like night inside the shed. Beams of light play with the stars of dust in the air, and Colin's skin looks lit from within, as if he's the different one now.

He curses under his breath, a sound of wonder, cupping her face and kissing her so hard, so hungrily, and then he's walking her backward, around, helping her down onto the air mattress, shoving aside the pile of blankets. Dust clouds up around them, leaves crumble beneath, but the setting doesn't matter. His skin, her skin, it slides and presses, hot and smooth. Not too much, not too little. Perfect.

They kiss, pulling away the last remnants of clothing, and then he's moving into her, moving over her and talking, and she doesn't care that it's going to end, because this feeling— *this* feeling—is what they've been missing. The connection and touch, the communication that words can never reach. Colin whispers his love into her neck as he shakes above her.

She clutches him, pressing her face against his skin and listening to the rustle of the blankets near her head as he releases them from his fists. Lucy doesn't want to move from this spot, maybe ever.

"Are you okay?" he asks quietly, his open mouth kissing a path across her throat to her ear. When she nods, he whispers, "Not sure how I feel that our first time was in a dirty shed."

She laughs. "I don't care about the setting."

He pulls back and looks at her, playfully bereft but obviously giddy, and then he blinks, languid, just for her. "I don't either."

The moment stretches. Colin hovers over her, kissing, eyes open, with an intensity that makes every muscle in her body tighten, makes her chest ache with how much he consumes her.

He doesn't need to say he loves her, but he does.

Then he's pulled from her body, flying backward again as if a band pulls at his chest, his mouth wide in an anguished cry in the shape of her name. He passes through the dancing bands of light and dust, he filters easily through the cracked walls and damp wood planks, and then Colin is gone.

Hours. It feels like it takes hours to get dressed and tear back down the trail, to where Jay pulled him out early, to where Colin will be awake. Lucy trips over roots and sticks in the snowy mud of the shore. She doesn't know how to manage these new, strangely heavy limbs.

And then she's there, falling on top of his blue-gray body and apologizing and kissing his unconscious face. "What happened? Why did you bring him back early?"

"I didn't, Lucy. I waited exactly an hour." Jay pushes her away, forcing air into Colin's lungs and smacking his chest. "Wake the fuck *up*, C."

Lucy's hands curl into fists, a wave of anger flashing along her skin, and she shoves Jay's arm away, causing him to cry out, stare at her for a beat in horror.

"What happened to you?" Jay asks, voice shaking. He squeezes his eyes shut and looks at her again before he reaches for another hand warmer to shove into the mittens covering Colin's fingers. "What happened to your face?"

"My face?"

He shakes his head. "Nothing. I must have . . ."

Lucy ignores Jay's rambling and bends over Colin, hugging him through the heavy layer of blankets. "I'm here. You're going to be okay. I'm here."

Chapter 28 · HIM

IT'S SO STRANGE TO BE IN THIS PLACE AGAIN, caught between life and life unraveling. Colin feels the faint burn of ice and snow against his skin, but he's not cold. Flashes of light pulse beyond his closed lids, and the echo of his name rings through the air in panicked voices, but he can't gather the strength to open his eyes. Despite the noise in his head, his chest is strangely silent. It's taking too long, and the instinct to return grows fainter and fainter.

He feels a mild tickle of fear, but it's gone quickly, the urge to slip back into darkness wrapping around him like a blanket. In a thick, creeping realization, Colin understands that his inclination to curl back into the lake is because it's *Lucy's* lake. He's less surprised to feel positive that Lucy is the ghost at the lake than he is to feel in his frigid bones that she's been waiting for *him*. For so long there hasn't been anything for him here, and there is everything for him in the lake. It would be so easy to go back in and walk down the trail to Lucy.

That's all he's ever had to do.

Chapter 29 · HER

HIS EYES OPEN AT ONCE. NOT THE CALM, fluttering awakening she expected, but one moment he's blue and unconscious, the next he's staring at her, gulping for air, his face burning red.

"Luce," he gasps. He inhales roughly, as if he's sucking oxygen through a straw.

She presses on his neck to feel his pulse.

"Colin." She has a million questions. *Can you feel me? Do you remember? Do you hurt? Can you move?*

"I think I know where you go," he mumbles thickly into her neck. His entire body has begun to shiver violently, and it takes him a moment to get the words out. "I think you live in the lake."

Her veins run cold at the thought that her home is in that deep, isolated world. That she is the one haunting this school.

But something about it rings true; she's more peaceful at the lake than she is anywhere else on campus. And there are no waters entering or leaving it; it's as landlocked as she is.

Sunlight steals the darkness from Colin's bedroom inch by inch and finally shines a spotlight on his warm, breathing body. For the hundredth time she memorizes his face, his neck, the way his hair curls and falls over his forehead.

"Wake up. Talk to me," she says. It's been one of the longest nights she's spent with him, waiting for him to come to and show that he's not hurt. Or sick. Or brain damaged.

He makes some groggy waking-up noises, turning to face her. "Your skin feels so different lately." He pauses, and Lucy hopes he's realizing that this conversation seems familiar. "Do you think it has to do with me?" he says instead.

She pulls back to look at him. Really look at him, as in try to see if his pupils are reacting to light and his skin has taken on his normal color. Does he not remember that they've had this conversation before, twice now? "Maybe."

"Do you think me being close to you, or even *like* you in the lake somehow makes you more . . . ?" He shakes his head, rubbing his face. "Like, more real?"

She smiles, trying to shake off the strange tickle in her spine she feels looking at his innocently wide-eyed expression. "I want to be a real girl, Geppetto."

"I'm serious."

"Me too."

"Maybe we can shift into some dimension that shows us how to make you human again," he says. "With more practice."

She gives him her best what-on-earth-are-you-talking-about look. "I don't think we'll be doing any more inter-dimensional Colin travel. I worry you've used up your last ticket."

He shakes his head, immediately riled up, and although her mind worries, her heart feels a silent, electric thrill. Something inside her begins beating. And it's this that worries her: If she's his Guardian, why does it feel so good that he's falling apart?

Lucy's never seen Jay rattled before. At least, that's what she assumes is going on outside at lunch when he's silent and fidgety. His usually piercing eyes are focused on his shoes, where he doodles with a black marker over older doodles. The fresh black ink stands out against the faded now-gray.

Over *"grenouille"* he writes *"eau."* Over *"papillon"* he writes *"froid."* Almost as an afterthought he adds CHAUD, in capital letters above it all.

Frog and butterfly become cold water, then hot.

She digs in her thoughts for more words in French but is

greeted by only a vast expanse of gray. She can't puzzle out her memories, how they seem to be vaulted inside until they get the smallest nudge and then spill forward. She wonders what other things will tumble out when prodded. Maybe something to explain where she goes when she's gone and what kind of Guardian lets her Protected dive into a frozen lake over and over just so she can touch him.

"I didn't know you took French," she says. Beside her, Colin is buried in a book about the acute effects of hypothermia.

"I don't," Jay says defensively, as if he's been caught somehow. As if he's the one who should be explaining himself.

They're an awkward threesome, with a secret the size of the Pacific Ocean between them, carrying on with their normal lives in the strange world of private school. Sneakers squeak on the asphalt of the basketball court in the distance. A short, chubby kid makes three baskets in a row from the three-point line. Lucy wants to ask Jay how he knows the French word for frog if he doesn't take French, but it also seems like the most inconsequential question she could ask after everything that happened this last weekend. "Are you okay, Jay?"

"My mom is French," he says instead of answering.

"So that explains *grenouille*," she says, and he grins, correcting her pronunciation under his breath. "But it doesn't explain why you're nonverbal today. Are you freaked out?"

His shrug is loose and slow. Jay is jerky and twitchy; the shrug is a decidedly non-Jay gesture. "Just thinking." He reaches for a magazine inside his bag. The front is creased and covered in scribbled notes, drawings, and watermarks. The pages are dog-eared and torn on the edges, DIRT RAG emblazoned across the top in jagged green lettering.

"Jay," Lucy begins, unsure of his mood and how to best phrase her thoughts. She looks over at Colin, satisfied that he's sufficiently distracted. "Don't either of you have that voice in your head saying that what you're doing is crazy?"

"I do," he says, then nods toward Colin. "He never has."

Of course Colin picks that exact moment to look up from his book. "I never have what?"

"The self-preservation instinct. You never turn back from a hill or a jump. I've never seen you look at something and say, 'I shouldn't try that.' It doesn't mean you always land it, but you always try. You have no good angel on your shoulder." Bending to his magazine, Jay adds quietly, "Only the devil."

Colin laughs, and it feels like a fist squeezes Lucy's heart.

Jay continues. "I can't believe it went like it did at the lake."

"How so?" Colin asks carefully.

Lucy starts to compile an apology to Jay, shifting words in her head to make the best, simplest statement, so he understands that she appreciates what he did more than he knows. She considers adding they would never ask it of him again, but the words feel slippery in her thoughts.

But instead of explaining his concern, Jay gives Colin a slow-growing smile. "It *worked*. I mean, look at you. You're fine. It's crazy that we can actually do this, and I'm over here just tripping out about it. I don't know why more people don't try. Makes *me* want to try."

Already nodding, Colin sweeps into the conversation, and the two of them are off a mile a minute, and although Lucy knows she should be worried, everything inside her surges with relief. Apparently, jumping into a frozen lake is like any other extreme sport. You think you're going to die, but what you get is the adrenaline rush of your life.

She hates her reaction, hates her calm. She hates how much she wants Colin in the lake. She hates not understanding.

So Lucy can't listen to their fascinated planning; it feels too much like condoning their insanity. Instead, she pats Colin's leg as she stands, telling him she's going for a walk. Despite her internal struggle, she feels strength wrapping solidly around her bones; her muscles zip with vitality at the simple thought of seeing Colin go underwater, of meeting him on their trail. She wants to hide this strange, bounding strength from him but knows she can't walk far enough to hide it from herself.

Was it because she died near the lake? Is that the connection for them? Maybe if she understood what happened to the other Guardians on campus, she'd know more about why she was back and why she can take Colin to her world. Colin's little sister died on the school road, and her mother drove them all over a bridge, possibly trying to find her. Now that Colin knows how to find Lucy's world, could it be different for them? Could they manage this strange balance in the world above and the one below? Where did Henry die, and is that where he goes when he's gone?

In the library, Lucy searches the archives for any information about Henry Moss. The name shows up in several places: for a dentist in Atlanta, a high-school football star in Augusta. And then a story about a nineteen-year-old college student from Billings killed by a hunter's stray bullet while hiking deep in the woods of Saint O's campus. Leaning back in her chair, she stares at the picture of Henry before he died, smiling at the camera with his trademark wide grin.

Caroline Novak was hit by a delivery truck heading into the school. Henry died in the woods. Lucy died in the lake. All of them returned and seemed to return *for* someone: a heartsick mother, a boy with cancer, and an orphan who kept a murderer from killing countless others.

"But *why* do we disappear?" she asks aloud, absently rubbing the firm shape of her arm. She's starting to suspect that she returns to the lake and had always been there. Is it true for the others too? Are they hovering in some mirror image of this world when they're gone?

She needs to find Henry. She needs to ask when he feels the most solid and permanent and whether he feels the polar opposite right before he vanishes. But she needs to do it without giving away that she feels the best when Colin is only barely escaping death.

It turns out this time he's easy to find, reading on a bench beneath a large naked maple near the arts building. When Henry sees her, he stands, shouting her name and gesturing for her to join him. They climb the stairs and walk through the massive doors together, right as the sky opens and the snow begins to fall.

"Where's Alex?" she asks.

Henry gestures to the quad at their backs. "English. I'm tired of the history class I've been sitting in on this semester. It's not like I remember anything about the past, but I still feel like I've heard it before." With a wink, he tugs on her hand, and she follows him into the auditorium, down the long center aisle, and into the deep orchestra pit. Although their footsteps echo in the small quasi cave, it's easy to tell that they're completely alone. They'd be able to hear a pin drop on the stage.

"I have to tell you something," she says, pulling at the sleeves of her shirt. "I know how you died, or, at least I know who killed you."

"Oh," he says. "Oh. I was . . . murdered too?"

"Yeah. Well, maybe 'manslaughter' is a better word. You were hit by a hunter's stray bullet. I think you were visiting the area on a break from college and that's when you were shot."

Henry stands, takes a few steps away before sitting down again, and Lucy bites back a smile at his familiar ignorance. If Colin hadn't told her about her death, she would probably still be in the dark about it all, too. Henry looks up to the ceiling, pauses, and then blinks back to Lucy. "I always half worried that I'd have that last piece of information and boom, the sky would open up and I'd be set free or sent back or whatever it is we're waiting for."

"That's why Colin didn't tell me how I died at first; he worried it would be the thing that would send me away for good." Lucy shivers, hating the ticking-time-bomb sensation beneath her skin, that bleak unknown. What *will* be the thing that sends her away? She hesitates. "But I think there's something about this school. Like it traps us somehow. Everyone I know of who died here, died on what was technically school grounds. I think there have been others, maybe there are others here *now*."

"Have you seen someone?"

She shakes her head. "No, but Colin's mother swore she saw the ghost of her dead daughter, Caroline. She drove them off a bridge, and I wonder if she thought she figured out a way for the family to be together again. Colin barely survived the accident. What if his mother *was* seeing her daughter? What if we're just ghosts, and we're just . . . *here*?"

"Without a purpose?"

Lucy nods. "Without a purpose. Haunting. Stuck."

Henry doesn't seem to like this idea, shaking his head sharply. "If Caroline were a Guardian like us, no way would she have led her *mother* over a *bridge*."

Unease tightens Lucy's chest. "I guess."

He stares at her in his intense Henry way, as if he can see her thoughts hovering beneath her skin. "How's Colin lately?" he asks.

"He's good," she says, not adding what a miracle that is.

"What else is on your mind, little sis?" Henry turns his chair so he's facing her, elbows resting on his knees.

"Do you sometimes feel stronger than other times?" she asks.

"What do you mean by 'stronger'? You mean more solid?"

She nods, picking at a thread on her sleeve. "I know this is personal, but sometimes Colin can barely touch me, and other times I feel like . . ." Lucy remembers the picture of

Colin at prom, his hands resting on a human girl's curves. "Like he can grab on to me. But I don't think I understand what I do to make it happen. I wish I knew so I could do it more."

"I have no good advice because it doesn't ever seem to change for me," Henry says apologetically. And then he growls, giving her a playfully dirty look. "Lucky."

"But when Alex touches you, can he, like, *touch* you?"

As if on cue, Alex walks into the auditorium. His boots clomp down the center aisle and down the steps into the pit before he collapses into a chair next to Henry. He looks back and forth between them, the bruises beneath his eyes almost black in the shadows. "What's up?"

Henry reaches down and pulls Alex's legs across his lap. "Lucy asked if you like to touch me."

She groans and buries her face in her hands. "That is not what I asked. I asked whether you *can* touch him. I don't need a testimonial."

Alex grins. "Yeah. But he feels like he's covered in static."

Henry watches Lucy for a beat before asking, "I'm sure you've already considered this, but what's going on when you feel strongest?"

She thinks back to when she's noticed it: at the lake, when Colin leaves for a ride. But also when Colin got back from the hospital. She wishes she could pinpoint a mood or even an event. "I notice it when we're outside together, or when he's riding his bike. I thought it was about him being happy, but then I felt it also when he was recovering."

"Even if he was recovering, I think he was probably happy to be alive, in his bedroom with his hot girlfriend, so I wouldn't rule out your theory."

Lucy ducks her head, grinning at her lap. "I guess."

"But *my* theory? You feel strongest when you're on the right path, when you're doing what you're supposed to be doing here. Maybe it's when Colin is happiest, maybe it isn't. Pick the one moment you felt strongest, most real, and do that again."

She looks up at the ornate ceiling overhead, painted deep scarlet and gold and decorated with intricate molding. She felt almost solid before Colin chose to go into the lake. *Is it wrong*, she thinks, *to keep this secret from Henry? Wouldn't he want to know that he could be with Alex like this?*

"I mean," Henry says, breaking into Lucy's internal debate, "I think I feel stronger every day. And Alex is still in remission. It tells me that whatever I'm doing for him is right."

That makes up Lucy's mind for her. She can never tell Henry what she's letting Colin do in the lake. "Okay."

"My point is, look at Colin. Watch him. If you do something to make him happy, you should feel that strength inside you build. If the strength is from something else, you'll notice. I saw your name on some chemistry plaques in the science building," he says with a wide grin. "Go do some experiments."

She stands, but decides to start right away. "Henry, what color is my hair?"

He gives her a tilt of his head before breaking into soft laughter. "Not the strangest thing you've asked me, but okay, I'll bite. It's brown."

Chapter 30 · HIM

I T'S COLD AS HELL, AND COLIN CUPS HIS HANDS
around his mouth and breathes, trying to warm them
up. The wind whips around the side of the library, chill-
ing him through a thermal, two T-shirts, a beanie, and his
favorite jacket. Colin shrinks farther into the warmth of his
hood and rocks slightly, forward and back on his skateboard,
watching Jay buzz his bike down the long flight of stairs.
Huge piles of dirty snow line both sides of the stairway, and
the sky looks heavy and swollen, like it's ready to crack open
and fall all around them.

The deicer scattered along the sidewalk pops and crunches
beneath Colin's wheels as he rides over to Jay.

"I thought it was supposed to warm up. Why is it so damn
cold?" Jay grumbles.

Colin doesn't answer, not wanting to think about what

will happen when the lake begins to thaw. Instead, he relishes the freezing temperatures, the way each breath burns cold in his lungs, and how the other students rush by, practically sprinting up the stairs to get inside.

"Thank God we're not at the lake today," Jay says, teeth chattering. "We'd both be freezing our balls off. Literally."

Colin laughs. "You're not the one that ends up naked and wet."

"Yeah. I'm the one sitting on the side of a frozen lake for an hour while you're having all the fun."

Colin snorts at Jay's use of the word "fun." Their idea of a good time has never made much sense to anyone else, but with Jay, it seems perfectly normal to characterize jumping into a freezing lake in January as fun.

"Think she'll want to go again?" Jay adds. "She got up and left kind of suddenly today."

"No clue." Colin exhales loudly into the cold, the condensation forming a small cloud in front of him. He remembers how, as kids, he and Jay used to think they were cool and pretend they were puffing on invisible cigarettes. He knows the tiny particles in his breath freeze when they meet the icy air, moving from a gas to a denser liquid and solid state, forming ice crystals before dissolving back into invisible particles. He sort of hates that this reminds him of Lucy, like it's some giant metaphor for what will happen when the days becomes dry and warm in the spring and there's nothing left in the air to hold her together. Is it possible she'll vanish along with the cold?

Jay pops his wheel and leans against the railing. "So that's it, then? We're done? Just when we're getting it down?"

"I don't know," Colin answers. "She says she doesn't want me to, but . . ."

"God, I still can't believe it worked. I mean, for all of my doubts, have you ever really thought about what you're doing? You're having an out-of-body experience and making out with a ghost. Never mind how insane that is. It's like you're cheating death, Col. Again! It's totally awesome."

"Do *not* say it like that in front of Lucy," Colin says. He climbs the stairs and looks out across the quad. He hated that phrase growing up—cheating death—as if he were somehow more life-savvy than his parents and managed to pull an ace out of his sleeve at the last minute, leaving him alive but his parents dead. "I'm not cheating anything. People get into cars every day, get on planes, get into boats. People hike and hang glide and ski down ridiculous mountains. Enough people have done those things and survived that we don't even think twice when we start the ignition on our car and head out on Route Seven with the drunk and methed-out truckers barreling down there every day. But what if what I'm doing isn't any more dangerous than skiing a black diamond? You don't know, Jay. No one does it, so you think it's wild. Maybe it isn't."

Jay is nodding almost the entire time Colin is ranting, and he puts his hands up in the air when he's done. "I get it. Like, at first I was doing this only because it felt like I never saw you anymore. But now I think it's cool. Leave it to you to find the fun in freezing your nuts off."

Colin stands on his board and kicks off the concrete, crouching and jumping upward as he leaps, popping the tail so the board leaves the ground. Even being as sore as he is, there's that singular moment of being airborne, where his head clears and the rush of adrenaline eclipses the wind in his ears and the cold on his face. His front truck makes contact, grinding the rail, and too soon, his wheels slam into the concrete. Colin weaves as he struggles to land steadily, gripping the handrail to stop from falling.

"Nice," Jay says, leaning back against the railing.

"Borked the landing."

"Dude, you were hypothermic yesterday. Cut yourself some slack."

Colin comes to a stop in front of him. "What you said earlier to Lucy about the devil on my shoulder . . . You know I'm not looking to get hurt, right?"

"I know. What I think is you have bigger balls than the rest of us."

Colin shakes his head. "No, listen. You know that feeling when you ride down a skinny from twenty feet up? Or look over a fifteen-foot drop to flat and think, 'Let's do this'? It only works if you never doubt that you can. Standing over that ice, I feel totally safe."

"Like you're in the zone," Jay says.

"Exactly."

"But you have to convince Lucy of that."

"Yeah."

"Well, hurry it up, you lucky bastard. I don't have a ghost girl. At least let me live vicariously through you."

Chapter 31 · HER

COLIN AND JAY ARE NEAR THE BACK OF THE library, jumping from rails to stairs, when Lucy returns. Colin approaches her slowly, as if she might roar, first inspecting her eyes and then reaching for her hand. "Are you mad?"

"I wasn't mad." She pulls his fingers up to kiss them.

"You totally were," Jay says, coming to a skidding stop next to them. "You just have to trust that we are completely legit. We are adventure experts."

"Legit?" She shakes her head at him, fighting a smile. "Don't do that, Jay. You can't pull off nineties gangster."

"Ignore him," Colin says, pressing a hand to Jay's chest and pushing him away. "I want to make sure you're okay."

"I needed to think. I went to talk to Henry."

"You told him about the lake?"

"No, no," she assures him quickly. "I wanted to know why I feel different lately. But it doesn't happen to him. He says he's always the same."

Colin's face falls, but he tries to hide his disappointment. "We'll figure it out." He kisses her cheek before turning to watch Jay grind down the stairs again.

In turn, Lucy watches Colin, thinking of what Henry said in the auditorium. She puts her hand on her opposite forearm, feeling the swirling energy beneath. "How do you feel today?"

He glances at her and then back to Jay. "I'm good. I swear. No tingling in my fingers anymore." He wiggles them playfully in demonstration, but Lucy only feels the tightness in her chest intensify. She's missing something. She's missing something and she can't disappear again.

"And you really do want to go back to the lake?"

He turns to her fully now, eyes bright. "Yeah, I do."

Lucy squeezes her arm. Nothing. Colin looks hopeful, bordering on giddy, but she basically feels the same: somewhere in between a solid and a gas. In that strange no man's land on the verge of the sublime. "And it works for you, going into the water alone? Having Jay pull you out?"

"Absolutely." Colin is practically vibrating with joy now, but Lucy doesn't register any change in herself. It can't be tied only to his happiness. There's something she isn't getting right.

"Is there a better way to do it?"

"Other than packing my bed with ice and curling up with me?" he says, laughing. "No. This works."

With him.

The idea sparks a realization so fierce it takes her a moment to see beyond it and into the present, where Colin has looked away again. She came back from the lake to be with him but has been sending him into the water alone. Every time he goes in, she's stronger. . . . She's grown stronger so she can *help* him.

"Do you want me to go into the water with you?"

Her fingers sense the shock of energy surging into place beneath her skin, and she pulls her hand back as if she's plugged her own fingers into a generator.

Colin reaches for her shoulders, steadying. She remembers the first day, in the dining hall, when she saw him and felt starved for details about his face up close, his voice, the feel of his skin on hers. She's been staring at his face at a distance for years. The face that is here, right in front of her, bending close and kissing her as if she's made from blown glass.

"Yeah," he says. "You would do that?"

"Of course I would."

"I'd follow you anywhere, Lucy. You just point the way."

"Then, let's swim." She's convinced she's smiling with her whole body.

"When? When can we go?"

She pulls away and looks behind Colin to where Jay is very much not looking at what they're doing. "Jay, you free tomorrow?"

Jay whoops and walks to Colin, bumping fists with him. "I'm in."

It's early, barely dawn. The sky clings weakly to darkness until clouds take their place and begin to drop fluffy snow. Colin and Jay shove peanut butter and jelly sandwiches into their mouths as they do a final check of the supplies.

"Still ready?" Colin asks her, heaving a large duffel over his shoulder.

Lucy nods, unable to open her mouth for fear she'll admit that she's never felt this strong or this sure of anything.

By the time they've arrived and hiked to the shore, the surface is blinding in the early-morning sunlight, brilliant white broken up by tiny speckles of fallen brown leaves. Colin's original site of entry, the jagged and thin section of ice in the middle of the lake, shines a brilliant blue, thinner than the ice around it. Now when she sees the sharp edges pointing like arrows to the center, Lucy's memory of Colin falling in is rewritten as something calm and idyllic. Like a reel of images, she sees him going under, his face relieved instead of terrified. She remembers hearing him call her name on the trail, of the first sensation of solid skin to skin, of the way his eyes begged her to not ruin it by pointing out that something was very wrong.

Their shoes crunch along the surface, and she hears Colin slip on the ice, and both guys laugh behind her. She doesn't even turn around because she wants *in*. It's different now that they've decided to go in together. Something heavy pulls inside her chest, a sudden tether to some unseen anchor underwater.

She turns and looks at him here and wonders if it's true that she lived in the lake for so long. Did she see him? Is that the hunger that takes over every thought? Beneath the blue ice there's something deeper, a space carved for them. It's all she can do to not pull him down to the opening with her. Her hands are magnets and his skin is iron and their place together is just below the surface.

While Jay unrolls the foil blanket and unpacks his kit of supplies, Lucy strips down to her underwear, unwilling to waste a single second. Boots, pants, sweater, shirt form a rumpled pile at her feet. Her skin is startlingly white in the sun, iridescent and more opaque than she's ever seen it.

She looks up at a surprised Colin, his eyes taking in every inch. He stutters a few sounds before fumbling with his own buttons to catch up.

"I've never seen you . . . like this," he says, eyes bright, cheeks flushed.

Lucy glances at the opening to the water and then back at him. "On the count of three?"

They dive in, arms stretching out into the clear blue water. It presses against every inch of her, cold and silvery. When they dip under a fallen tree, a fluff of moss waves in their wake, releasing a million tiny bubbles to travel the surface. Lucy doesn't know exactly where she's going, but she's pulled toward the deep end of the lake, under the shadows where the ice is thick and dark.

She feels Colin's fingers brush the skin of her ankle, his hair on her thigh as he pushes to catch up and swim beside her. As she turns her head, she sees him trying to hold his breath. Behind them, his unconscious body floats to the surface.

"Let go," she says as clearly as if they were on dry land. She takes his hand and pulls him closer. It's warm in hers, solid and familiar. At the surface, Jay pulls Colin's body out of the lake. "Jay's got you out."

He struggles for a moment, a look of fear passing through his wide eyes as he works to let go of the instinct to breathe. Tugging his arm, she leads him forward, where the deep blue slowly morphs darker and darker, turning into a tunnel of soft black.

"Luce," Colin whispers from beside her. "Where are we?"

"I don't know exactly," she says. And she doesn't. Even

though being back in the lake feels familiar, she realizes she's never known what this world is. It's not heaven or hell. It's not a different universe.

Light shines above, and they both look to the whiteness over them and push up through the crystal-blue water until they break the surface on this strange, other side. It's unlike anything Lucy has ever seen since her return, but the space is so familiar and tugs at something in the back of her mind, some instinct that she's finding the world she retreats to when she vanishes.

There's a brief flash of disappointment: Everything is the same—trees and boulders and the trail—but then Lucy realizes that it's not at all like the shore they just left.

Instead, it's a mirror image, a replica of the icy earth aboveground, but it's so much *more*. More color, more light, more reflections on every surface. Entering this world feels like stepping into the center of a diamond.

Lucy and Colin climb out of the water onto a shore of sand so crystalline, it glimmers in the indirect sun filtered through the trees. Branches of amber, leaves of a silver green so bright Lucy has to blink away, let her eyes adjust.

Beside her, Colin is silent, and when she looks to him, she registers that he's watching her reaction, waiting. *"There was something different about that world, something perfect,"* he'd said. He's seen this every other time he's been here, and it's she who's forgotten what it's like, because, until now, she didn't go under with him.

"You can see this?" she asks, looking up at a sky so blue it almost needs another name. It's the lake reflected, an entire galaxy, a massive ocean in a single glimpse of sky.

He nods, taking her hand and pulling her toward the trail. But when she expects him to pull her in the direction of the shed, he surprises her, walking the other way, away from the field and the school buildings and deeper into the woods instead.

Beneath their feet, amber leaves crunch like splinters of precious stone. The snow is mesmerizing, winking back a hundred shades of blue reflected from the lake and sky. It's like she can see every frozen, glittering crystal that blankets the ground and trees and hills beyond.

Lucy's memories come back slowly, giving her mind time to adjust the same way her eyes adjusted to the light: first recover. And then *see*: see the world that must have been her home for the past ten years.

"It's like a reflection," she tells Colin, following his lead at a fork in the trail. "Everything up there is down here. Buildings and trees. Even the lake. Like Wonderland." She points back at the water behind them, looking like a sapphire planted in a bed of quartz.

He must hear the awe in her voice because he stops, turning to face her.

She shifts where she stands. "Except people. I mean, I think I've been alone, watching."

His dark brows pull together, and he whispers, "I hate that."

Not wanting to worry him, she adds, "I don't think time passed the same way. I mean, I remember being here, but I don't feel like I was sitting around, bored out of my mind for the past ten years." His face relaxes, and she says, "I remember looking up, as if I could see everything through a glass. I think I was waiting. And I remember watching you."

"Really?"

Nodding, Lucy takes his hand and leads him down the trail this time, feeling a pull to go forward, to keep *moving*. "I remember watching you on the hill during a winter social. You and Jay swung from a tree branch and jumped down onto the lake."

Colin laughs, shaking his head. "I'd forgotten about that. We were twelve. I broke my ankle." There's a hint of pride in this admission that makes her smile.

"I saw you ride out here the first time," she says, the images unrolling in her head like a reel of film. "You were a little scared but a lot more excited." She grins as she remembers his pink cheeks and smiling face, the way he kept glancing back over his shoulder as if he expected to be caught any minute. "You two were the only ones who came out here at first, but you didn't seem to be looking for me."

"I remember that! Jay dared me to walk out on the ice when we were seven. The joke ended up being on him because he cut himself on the dock and needed a tetanus shot. Man, we got in trouble for that."

Their joined hands swing between them as they continue to walk along the trail. Every few minutes Colin lifts the back of hers to his mouth, kissing it. His lips are warm.

"And obviously it didn't stop you."

He grins. "No way. We've grown up hearing stories about this place. About Walkers and disappearances, of people claiming to see a girl slip along the shore or hearing voices." He bends to pick up a leaf, spinning it in front of him. "I mean, it was creepy, yeah. But not everyone bought into it. Just adults discouraging crazy kids from drinking and fornicating at the lake. Made it sound cooler, really."

Lucy snorts and shakes her head. "Of course the prospect of danger *would* make it more appealing to you. And even before I died, I don't think we were supposed to come out here. Too far from the main buildings, too many ways to get in trouble."

They stop walking, and he bends to her, whispering, his smiling kiss covering her lips, "I can think of lots of ways to get in trouble out here."

"How long have we been gone?" she asks, tilting her head back as Colin kisses a path from her chin to her neck. He mumbles something unintelligible, and she means to ask him what he said, but a bird cuts through the air over his shoulder. A raven. It's beautiful, with wings like shards of ebony. It flies overhead, calling out into the silence before circling back and landing somewhere in front of them.

Lucy turns to find it, to point out the hauntingly beautiful bird to Colin, but she freezes, the words lost in a gasp when she realizes how far they've walked.

She can see the hulking shape of Ethan Hall behind them in the distance, and ahead of her is the raven, its talons wrapped around the highest arch of the imposing metal gate that surrounds Saint Osanna's.

But something is different. Instead of feeling an invisible bubble pushing against her chest and sending her back to the trail, she feels like a fish caught on the end of a hook. Pulled. Slowly reeled in.

She takes a step forward.

"Luce?" Colin asks. "You okay?"

"I don't know," she says, continuing on, her steps quicker now. Purposeful. As she nears the iron fence, she looks up and meets the raven's watchful stare, can see her own reflection in the luminous black of the bird's eyes. "Something . . . something's different."

She hears the crunch of snow as Colin jogs to catch up, feels the beat of a pulse in her hollow veins. When Colin stops at her side, the pull gets stronger. "Do you feel that?"

"Feel what? Lucy, what's going on?"

"Like suction? Like I'm metal and there's this giant magnet on the other side? You don't feel that?"

Colin shakes his head, eyes wide as he blinks from Lucy to the gate and back again. "Do you think you can get through?"

"I don't know." Her mouth is suddenly so dry, drier than she can ever remember. For the first time since waking, she wants something to drink, can almost imagine the feel of cold water as she swallows.

"Touch it," she hears Colin whisper. "Lucy, touch it."

She licks her lips, shaking as she lifts her arm, fingers trembling as they find the icy metal. There's no resistance. She holds her breath, watching as her hand passes between two of the ornate balusters and to the other side.

"Oh my God," she gasps. "Oh my God!" There's the faintest hint of a tan; blue veins form a map across her palm and up her wrist. There's a scar. Freckles. Imperfections. She forms a fist, feeling the warmth of her own skin. "Colin!"

But he doesn't answer. Colin is gone.

Chapter 32 · HIM

SOMETIME DURING THE NIGHT, COLIN FEELS Lucy slip into bed behind him. The mattress shifts with her weight as she burrows under the layers of quilts and electric blankets to wrap her arms around his chest. He's not sure how, but Lucy and Jay have managed to move him from the lake to the dorm and up to their room without anyone noticing. He's wearing a set of old flannel pajamas and is in bed beneath a pile of blankets. Jay is gone, so Colin assumes he must have had the first watch. He doesn't remember anything after leaving Lucy's underwater world.

"Hi," she says, her voice muffled against his back.

"Hey." It comes out as a croak, and he closes his eyes tight against the burn. His throat feels swollen, scorched, as if he ate a meal of solid fire. "Have you been lying here for long?"

"No. I got here a few minutes ago. I've been waiting for

Dot to go to sleep. She's been down in the common room stirring the same cup of coffee and staring at a blank TV for more than an hour."

He doesn't want Dot to see him like this, and the guilt he's been trying to ignore flares inside his chest. "She didn't see you, did she?"

"No," Lucy assures him. "She never would have let me get past the stairs."

So Dot came to his dorm to be close to him? He rubs his face, groaning quietly. "She's worried. She feels so responsible for me."

"Yeah."

"I think she knows I'm doing something crazy. She knows about you." He shivers and presses the heating pad closer to his chest.

"I thought she might." Lucy ignores the way anxiety burrows into her skin and tucks the blankets more securely around his body. "Are you warm enough?"

"Mm-hmm. But if you want to seduce me, you might have to leave on my socks," he says, trying to lighten the mood. He doesn't want to think about the downside to any of this. Only wants to feel her curled behind him and remember the world underwater. A fraction of his mind registers how crazy this is, that from the outside looking in, he might even appear suicidal. And with a piercing stab to his chest, he realizes this is how his mother must have felt. Doing whatever she could do to have even one more day with her daughter. Colin has never been more positive that his mother wasn't insane after all. She simply wanted her family back.

It's early—hours before the sun comes up and the students flood campus—and Colin can hear one of the delivery trucks outside, dropping off supplies at the kitchen. The steady beep as it backs up echoes off the stone buildings and fills the empty quad. "Hey, how'd you two get me up here anyway?"

"That would be Jay. Turns out he's excellent at distraction and a lot stronger than he looks."

"How is he?"

"He's okay," she says, and he feels her shrug slightly. "I mean, he seems to thrive on this kind of thing. I don't get it, but I'm glad he's like that. What he's doing for us is amazing."

"I know."

"I wonder if we'd be able to do it without him. I wonder if I could get you out of the water somehow." She pauses, watching him. "I wonder if that's why I'm so strong now."

Colin is silent in response to that. He's given this some thought. If the lake is where Lucy was before she found him and where she goes when she disappears, Colin wonders if he could simply go find her there. He's not exactly sure how they got to the other side because his head is still a bit foggy, but he likes to think if he had to, he could find it alone.

"Tell me what happened," he says. "It's true, isn't it? You got past the gate."

"You remember that?"

He nods.

She shivers beside him. "Other than finding you, I don't remember ever feeling so drawn to something. I saw my hand, and it looked alive, Colin. I felt like I needed to be on the other side of the gate."

"Do you think that's how it works? We need to get you off campus? Like, unlocking some puzzle?"

"I don't know. Somehow I don't think it's that simple. It can't be."

"Maybe you're overthinking it."

She doesn't answer, just presses her cheek into the back of his shirt, reassuring herself that he's warm and really here.

"It's where you were before you came back?" he asks.

"I think so. I feel like I'd been pacing inside a cage, looking out through the lake, waiting to come be with you."

"And you think it's where you go when you disappear?"

Her arms tighten around him when he says that. "Yeah, but I don't plan on disappearing again."

Maybe not, he thinks. *But at least I know where to find you.* Colin relaxes. This knowledge makes the prospect of the approaching spring much less terrifying.

Chapter 33 · HER

THE DEEP PURPLE WATER-SKY TREMBLES ABOVE them, with stars made out of a million of the smallest bubbles. The illusion of earth and lake bottom turns into the soft, inviting blackness. An instinctive burst of energy courses through Lucy's system, and she pushes forward faster.

"God, I can't wait to get there," Colin says, floating behind her. "I hope we can stay longer this time. I want to try the gate again."

Lucy doesn't respond, simply kicks her feet through the icy clear water. It's all she's been able to think about: how her skin looked like real flesh, that she felt the sting of the cold air on her fingertips, but she's worried there's something they haven't considered yet.

It's strange to not be able to see but to know exactly

where to turn, like the directions are embedded in her muscles. Does he feel it too?

"Can you find it?" she asks, stilling.

"What?" He stops next to her, his arm pressed along the length of hers.

"Do you remember how to get there? Could you find it on your own?"

He looks behind them, to where the water has simply emptied into blackness, and then forward again. "Not like this. I can't see anything. I don't think this is how we got here before."

"Never mind," she says, grabbing his hand to pull him closer. "I guess it's a feel thing. Maybe after you've been here a few more times."

"Maybe," he says, though he sounds unsure.

A few seconds later, she instinctively turns. A light in the distance grows brighter and brighter.

It takes a moment for their eyes to adjust, but everything is exactly as they left it. A canopy of crystalline leaves sparkles above them. The sun is a trapezoidal beam of yellow sweeping across the frozen shore. Orange, blue, red, and purple flowers bloom in small pops before they freeze, leaving waves of stained-glass color in their wake. A light snow is falling, and Colin holds out his hand; intricate, lacy snowflakes land in his palm.

She grins at him, watching him look around. It's everything at once: vibrant color and glistening ice. They can smell the wet earth beneath the snow and hear the water freeze across the lake. It becomes disorienting and overwhelming, and she can see the moment it becomes too much for him when he sits on the bank and covers his eyes.

She sits next to him, resting her hand on his bent knee. "Are you okay?"

"I love you," he says quietly, slowly blinking up to the sky.

She breaks into a grin so wide it takes her several seconds to respond. "I love you back."

He picks up her hand and massages her fingers. "I thought I knew what love was before."

"I didn't." She leans down, kisses the back of his hand.

Colin looks over at her, his eyes as hungry as she feels when she pushes him onto his back in the snow.

"Cold?" she asks, moving over him.

He shakes his head, hands running up her sides, lifting her shirt up and off in a single movement. "Not even a little."

Her hair falls in a curtain around them, and he pushes it back, kissing her like she's a normal girl he can grip and feel and not worry about breaking.

Lucy wonders if time moves down here at all because before she knows it her clothes are gone and Colin is smiling down at her, snowflakes in his hair and clinging to his lashes, disappearing into the skin of his bare shoulders. He bites his lip as he moves above her, fingers memorizing every inch and finding where they come together.

Frost gathers on their skin and disappears as quickly. Light explodes behind her eyes, and Colin holds her shaking hands with his. He says her name against her mouth, that he loves her, that even having all of her will never be enough. He groans into her neck, and when they still, his heart silent against her chest, she can hear the sound of feathery snow falling around them.

"How's it possible to feel like I want to be here with you but I shouldn't be?" he asks. They're on the trail again, hand in hand as they make their way toward the front of the school. Lucy tried to say no—to distract him—but there wasn't any conviction behind her words.

"I don't know," she says, "but it's how I feel bringing you here too. It feels selfish."

"Lucy?" he says, and she watches a cloud of anxiety pass through his eyes. "I think this is what we've been missing. Don't you?"

She looks up, watches how fast the sun seems to move across the snowy sky. She can feel it with every step: the need to keep going, to escape.

They stop with the iron gate in front of them, its hulking

mass like a scar blooming out of the pristine snow. Lucy notices Colin rubbing the spot over his sternum. "Jay's bringing me back. My chest hurts," he says. "We don't have much time, Luce."

He reaches for her then, pulling her to him with a smile that doesn't completely fill his eyes. His mouth is soft but insistent, wet and warm.

She turns, a sense of longing filling her chest like a warm bath, a tug behind her ribs pushing her toward whatever is on the other side of the fence.

The same feeling of anticipation coats her skin, and she reaches out to lift the latch. The old gate groans, the hinges squeak, and Lucy steps back as it swings open.

She twists her fingers with his, and as if acting on instinct, steps through first.

She hears the gasp before she's even turned around. He's smiling. Tear tracks line his face, and he's looking at her as if she's the most beautiful thing he's ever seen.

"Your hair," he says. She looks down. It's brown, every shade of brown at once. "And your eyes." He's laughing now, disbelief etched in every part of his face. "They're green."

"Come here," she says, and pulls him forward.

She's on the old trail again. Her feet dig easily into the snowy earth, but she almost trips on a bank of snow when she catches sight of Jay, curled in half and throwing up the contents of his stomach several feet away from where Colin's body lies.

Colin's lips are blue, and when she gets closer, she can see that his eyes are open, but hollow and staring straight up at the heavy gray sky. His chest rises and falls in shallow pants, but when he hears her feet crunching across the ice, he turns his head to her and tries to smile. His breathing grows more ragged; his eyes roll closed.

"GET AWAY FROM HIM!" Jay screams, wiping his mouth on his sleeve and stumbling to Colin, shoving Lucy out of the way. "I just got him back, Lucy. Stay away from him!"

Jay's eyes are squeezed shut. He refuses to look at her.

"What happened, Jay? Why is he so bad?"

"I don't know. I don't *know*," he mumbles. "It's not working." Still, he keeps his eyes down, frantically shoving hand warmers under the blankets and against Colin's cold skin.

Dread trickles along her arms. "Are you afraid of me?"

"When he comes back, you look fucking terrifying," he says, voice shaking in the cold. He points without looking. "Grab that bag; it has gloves."

She walks to the bag numbly, Jay's words echoing over and over. He's said it before: *When he comes back, you look terrifying.*

It's the same reaction Joe had when he fell through his porch. He told Colin she looked like a demon. Lucy feels the high of her time with Colin underwater begin to evaporate.

"Here," she says, carefully handing Jay the gloves. "What can I do? Is he going to be okay?" Her voice is so flat, sounds so indifferent. She squeezes her eyes shut, unable to get rid of the image of Colin in front of her, smiling up into the sun right before he slipped away.

"He's been under for more than an hour, Lucy! He's nonresponsive with a pulse of thirty. Thirty! His normal resting pulse is sixty-four. Do you even know what that means? He might die!"

"Just let me closer; he'll be better when I'm there." She's so sure of it that at first she doesn't register that when she puts her hand on his arm, the small monitor at his side lets out a steady, flat beep.

"Lucy!" Jay gasps, pulling at her arm and staring where his hand wraps firmly around her flesh. "Go away. Go away. Go away," he whispers over and over. She realizes she was completely wrong when she assumed a silent Jay is a panicked Jay. This Jay is panicked, and he's unable to stop whispering to himself. He's a rubber band pulled taut, about to snap.

"Let's get him to the dorm," she says. "I think I can help you carry him. I feel so strong."

"No. Don't touch him again. I don't think you're helping."

"Of course I'm helping. Jay, we have to get him out of here. You can't carry him alone!"

Sirens wail in the distance, and Jay meets her eyes, apology and fear and anger and fresh tears brimming inside. "I called nine-one-one. I didn't know what else to do."

The ambulance crunches along the trail, coming to a skidding stop. Paramedics burst from every door, rushing to Colin's body, pulling away the blankets and heat pads, checking his vitals. They wrap him in some type of bag and pepper Jay with questions. How did he go in? How long was he under? Has he said anything? Jay answers, wooden. No one even looks at Lucy.

She watches as the two men lift Colin onto a stretcher. His hand reaches out weakly, and she waves.

"I'll meet you there." Somehow, she thinks. Her thoughts grow panicked and jumbled as the ambulance starts up, beeping loudly in the echoing quiet of the lake as it backs down the trail. How can she possibly follow him?

She runs toward the school, and in the distance, sees Joe and Dot begin jogging to the parking lot. Brake lights flash on a shiny blue pickup truck as Joe unlocks the doors with a remote.

Without thinking, Lucy sprints to the truck, crouching behind the back gate. Just as the two passengers shut their doors, Lucy throws her body over the side, into the open bed.

Gravel spits up behind them as they peel out of the lot, chasing the ambulance down the dirt road leading out of the school.

It's only when they pass through the iron gates that Lucy realizes she hasn't been bounced back to the trail. Ahead of them, the ambulance wails down the two-lane highway.

But why now? What's changed? She looks up to the flashing lights down the road, to where her heart lies, strapped into the back of an ambulance. *Where you go, I go,* she thinks.

Always.

"Eighteen-year-old male, severe hypothermia. BP ninety over fifty-four. Current temp is ninety-four point eight, respiratory rate fourteen. Lactated ringers pushed at one hundred fifty milliliters an hour. EKG stable with normal sinus rhythm. Chest X-ray results are here for your review. Blood work was sent to the lab for stat processing."

Lucy pushes her way into the corner about ten feet from where a physician is looking down at Colin's chart while one of the paramedics ticks off the vitals. Lucy has managed to walk into the triage area without anyone saying a single word to her.

The attending physician listens to the account of the scene: The kids were playing on the lake, Colin went in, they had equipment to revive him, and it seemed intentional.

"Isn't this the kid they were talking about on the news? Around Christmas?"

"Colin Novak. From Saint O's."

"Yeah." The doctor gently pushes hair off of Colin's fore-head. "That's him."

Lucy turns as they wheel him away and through two wide doors. She wanders the halls until she can't take the beeping and antiseptic smell and chatting nurses. She's glad for them that the stress of the ER becomes as tolerable as with any other job, but their conversation about the recently passed Valentine's Day is too far removed from the updates on Colin she wants to be hearing. She wants news about him blared through the intercom.

She wishes she were a ghost like on television, only as solid as a hologram. She'd be able to walk through walls and into any room, peek her head through and watch the color return to Colin's skin.

On her seventh circuit of the halls, she peers into the family waiting room. Jay is gone, but Dot remains and stares, unseeing, out of a large window that overlooks the parking lot. There's no one here to comfort her, and there's no one here to comfort Lucy. She steps into the dark, silent room, ready to share her loneliness.

Dot is so lost in her misery that she doesn't even look up when Lucy walks in. She simply stares down at the book she clearly isn't even reading. Lucy wants to talk to her, to explain what happened and assure her that Colin is okay and they've almost got this whole mystery figured out, but the words turn into dust in her throat. Instead, she sits down on a couch in a dark corner and waits.

Over the next twenty minutes Dot asks the receptionist to let her see Colin four times, paces the room seven times, sits and stares at her book the rest of the time, but never once does she turn the page.

Dot is tall—some might even describe her as formidable—with surprisingly young skin and hair that has been left alone; silver dominates the deep brown. It's bundled back in a messy ponytail, exposing her large blue eyes. Even with her striking physical presence, Lucy can tell Dot feels small. Helpless. She's a mass of constant movement and anxiety.

And then Dot stills. Her hands freeze midway up her thigh as she's rubbing them worriedly, and she turns to look at Lucy. To her horror, in Dot's face Lucy sees a mixture of understanding and fear.

"I remember you, you know." Her soft voice carries a bite of accusation. "You're the girl I saw in the dining room, covered in dirt." She lifts a shaking hand and pushes a loose thread of hair behind her ear. "But I remember you from before that too."

Lucy feels the layers to the statement and looks away before nodding, unable to face the worry and accusation she can see in every line of Dot's expression.

Many minutes pass before Dot speaks again. "Say your name."

"Lucy."

Dot says her name again, and then adds, voice shaking, "Lucia Gray."

"Yes, ma'am." Something cold and leaden thunders in Lucy's limbs, brought on by Dot's expression: fear. Beneath it, anger.

"You care about him?" Dot asks, leaning forward to get a better look at Lucy in the dim room.

Lucy nods again but turns her eyes to the floor.

"Tell me."

"I love him."

"That isn't what I meant."

"I'm sorry," she says, finally looking at Dot's face. "Yes, I care about him. I want him to be safe. I don't know anything else about what I'm doing here, other than I'm supposed to protect him."

Humming, Dot closes her book on her lap and stares at the wall. Lucy can feel her unease rise like a curtain between them. "You care about him enough to let him take blankets and resuscitation equipment to the lake?"

"I didn't ever want anything bad to happen to him," Lucy begins, but her words ring false with the sound of hospital equipment behind them. "We were trying to figure out how to bring me back."

"Bring you *back*?" Dot lets out a confused breath and shakes her head. "I always knew it would catch up with him eventually. Just didn't think it'd be so soon, or he'd be the one chasing it."

Before Lucy can ask what she means, the nurse steps into the room with Joe, beckoning to Dot. With one last, lingering glance to where Lucy sits in her stiff chair, Dot leaves her alone in the waiting room.

Lucy waits five minutes before following. She'll never believe she's worthy of being Colin's Guardian. It's what she should have told Dot. She should have told her she'll do anything to deserve him and to tell her what that is.

Dot's in his room now, speaking in soothing tones as Joe walks down to the end of the hall, head down, tired eyes on the shiny linoleum floor as he disappears into the elevator. Lucy perches in a vinyl seat just outside Colin's door, waiting until she can see him, feel him, apologize.

"Colin," Dot says, apology thick in her voice. "I met your girl."

"You met Lucy?" His voice is worse than she could have imagined. Raw and weak.

"Yeah, sweetie." She's silent for a beat, and Lucy hears a quiet tapping sound, as if she's holding his hand and patting it reassuringly. "I don't know what's going on. I don't need to. But I do need you to promise me this is the last time you're going near that lake."

The only sound Lucy hears for a long time is the steady beep of his monitors and the garbled voices and laughter from the nurses' station.

Finally, Colin clears his throat. "Dot." He sounds like he's swallowed crushed glass. "I can't promise that."

"I knew you'd say that, but I'm afraid I need you to promise anyway."

"It's not what you think. I know what I'm doing."

"I don't know what to think, baby. All I know is this was no accident. I don't trust that girl."

Lucy hears sheets rustle and Colin saying something that sounds like, "Please don't cry."

"Are you trying to kill yourself?" Dot asks.

"What? Dot, no. No. I'm trying to help her come back. It's making a difference, She's stronger and I—"

"No more, Colin. Because it *will* kill you. You understand that, don't you? You're meant to be here, not there. You can't bring her back, baby. You aren't meant to die."

Lucy feels her heart begin to beat to the rhythm of the monitor in his room. The familiar tick of a clock seems to pulse beneath her skin.

Minutes pass.

Don't make me leave him. Don't make me leave him.

She remembers the feeling of his hands on her arms, the soft exhale of his kiss against her shoulder. She's traced the constellation of freckles across his nose, felt the cold press of his lip ring. She remembers his first tentative touch and his most recent fevered ones.

She's silently begging him to not let her go. Not to promise, never promise, and hating herself at the same time.

"Okay, okay, Dot. Don't cry. Please." He exhales in a quiet, defeated hiss. "I promise I'll stop."

The ticking stops and Lucy closes her eyes, feeling like she's unraveling at the seams.

"I promise I won't go back into the lake."

Chapter 34 · HIM

COLIN SLEEPS FOR WHAT FEELS LIKE DAYS. HIS eyelids are like sandpaper when they finally open. The room is too bright: Daylight streams in through an opening in familiar curtains, washing the foot of the bed in blinding yellow sun. There's a vase of flowers on a table, his duffel bag and a haphazard stack of schoolbooks on the couch.

"There you are," Dot says, standing from a chair by the door. She tucks a well-worn paperback into her bag and crosses the room toward him. She seems lighter, happy, and for a single, oblivious moment, Colin almost forgets why. "I guess you really needed your sleep, didn't you?" Her smooth hand touches his cheek and tries to make some sense of his hair, like she's done a hundred times in his life.

"What time is it?" he asks, wincing at the feel of words

in his throat. It takes some effort, but he manages to sit up a little. Dot brings a green bendy straw to his lips and he drinks. His empty stomach revolts, clenching tightly. The room shifts and weaves around him.

"Around eleven. Now, lie back down," she tells him.

"Eleven a.m.?" he asks, wide-eyed.

She smiles. "Yes, eleven a.m., Friday, February eighteenth."

Colin tries to remember what day it should be, feeling sick when he finally does. He's been asleep for two days. "Where's Lucy?" he asks, heart racing, the color of dread bleeding into the edges of everything around him.

"I don't know, honey," Dot answers, the relief slipping from her face. "I haven't seen her since the night they brought you in."

Colin is released from the hospital the next day. Joe and Dot don't talk much to him or each other on the drive back to campus, and for a long while there's only the sound of tires on asphalt to break the silence. It's a strange tension and one that Colin has no idea how to reframe, even with his side of the story. Joe and Dot couldn't understand what he has been through even if they tried. Colin's pretty sure they both think he has some sort of a death wish by now, that he was trying to hurt himself on purpose. He's glad Joe doesn't ask, though; it's almost impossible for most people to understand how much space there is between craving danger and craving death.

When Joe finally does speak, their conversation is short. Joe asks how he's feeling, lets Colin know that he won't be returning to school for a few days and that he'll be staying with him until further notice. Colin grunts something resembling a response in the appropriate places. He's disappointed, but not surprised.

He hasn't seen Lucy since he was pulled from the ice and doesn't hold much hope that she's waiting for him in his room, even less that she's at school or the shed. Somehow he knows she's disappeared again. It's almost like he can feel her absence in every particle of everything that they pass. The trees look emptier; the air looks bleak.

He closes his eyes and imagines her in the blackness just before she breaks the surface. He can see her on the trail beneath the mirror sky and wonders if she managed to get through the gate without him.

At first Colin tells himself that he needs to be patient and wait. She wouldn't stay away, not now. So he does as he's told: He goes to class and comes home right after. He spends an entire afternoon talking to a counselor because Dot says it's important to her. He stays away from any trouble. He waits.

But the storm is always there, gathering. He feels it spread like the wind that creeps across the lake, like icy fingers that close around his lungs until he can barely breathe—until he's nearly frantic with the need to find her.

Days turn into weeks, and the ice begins to thin, and though it sounds cliché, he feels like he's drowning—melting into the lake right along with it. He does his best not to let his growing frustration show, not to take it out on Dot or Joe, both of whom now watch him like a hawk. Colin wonders what they've said to Jay, who seems to have been scared straight, immediately shooting down any discussion of going to the lake.

Three weeks after he woke up to find Lucy gone, Colin knows he can't sit still anymore. He makes a show of cleaning his room, studying at Joe's kitchen table, and volunteering to help Dot finish up dessert prep.

The sky has grown dark, and Joe raises an eyebrow when Colin settles into the couch beside him. A few distant shouts carry in from outside, as students start making their way across campus.

"It's good to see you busy," Joe says. He drinks from a steaming mug before setting it carefully on the table at his side.

"If feels good," Colin answers, and they're silent for a few minutes, Joe's eyes on the evening paper and Colin's on the TV. "I was actually wondering if I could get a suspended sentence tomorrow, maybe get off campus for a few hours." There's hope in his voice, something he knows has been noticeably absent the last few weeks.

Joe eyes him skeptically. "And what exactly would you be doing?"

"Nothing," he says, easing off a bit and trying to sound nonchalant. "See a movie, maybe stop by one of the bike shops in town." He shrugs for added effect. "It'd be nice to get away."

Joe considers him. Colin can almost see the release of tension in Joe's shoulders, his relief at hearing him talk about things that are so normal.

"Actually, I think that sounds like a great idea," Joe says, surprising him. "Your grades are good. You haven't been in any trouble." He glances at Colin over the top of his paper, expression serious now. "But back here by dark. No exceptions."

"Yes, sir," he says, smiling. Joe shakes his head, but Colin doesn't miss the way his lips twitch at the corners.

"I'll get you your keys in the morning."

Colin leans back, happy, his eyes on the game but his thoughts somewhere else completely.

Slush covers the walkway leading to the door of the infirmary, and Colin laughs quietly, realizing this is the first time he's climbed these steps without A) the aid of someone else, or B) blood gushing from some part of his body.

He lets the door close softly behind him and wipes his feet on the rug, walking toward the sound of movement at the end of the hall. It's too quiet, and his sneakers squeak on the linoleum, the sound bouncing off the walls around him. Colin's been here so many times he knows exactly where he's going, knows what each piece of equipment is for and which room has the bed with the spring that pokes you in the back. He also knows Maggie won't be thrilled to see him and that his footprints are probably mucking up her clean floor.

Right on cue, she peeks her head out of an open doorway, scowling in his direction. "You better be bleeding," she says, looking behind him.

He smiles. "I'm not."

"What're you doing here?"

He follows her into the room where she's changing out one set of sheets for another. A kid he's never seen before sleeps in a bed on the other side. "I need to ask you about Lucy," he whispers.

She glances to the sleeping boy and back to him. "I don't think so."

Maggie picks up the basket of sheets and walks into the next room. He follows again.

"Please." His voice cracks, begging. She won't look at him. There's a hardness in her expression, something that tells him she's building a wall to keep tears from leaking out. "Please."

After a long pause, she finally meets his eyes. "Why today?"

"Because I can't find her."

She watches him, eyes narrowed. "Heard you did something pretty stupid. Stupid enough it landed you in the hospital. Stupid enough you're lucky to even be here."

Colin tries to laugh it off. "What's new, right?"

Maggie clearly doesn't find it funny. "This is . . . You've done some stupid stuff, but this . . ."

He nods, guilt and shame warring with the unrelenting need to find Lucy. "You heard the details, huh?"

"Ain't nobody around here who didn't hear."

"Maggie, you knew about Lucy. When will you tell me how?"

She keeps working, and Colin rounds the bed, taking the other side of the new sheet and fitting it over the mattress.

"Almost died and didn't learn a damn thing. Fool-headed child," she mutters.

Colin waits; it's not exactly like he can argue with her.

"There's only one way this can end, Colin. You know that, right?"

"I can't believe that, Maggie. I don't."

"Of course you don't." She sighs, defeat written in the slump of her shoulders. Maggie straightens, looking out into the hall before closing the wide door. "You're lucky I don't kick your skinny butt out of here."

Colin tastes salt water and the thick, choking tide of sobs, but pushes it down. "Thanks."

Perched on the edge of the bed, she swallows and says, "I met Alan here when I was nineteen. I wasn't always the person I should have been, Colin. I was young and stupid and did a lot of stuff I'm not proud of. I was on my own, trying to keep up with nursing school and homework and a full-time job. Right before I started here, a friend noticed I was having a hard time and gave me something to get me through it all." She pulls a pillowcase into her lap, tugs on a loose thread. "Not long after, I was walking from the dorm to my car, and he was there. He was sweeping the sidewalk, and he looked up, smiled like I was a rainbow after the storm. I saw him like no one else did. Saw those crazy eyes and felt something I'd never felt before. He was mine; you know what I mean?"

Colin nods, knowing exactly the feeling she describes.

"He found me for a reason," she continues. "I was alone at this big school and needed someone. He was so lonely. No family, no friends, practically invisible to everyone here. He took care of me, saw me stressed and understood why I needed something to get me through the day."

Colin nods and isn't even embarrassed to realize he's crying.

"And when I realized what he was"—she laughs, shaking her head—"when I found out that he'd died? Here? That he haunted this place? I could handle that. But the disappearing? That's what broke me," she whispers. "How long has your Lucy been gone?"

"Twenty-four days."

She pushes a skeptical exhale through her lips, shaking her head. "Twenty-four days you get used to. Twenty-four days you can live with."

Bile rises in Colin's throat at the idea of even one more day. "Did he disappear because you were unhappy?" he asks.

"Don't know why he left. I went to rehab, and he didn't visit me once. I started using again and he was back. Telling me it was okay, that I needed it. Almost encouraging. First time he was gone for six days. Second time, I didn't see him for forty-three. And that wasn't even the longest."

Colin wants to move somehow, to release this discomfort that's burrowed into his stomach. He paces to the other side of the room, pushing his hands into his gut, hoping something inside him untangles. "How long?"

"Two years. I had two years with him and then he was gone for two. I'd been clean for a while but going through a rough patch." Maggie pinches her eyes closed, takes a deep breath. "I took some pills from the infirmary. When I got back to my room, there he was, sitting at the kitchen table like he didn't have a care in the world. Like I'd gone out for a cup of coffee and he'd been waiting for me to come back. But it'd been too long, Colin. I couldn't do it."

"Two years?" Terror wraps a cold fist around his lungs, pulling down, and the sensation of caving in on himself takes over. He would chase Lucy anywhere. He doesn't know how to function without her anymore. Maggie stays put in front of him, but she weaves, his vision blurry.

"He still felt the memory of the night before. Meanwhile, I'd lived two years—going to school, coming home, looking for him, trying to stay clean. Going to school, coming home, looking for him again. Every day, for two years. And there he was. My life was falling apart and he looked like he'd won the lottery. So, I left him. I wish I'd told him to stay away long before that. I wish I'd told him to leave me alone the first time he came back."

Colin doesn't know if he could do that. He doesn't think he could ever give Lucy up.

He doesn't realize he's said it out loud until Maggie responds, her voice deep with sadness. "You'll get there. You'll find that point. Maybe it will be the first time she's gone for more than a month. Maybe it will be that time she comes home for an hour and then is gone again for days. Or maybe she'll get her way and you'll do her dirty work for her."

He can hardly process what she's saying, but forces himself to speak anyway. "Did he disappear for good?"

Her eyes close, and a few tears escape. "I don't know."

"But when did you last see him?"

"Pretty soon after he came back. There were stories, always have been. I didn't figure out till later that the dead around here are bound by the gates. I . . . stopped looking." She straightens, shaking her head and reaching for a tissue in the front pocket of her scrubs. "I don't know what takes more strength. Staying through it or letting him go. I don't know. I just don't."

A phone rings somewhere and the bubble pops; the bleak light seems to give way again to bright fluorescent and echoing silence.

She walks past him, returning to nurse mode and telling him to take care, but he stops her with a hug, thanking her, squeezing her tight.

The entire way to Hillcrest Cemetery, Colin reminds himself that seeing Lucy's tombstone is not the same thing as seeing Lucy. But he's got a lot to talk out, and right now, she's the only one he knows will understand it all.

He parks and steps onto a trail that leads through stretches of manicured lawn, which, in the coming months, will shift from sleeping brown to vibrant and green. He looks down a familiar narrow path through a thatch of bare, spindly trees. The graves that way lie under an enormous oak tree; the earth is covered with acorns in the fall and dappled sunshine in the summer. Even when the sun is shining and the grass is brilliant and alive, Colin feels a strange vacuum there. He hasn't been down that trail—the one that leads to his parents' and sister's graves—in more than two years.

But the pull to find Lucy is different; it's a hot urgency in his chest. Following the map, he continues straight and turns at a fork, to a plot sectioned off from the others and surrounded by an iron fence. He's not sure what he's expecting to find, but his heart beats heavier in his chest with each step, his boots making squelching sounds in the soggy ground.

He matches the markers to the map as he goes:

Mary Jorgey Stevenson, loving wife, mother, sister. 1923–1984

Jeremiah Hansen, our father. 1901–1976

Harry Hawkins, cherished son. 1975–1987

Names, words, dates. Entire lives summed up in a few lines.

And then, in a wide plot encircled with a crooked ornate gate, is a single headstone. It seems strange to see her alone, set away from the other graves. But he realizes the spaces next to her must be empty, waiting for her parents.

He stands, hands clenched into fists at his sides, eyes moving over the simple script, the delicate flowers etched deep into polished granite. His fingers itch to touch the letters of her name, to see if they feel as real as she did, to see if there's any of her left here at all.

"Hey," he says to the slab of stone. "'Lucia Rain Gray. 1981 to 1998. Beloved daughter and friend.'" He feels irrationally angry at the generic memorial on her tombstone, letting out a few choice curse words before glancing behind him. Still alone, though he's sure he could be heard from clear across the hillside. "Seriously? I think they could have done better than that."

He shoves his frozen hands deep into his pockets and looks out over the other graves. The cemetery seems to stretch on for miles. There are no trees, no buildings, nothing to stop the wind from tearing through this side, blowing dried flowers down the hillside and away from the intended recipients. It's brutal and cold but eerily silent. Colin sits down on the damp, scratchy grass covering her grave.

"There was a dance last night," he says. "Jay took Amanda." He smiles, knowing exactly how Lucy would react. "I'd been planning on asking you, but . . ." He picks up a stone and turns it over in his hand. The bottom is wet and looks like shiny onyx, but the top is dry and almost white in the light. It's strange how water can make a simple rock look like a gem on one side and like a slab of concrete on the other. Just like the lake.

"This is my first time on this side of the cemetery, and yeah, it's creepy. You know my parents are right over there? How weird is that? I had a family plot already waiting for me when they buried you." Colin shakes his head, and a chill makes its way beneath the layers of his clothes. "They weren't kidding about cemeteries being creepy. You'd think they'd feel full of ghosts and death, but they just feel empty. That's the weirdest part, to be in a place that feels completely hollow and deserted. Why would anyone stick around here? What's there to see? No wonder you decided to come back on a trail with trees and water and . . ." He trails off again, eyes lifting to the ominous white sky. There's a patch right above where the clouds have drifted apart, and it seems like a vortex where he can imagine souls are sucked up and away.

"Is it strange that I'm glad I was the one who saw him . . . ? I mean, I don't remember any of it, and I know this sounds all kinds of wrong, but I like that I saw him take you. I want to feel like him getting caught that night made a difference. The universe owes you, Lucy. You deserve to come back."

He clears his throat, taking a much-needed breath to soothe the knot in his stomach. "So, I realize I'm talking to myself. You're not here, in the dust and the grass and the air, because if you were, you would have figured out how to create a body from all of that. I know where you are, though. Is it weird that I think these people in this cemetery are really gone but can't accept that you are? Like, I've never said a word at my mom's grave, because what's the point? She left a long time ago. You know I hardly remember her face?" He shrugs, tossing the rock to the ground. "But not you. I remember every one of your smiles, and I spent probably a half hour last night trying to picture the expression you make when you're braiding your hair. I know how you grip a pencil and that you cross your right leg over your left and almost never the other way around. And I know where you are, Lucy. I've never felt like anyone was waiting for me before, not my sister or my mom or my dad. It's only ever been you."

He stares down at the dead grass near his legs and picks out a single blade. The root is tender and green even if the exposed section is dried and yellow. Beneath the ground, it was still alive.

"I've spent the last few weeks trying to figure out how this happened, and I think I understand it now. I shouldn't be here. Dot's told me that enough times—joked that I have nine lives—but I never thought about it that much, you know? I should have died with my family—and at least a dozen times after that. Even the quarry didn't scare me. When I fell and broke my arm? For the first time ever, I thought, that's it. This is the end. But it wasn't. You'd been watching me, waiting, and I think that thought was enough to finally bring you here. If it wasn't over for me, it's not over for you either.

We're connected in a way that no one else is. I didn't let the man who killed you get away with murder, and you came back because you knew how much I'd lost."

He drops the blade of grass and runs his hand over the other yellowed blades, still firmly rooted in the soil. "I guess what I'm saying is that I hope you're waiting for me, Lucy. Because this time, I'm taking you through the gate, not the other way around."

Chapter 35 · HER

LUCY TAKES A BREATH AND BLOWS IT OUT, HER eyes opening to the bright yellow glare of the infirmary hallway.

No voices come from any of the rooms, and panic seizes her immediately; she's disappeared again.

How long has it been?

She stands, moving silently toward the closest doorway.

When she peeks in the room, she finds Colin asleep on his side. Her relief is a warm, tangible thing. A tangle of tubes dives down underneath the blankets, and only a tuft of hair is visible outside the bundle. She feels like she can finally breathe again, knowing he's well enough to be here and no longer at the hospital.

Instead of waking him with her cool skin, she sits near his bed and waits.

She promises not to go into the lake again. She promises not to let Colin go in either.

It's okay, she tells herself. This is what she wanted, for Colin to be safe above everything else. She feels stronger with every deep breath, as if the air simply bypasses her lungs and builds into her, cell by cell.

"Excuse me?" The words and voice don't mix; it sounds like courtesy dripping acid.

Lucy looks up to meet the familiar deep brown eyes of Maggie. She can't imagine the nurse is particularly thrilled to find her here, but the look on her face seems downright angry.

"What the hell are you doing?" she asks in a hiss, glancing at the bed.

"Waiting for him to wake up."

Maggie looks to Colin's huddled figure and then back at Lucy as if she were sitting naked in the chair. "Girl, are you out of your mind? That's not Colin."

The chair clatters backward as Lucy stands. "Where is he? I left while he was in the hospital but woke up here. I thought—"

"Left?" the nurse asks in an angry hiss, pulling Lucy toward the door. "As in, stepping out for a moment? As in getting some fresh air? Lucy, Colin left that hospital three weeks ago."

"Three weeks?" she asks, a lead ball of fear crashing through her insides. Maggie nods and moves to pick up the chart at the foot of the stranger's bed. Her words click into place in Lucy's head. "What day is it?"

"It's a Sunday. And he was just here, came by looking for help finding you. That boy had a look on his face like he was going to search under every rock if he had to." When she shakes her head, Lucy can tell she thinks his effort is wasted. "As if that'd matter. I told him this would happen, that you'd leave without a trace and he'd be left here, trying to pick up the pieces. Your kind ain't good for nothing but heartbreak. Don't want us safe and happy. No, you want us on the edge and broken, taking us somewhere we ain't got no business going. Let's hope he's smarter than I was." Maggie walks out of the room and toward a back office.

"How long ago?" Lucy asks, following, a wave of anger building deep inside her chest.

"I have things to do," she says over her shoulder. "If you'll excuse me."

This time it's Lucy who reaches out, grabbing Maggie's arm to stop her. The woman's eyes widen, and Lucy can tell right away that something is different. Maggie looks from where Lucy grips her—knuckles white, skin solid and warm—up to meet her gaze. "You leave that boy alone." There's anger in her voice, but more than that, there's fear.

Red clouds the edges of Lucy's vision, and the air moves in waves around the room. Maggie gasps, reaching up just as a small trickle of blood begins to run from her nose.

"How long ago!" Lucy shouts, startling herself.

Maggie pulls herself free, looking frightened and disoriented. "About . . . about a half hour," she says, staggering on her feet.

Just as quickly as the rage appeared, it's gone, and Lucy looks down at her own hands, terrified. She reaches toward Maggie. "I'm sorry," she begins, wanting to help. "I don't know—"

"Get away from me," Maggie says, staggering backward before crumpling to the floor. The color has fled from beneath her dark skin, and the bleeding has increased, now running in scarlet rivulets down the front of her teal uniform. She knocks over a small metal table as she falls, sending it and the items on top tumbling loudly to the floor. It's loud enough to get the attention of the woman in the hallway. She's wearing her coat and gloves, as if she'd just walked in the door.

"No, no, no, no, no, no," Lucy says, shrinking back into the shadows and watching as the woman fumbles with her cell phone while trying to help Maggie, who's lying in a growing puddle of blood.

Nobody even notices Lucy as she stumbles from the room,

tripping over a chair in the hallway and sending it skittering across the linoleum.

What's happening?

What they say about riding a bike is true. With no money for a cab or a phone call, Lucy steals a bike from outside the infirmary and has no problem remembering how to balance and take off. As she crosses the quad, she realizes she doesn't even know Colin's cell number. Her hands shake violently where she grips the handlebars, too afraid for a second glance behind her, to even consider what just happened. She has to get to Colin.

Lucy feels almost winded by the time she reaches the dorm. Two state police cars are parked in the lot, and she sees Dot's car a few spots down, but Lucy doesn't risk going to the kitchen to find her, to ask if she's seen him.

Continuing on, she notices the sidewalks seem busier than usual. Students stand together, trading hushed but anxious voices, and Lucy moves around them, leaning the bike against the side of Ethan Hall. She freezes when she spots the campus security guard standing at the door and talking to a teacher she recognizes. It seems impossible, but her guilty mind races, and she can't help wondering if he's looking for her. Lucy feels so alive right now—like every cell is pulsing with a heartbeat of its own—that she worries there's no way she could hope to sneak by. She feels like an illuminated billboard.

A group of chattering girls approaches the entrance. They move like a school of fish, lost in a torrent of whispered conversations. Lucy tucks herself near the back and must manage to look like she belongs, because soon she's through the door and racing up the stairs, praying that Colin is in his room. She can hear the music pulsing before she's even reached the landing.

She runs down the hall, and not waiting to knock, bursts through the door. Jay is sitting at his computer, his head in his hands.

"I heard," he says, with gentle gravity.

Lucy pulls up short, searching the small room for Colin. "What?"

"He died last night."

She shakes her head, confused. "Who died last night?"

"Your friend Alex."

Lucy no longer has legs. They buckle beneath her, and she sits on a pile of laundry as the world starts to spin too fast for her to hold on to any single point. "What?"

"He collapsed last night. He was never in remission; he just didn't tell anyone." Jay points to his monitor, to the news article he was reading as she came in, but she's crawling to the door as dread and sickness and terror wash over her. Fear is freezing her limbs, because if Jay is here and Colin is not . . . Lucy looks down at her arms. She is so solid she can see her skin roll firmly between her fingers as she pinches herself.

My presence is fighting the cancer, helping make him healthy again. And I feel stronger every day.

Kids like you? They always take someone with them. Try not to, Lucy.

"Where's Colin?" Jay asks, looking behind her. "I'm not sure he knows yet. But maybe, because he's been camped out at Joe's and—"

"Jay, I think Colin went to the lake to find me."

Jay begins throwing supplies in a bag, shouting for Lucy to wait just a second, to let him call 9-1-1. But she can't. Every particle of her body propels her out the door and down the stairs, sprinting to where she knows Colin is.

Her chest burns from trudging through the snow at this pace, and looking down as she runs, she sees two sets of footprints, converging. Colin's and hers. Equally deep. The ice groans in warning beneath her weight, and she slips for the first time, cracking her solid hip on the surface. Closer, closer.

Lucy hates how strong she feels. The only thing keeping her going is that she's still here. If Colin died, she would vanish, right?

"I'm almost there. Please don't go looking for me. I'm here."

At the edge of the ice lies a pile of clothes. Jeans, boots, his favorite blue hoodie. In the water, there are no bubbles, no ripples, no movement. Just blue water that slips into darkness.

Her scream carries through the trees and echoes off the surface of the water. The force of her anguish tears her in two and pulls her down to the brittle, thinning ice.

Every piece finally fits.

I'm no Guardian; I'm a lure.

She feels the streak of hot tears falling down her cheeks—the first ones she's cried since waking. In the distance, sirens fill the air, the sound ringing in the empty silence of the frozen lake. Closer. Closer.

As she stares at the pile of clothes, they become covered with fluffy flakes of snow. When she looks to the sky, she finds only brilliant blue above. Holding her hands up in front of her, Lucy watches her skin disintegrate into snow and ash and air. She watches as she's blown into the wind.

Epilogue

I T WASN'T AS SIMPLE AS SLIPPING INTO THE BLACK-
ness and finding him there waiting. She expected it to
be simple. She moved with the same instinct as before.
But instead, she was back in her mirror world, alone, and
more aware this time. She'd never been lonely there before,
because she'd needed only to look out into the other sky and
see him. But when she returned alone, she remembered every
minute with Colin, every smile, every sensation of him.

Time was her sole, begrudging partner. It twisted and
slept, lingered interminably and then would burst past her in
the few moments Lucy let herself enjoy her lush memories
of togetherness. Minutes passed differently under the lake
than they did above it. A minute here could be a second or a
year to anything on earth. How long would it take him to get
here? How long had it been?

Every time the strange sun rose, she thought, *Today is the day we'll be back together.* Every day she walked to the gate, but the longing to walk through was gone, like it had drifted off with her body into the snow.

And then everything changed.

It was a different sort of morning, cold like the first day he went into the lake, with air so sharp you hesitate before taking it into your lungs, even if it gives you your shape and its coldest elements are your only essence.

She had a good feeling that morning, one she couldn't explain. It was weather that would make Colin's eyes flame golden and she would know he was thinking about falling into the water, about touching her with same hands and same lips and same skin.

The trail was deserted, of course. Downy snow buried the dirt and grass. Apples that hung ripe and round the day before lay like glittering rubies in the snow. And then he was there.

His eyes were full of confusion. He looked at his arms, at the apples in the snow, at the ice-blue sky, and at the path in front of him. When he saw Lucy, his face relaxed and he blinked once and then twice for her, the second one bringing with it a smile.

TAKE A SNEAK PEEK AT CHRISTINA LAUREN'S
NEXT BEAUTIFULLY HAUNTING NOVEL

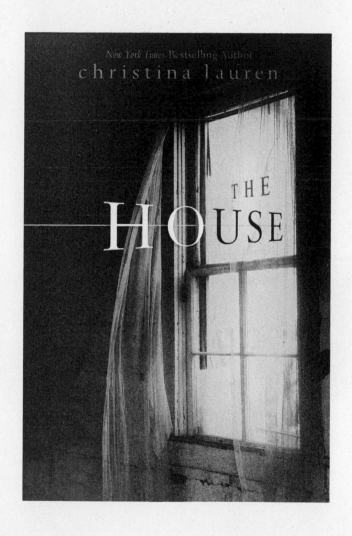

P LACES WITH BOYS ALWAYS SEEM SO DIRTY. As soon as Delilah had the thought, she hated herself for it because it was exactly what her mother would think. Girls were just as dirty after all, with thick, sticky makeup and every flavor of perfume clouding the locker rooms. The public high school seemed to have a dim film layered over the lockers and floor, walls and windows. It was the first day back after the winter, so Delilah assumed that everything had been cleaned vigorously over the break, but maybe the fog of girl and boy hormones mixing together had permanently dulled every surface.

All around, students pressed past her and lockers slammed near her head, and she struggled to appear unaffected by the public-school chaos. Delilah looked down to the piece of paper clutched in her hand. Before she'd even been dressed and fed this morning, her mother had already begun highlighting all of the important information for her:

locker number, locker combination, class schedule, teacher names.

"I should have printed a map for you," Belinda Blue had said as the highlighter squeaked across the page. Delilah had looked away to the neat rows on the carpet left by the vacuum cleaner, had waved politely to her father as he'd walked into the kitchen wearing his standard outfit of tan pants, a short-sleeved white collar shirt, and a red tie. Even though he wasn't going to work and maybe didn't even have a job interview today, she couldn't fault him for dressing the part. She, too, was still more comfortable in clothes that resembled her private-school uniform than she was with having this new freedom to wear whatever she wanted.

"Mom, it's only two main buildings. I can handle it. Saint Ben's had seven."

Morton City High was smaller than Saint Benedict's Academy in pretty much every way possible, from the size of the classrooms and number of buildings, to the minds of the student body. Whereas—perhaps unexpectedly—imagination had been embraced and nurtured in her beautiful Catholic school, there had always been a single way of thinking in her small Kansas hometown, a tendency to embrace normal and disregard anything else in hopes that it might simply go away.

It was what had happened to Delilah six years ago, after all. Her parents had tolerated her strangeness with shared looks of exasperation and long-suffering sighs, but then had shipped her off to Massachusetts as soon as an excuse presented itself.

"Still, you're used to calm. This school is so big and *loud*."

Delilah smiled. When her mother said "loud" she really meant "full of boys." "I'm pretty sure I'll make it out alive."

Her mother had given her the look Delilah had seen countless times over winter break—the look that said, *I'm sorry you can't finish your senior year in a fancy school. Please don't tell anyone your father lost his job and your nonna's money is all tied up in her nursing care.*

The look also said, *Be careful of the boys. They have* thoughts.

Delilah had thoughts too. She had a lot of them, about boys and their arms and smiles and how their throats looked when they swallowed. She had infrequent contact with these things, having been sequestered away for the past several years at an all-girls boarding school, but she certainly had *thoughts* about them. Unfortunately, the schedule in her hand didn't mention a thing about boys, and instead read: English, Phys Ed, Biology, Organic Chemistry, World Studies, AP French, AP Calculus.

She felt her enthusiasm wilt a little before the day had even started. Who wants to have PE so early in the day? She'd be a sweaty mop and would never factor into any *thoughts* anyway.

Delilah successfully negotiated her locker combination, stowed some books, and headed to English. The only empty seat in the room—Room 104, Mr. Harrington, highlighted in yellow, *thank you, Mother*—was of course in the middle, up front. Delilah was a bull's-eye for the teacher and for the fellow students. But even if she sat in the back of the room, it wouldn't have made a difference: She was a target anyway.

Delilah Blue was back from the fancy East Coast boarding school.

Delilah Blue had come home to go slumming.

Although she spent some of each summer back in Morton, being at school here was different. Delilah had forgotten how many teenagers could come out of the woodwork, and all around her they were yelling, throwing notes, whispering across aisles. Was this how they always behaved while waiting for the teacher? *When your time is yours, use it to create something,* Father John had always told them. *A picture, some words, anything. Don't rot your brain with gossip.*

Having seen only her best friend, Dhaval, with any sort of regularity—and maybe a handful of her classmates around town during breaks—Delilah's memories were an old stack of pictures of her eleven-year-old peers. She struggled to place the faces she remembered from six years ago with the reality of the faces now.

Rebecca Lewis, her best friend from kindergarten. Kelsey Stiles, her archnemesis in third grade. Both were looking at Delilah as if she'd kicked a puppy before class. Rebecca probably glared at her because Delilah had left Morton so successfully. Kelsey probably glared at Delilah for having the gall to come back.

Not everyone had been hostile when they recognized

Delilah; some girls had greeted her in front of the school with hugs and high-pitched welcomes, and Delilah knew that she had a completely blank slate there. She could be anyone she wanted to be. She didn't have to be the girl whose nervous parents sent her away when she was only eleven for getting into a fistfight defending her unrequited first crush.

Delilah took her seat next to Tanner Jones, the only person to ever have beaten her at tetherball in sixth grade, her last year of public school.

"Hi, Delilah," he said, eyes on her legs and then chest and then mouth. Six years ago he'd been looking at her pigtails and skinned knees.

She smiled to hide her surprise. Delilah hadn't expected the first boy to speak to her to also have *thoughts*. "Hi, Tanner."

"I heard you had to move back because your dad lost his job at the plant."

She kept her smile and stayed quiet, thinking of her mother's innocent-at-best, naive-at-worst hope that people would assume Delilah came home for a single semester for educational purposes, and not because Nonna's well of money had dried up. Clearly the town knew better.

Your business is only yours until you share it, Father John had always told them.

Just as Mr. Harrington was closing the classroom door, a boy slipped in, mumbling an apology and staring with determination at the floor.

Delilah's breath grew trapped in her throat, and the old protective fire flickered to life between her ribs.

He was the same, but not. His shirt was black, jeans were black, and shaggy black hair fell into his eyes. He was so tall he must have been pulled like taffy. When he looked up at Delilah as he passed, the same eyes she remembered from all those years ago—dark and stormy and shadowed with bluish circles—seemed to flicker to life for a moment.

Just long enough for her to lose her breath.

He looked like he knew every one of her secrets. Who would have guessed that after six years Gavin Timothy would still seem so perfectly dangerous?

Apparently, Delilah was still smitten.

I T WASN'T UNHEARD OF FOR GIRLS TO WATCH HIM,
but usually it meant one of two things. Either they were
terrified that Gavin might pull a knife from his shoe
(which had never happened), or they were building up the
courage to ask him out, with hopes of bringing him home to
terrify their parents into buying them a car (which had happened twice).

Delilah Blue was back in Morton and was watching Gavin
in a singularly different way. She looked like a wolf stalking
a rabbit.

He spun a pencil on his notebook and blinked up, looking
right into her eyes and causing her to whip around in her seat,
sitting ramrod straight. Her caramel hair was braided and
secured tightly with a red elastic band, swinging into position
at the middle of her back just below her shoulder blades. Her
foot tapped impatiently under her desk. For the remainder of
class, she was obviously attentive, maybe overly so. But what

she was attending to was definitely not at the front of the room. If she were a cat, she would have her ears turned back, facing *him*. Gavin was sure of it.

He could still remember the way she'd looked the last time he'd seen her: scraped knuckles, bloody nose, and an expression of protectiveness so feral it made his stomach twist. He'd never even had a chance to say thank you.

The end-of-period bell rang, and Delilah jumped, looking frantically for the source. Did they not have bells at her fancy private school? Because yes, Gavin knew enough about Delilah to know exactly where she'd been. But why she was back was an entirely different question.

Just as she appeared to spot the bell, perched above the whiteboard, the door flew open and Dhaval Reddy swept into the room, pulling her up and wrapping his arms around her.

"My girl is back!" Dhaval sang loudly to no one in particular. As everyone gathered their things, Gavin felt the room settle: Delilah's return had been approved by the in crowd.

Gavin collected his books and papers and slipped past her, but not before he felt her hand reach out and touch his, or before he saw the tiny drawing on her notebook: a dagger dripping blood.

WHAT IF

ALL YOUR CRUSHES
FOUND OUT HOW YOU FELT?

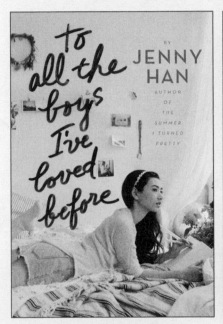

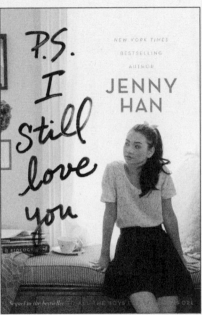

From bestselling author

JENNY HAN

There is a **universe of possibilities** in all your choices.

You never know where they will lead . . .

or whom

they will lead you to.

A sacred oath, a fallen angel, a forbidden love

YOU WON'T BE ABLE TO KEEP IT *HUSH, HUSH.*

PRINT AND EBOOK EDITIONS AVAILABLE